One Good Thing

ONE GOOD THING

A NOVEL

Rebecca Hendry

Copyright © 2018 by Rebecca Hendry

All rights reserved. No part of this publication may be reproduced, stored in a retrieval system, or transmitted in any form or by any means, electronic, mechanical, photocopying, recording, or otherwise, without the prior written permission of the publisher. For more information, contact the publisher at:

Brindle & Glass
An imprint of TouchWood Editions
touchwoodeditions.com

Edited by Kate Kennedy
Cover design by Tree Abraham
Interior design by Colin Parks

LIBRARY AND ARCHIVES CANADA CATALOGUING IN PUBLICATION

Hendry, Rebecca, 1972-, author
One good thing : a novel / Rebecca Hendry.
Issued in print and electronic formats.
ISBN 978-1-927366-77-6 (softcover).
I. Title.
PS8615.E539O54 2018   C813'.6   C2017-906580-7   C2017-906581-5

We acknowledge the financial support of the Government of Canada through the Canada Book Fund and the Canada Council for the Arts, and of the province of British Columbia through the British Columbia Arts Council and the Book Publishing Tax Credit.

The interior pages of this book have been printed on 100% post-consumer recycled paper, processed chlorine-free, and printed with vegetable-based inks.

This book is a work of fiction. Names, characters, places, and incidents are either products of the author's imagination or are used fictitiously. Any resemblance to actual events or locales or persons, living or dead, is entirely coincidental.

PRINTED IN CANADA AT FRIESENS

22 21 20 19 18   1 2 3 4 5

For my father, David,
who always came back

✳︎✳︎✳︎

> We are, each of us, a multitude.
> Within us is a little universe.
>
> —CARL SAGAN

may 1977

WHEN DELILAH FIRST LAYS eyes on the great white north, she isn't thrilled about it. As she stands on the banks of the Mackenzie River in her hand-knit rainbow-striped sweater, her mother, Annie, sits in Bessie, their VW van with the little checked curtains, head back, eyes closed. There's no one else in the muddy parking lot of the Fort Providence ferry. Annie and Delilah have already been told what everyone else must know. A guy had pulled over in his pickup and asked them what they were waiting for. He told them they couldn't cross. The winter road had closed weeks before, and the river was now a soup of open water and small, deadly icebergs the ferry would not navigate for days. He said they'd probably get a deal on a weekly rate at the motel if they explained their situation. For now, they're trapped.

Delilah doesn't want to get a room in some motel and eat trail mix and her mother's homemade seed bread with peanut butter for another week. She wants a cheeseburger, tacos. Something cooked. They hadn't stopped at a single restaurant the whole drive up from Vancouver. Annie said the last of her student loans had dried up and they only had enough for gas.

Delilah needs to see her dad. She imagines him on the other side, shouting above the cracking ice, "Come on! I'm waiting."

Of course, this isn't true. He isn't there. He's probably in his little cabin having a beer or playing some Zeppelin or snoring away. How could he know his family was stranded across the river in the van loaded to the roof with boxes and houseplants and garbage bags full of clothes? He doesn't even know they're coming.

As Delilah watches that strange horizontal avalanche of ice roll and crack its way toward shore, she is aware of the power of nature in a way she has never been before. There's something angry about the way the ice gathers, rises, and then crashes in a jagged heap of snowy crust and aqua-tinted chunks. It's as if a giant hand were ripping it from the surface of the water and shoving it aside, uprooting everything it touches. When she closes her eyes, she hears an amplified tinkling like hard rain turned to glass.

It isn't exactly welcoming.

FOUR DAYS LATER, BESSIE sputters into Yellowknife, low on gas and leaking some sort of fluid that Annie doesn't seem interested in investigating. Seven of their nine plants are dead, frozen overnight when they hadn't thought to bring them into the motel room with them. The one surviving spider plant is wilted at Delilah's feet, the leaves gone transparent from freezing and thawing. She rests her legs on either side of it, gently, to keep it warm.

To her, this new town looks like any other town in Canada. Aside from Vancouver, they have lived in Toronto, Winnipeg, Thunder Bay, Victoria, and, for about six months, Regina before Annie insisted they leave. Cold was bad enough, she had said, but she was not going to be slapped around by the Saskatchewan wind.

Now Delilah can feel her mother's tension like a thin, humming wire. Snappable. They drive slowly through the streets, Delilah scanning the unfamiliar low buildings of downtown. There are small piles of grey snow on the sidewalks, people still wearing heavy boots, some even wearing parkas.

They stop and Annie cranks her window down. "Hey," she shouts to a group of men coming out of the Gold Range Hotel, a three-storey building with a faded yellow awning. "You guys know where Old Town is?"

One of them steps forward, lighting a cigarette. He's well over six feet, his thick black hair fastened into a ponytail with a strip of leather. He comes so close to the van window Delilah thinks he's going to open her mother's door and hop in. He peers in, his head and wide shoulders taking up the whole window.

Delilah is used to men staring at her mother, but he isn't looking at her like that. His eyes are like those sparklers Annie puts on birthday cakes, bright and crackling.

"Old Town?" he says.

Annie smiles. "Yeah. Do you know where I can find it?"

He steps back, takes a drag of his hand-rolled cigarette and points toward the main road they were travelling on before they turned down a side street. "Back that ways. Turn right and keep driving down the hill till you hit the bay."

"Thanks," Annie says. "Any chance you know where James MacIntyre lives?"

The address they have for him is just a mailbox number, so Annie's master plan had been to ask around until they found him. Delilah shrinks down in her seat a little, embarrassed at their overstuffed, rusty van, Annie's thrift store fur coat that still reeks like some rich old lady's mothballs.

"Mac?" the man says. He seems amused. "Sure do. Green shack on Old Stope Hill. Can't miss it."

"Great, thanks. We've had quite the adventure. Looking forward to being on solid ground. Although I'm not sure how I feel about the snow here. Don't you people know it's spring?" Annie is watching him languidly, one fur-clad elbow resting on the windowsill.

"Mom," Delilah says.

The man grins. "Well, like I say, can't miss it. Green shack on Old Stope." He steps back and salutes Annie before shifting his eyes to Delilah. "See you around, kid."

She raises her fingers in return.

They drive in silence, passing unremarkable houses and small businesses. A laundromat. A Chinese restaurant. "Everything looks so dead," Annie says. "So white and cold. It reminds me of Ontario."

She rests a hand on Delilah's leg. Delilah shifts away slightly.

"Come on, little bird, enough of the silent treatment."

Annie squeezes Delilah's thin knee. The spring sun has come out. It's streaming in on Annie's side of the van, lighting her long hair into fiery wisps.

"Okay," Delilah says.

"Okay what?"

"Okay, I'll talk to you?"

"Good. Otherwise I would get pretty damn lonely. You're the only one I know here so far."

Her mother's amethyst ring has snagged Delilah's tights, pulling a tiny thread loose.

* * *

THEY FINALLY STOP BESIDE a lopsided, peeling green shack on a hill between two half-frozen bays. There are wind chimes hanging under the eaves by the front door, what seem like hundreds to Delilah, some made of metal, some of coloured plastic, some of carved bone.

"We made it," Annie says. "We're here."

Delilah opens the door and hops down, her body flooding with relief.

"I'll meet you in there," Annie says.

She's still staring at the cabin, and Delilah isn't interested in what she might be thinking. She shuts the van door and walks past an old red pickup with a Ski-Doo parked beside it. There's a small, crooked porch with beer bottles lined up against the side of the house. She can hear the faintest shimmer of sound from the wind chimes though there's no wind she can feel. She thinks of dogs, how they can hear sounds humans can't.

She pulls opens the creaking screen. Should she knock on her own father's door? She steps inside. Music is playing. Led Zeppelin's "Ramble On." She's heard it a million times before. He appears through a dark doorway at the back of the cabin.

"Holy shit!" His hair is wet, shaggy, and he has a beard that reaches almost to his chest.

He takes the room in three strides and wraps Delilah in his arms. Tears sting her eyes as she lets her weight sink into the familiar muscle and warmth of her father. She can finally relax.

"Lila," he says as she buries her face in his shoulder, inhaling the clean-shirt smell, the Ivory soap, the minty toothpaste on his breath. "What the hell are you doing here?"

***

THERE IS ONLY A yellow wool blanket for a door on the closet-like alcove she will sleep in. Her bed is a lumpy, shiny green couch. She lies on it, taking in her new surroundings. She feels the springs under her back, coiled like hard snakes. Her dad says he will get her a bed as soon as he can. He knows a guy who's moving away, and he can get it for cheap. There are only two bedrooms in the shack, and this one is filled with junk her father says was abandoned by the last guy who lived there. He left in a hurry, flew home to Alabama when his father had a heart attack. There is mining gear stacked in the corner, heavy boots, a wooden blasting box that Mac assures her is not dangerous anymore. She still eyes it suspiciously.

Her parents are laughing in the kitchen as they clean up from supper, a thick stew that Mac made from caribou meat. He told them his friend Will had killed the caribou. He said he had been there and tried to shoot it but lost his nerve at the last minute. Will had been the one to pull the trigger.

Delilah lets the sound from the kitchen absorb into her cells, soothe the aching exhaustion she has been feeling since Vancouver. She hadn't slept well at the motel with the strange northern sun blazing until after eleven each night. She listens to her parents tell each other stories, tease each other, her mother light and bubbly as though nothing had happened at all. *Look how fun I am*, she seems to be saying. *How spontaneous. We just up and decided to come see you.* When Delilah breathes in, there is a faint wheezing rattle in her chest. She reaches for her inhaler, which is stuffed in her jeans' pocket, and takes a deep puff of the metallic spray. Waits until the kindling fire in her chest subsides to embers.

When Delilah comes out, Annie has started unpacking their boxes in the tiny living room and is sorting through a carton of black and white photographs. She sits on the floor, holding up the prints and squinting at them in the dimming light. There's no electricity in the shack, which her dad has pointed out almost proudly. Something to do with ancient, faulty wiring he hasn't bothered to fix. They'll light kerosene lamps when it gets too dark to see.

Mac walks over and kisses the top of Annie's head, then beckons to Delilah. "Come on," he says.

They put on boots and walk out into the early twilight, climb the steep stairs up the clump of grey rock beside the house. At the top is a pillar made of concrete with a propeller resting on it.

"It's a memorial to all the bush pilots. They've been flying planes here since before there were even any roads," he says. "Transporting bushworkers, bringing supplies to mining camps. Dangerous job, flying through bad weather in the middle of nowhere."

They sit on the rock. There is a street below them with buildings and old warehouses facing the open lake. Her dad points out to the water.

"That's Great Slave Lake," he says. "This side is Yellowknife Bay. That small island out there in front of us is Joliffe. You can walk to it when the lake is frozen. It's mostly thawed now." On the silver horizon, she sees small sheets of thin ice drifting free like rafts on the water. He twists and points behind them to the smaller bay. "That's Back Bay. Leads out to Giant Mine."

He leans against the base of the monument and lights a cigarette. His long hair and big beard make him almost unrecognizable. Only his soft blue eyes seem familiar. She shivers in the breeze. He's looking far off down the long arm of lake. "We'll have to get you a proper jacket. That sweater might be good for Vancouver, but you'll freeze to death here." He takes a drag and lets it out. "What happened?" he asks.

She shrugs. The rock is hard and cold under her cotton pants. She can't tell him about the night her mother woke her to tell her they were leaving Vancouver. How when she opened her eyes, startled, Annie was kneeling by the bed in the glow from the street light. "Come on, little bird," she had said, shaking Delilah's shoulder gently. "Wake up.

Let's go." She was whispering, breathless, like she was saving Delilah from some delicious emergency.

"Go where?" Delilah had asked.

"Yellowknife. Tonight. Let's pack up our clothes and go." Annie was crackling, her eyes snapping and restless.

"What? Why?"

"What do you mean, why? You're the one who kept saying you wanted to go up there. Don't you miss your dad? We can surprise him. Just get in the van and drive. It takes three days. We'll show up at his doorstep. Knock knock, it's your family."

She had wanted to go, it was true. For months she had asked Annie if they could join Mac, but her mother kept saying they had roots in Vancouver, that she needed to finish art school but they would all be together soon. Delilah had finally resigned herself to the big, rundown house with its revolving door of drifters and roommates, people sleeping on camping mattresses on the living room floor. But that night she thought about the school talent show on Friday. She'd been working out a routine to "Jive Talkin'" by the Bee Gees with Dana and the two Jennifers. And her Grade 7 grad was in three weeks. She had already bought her dress at the Bay with money her father sent. Blond Jennifer helped her pick it out. It was candy-striped with little white hearts for buttons.

Delilah knew better than to try and reason with her mother. And she had seen it coming. All that shouting the night before. Annie slamming a pottery dish on the counter so hard it exploded into shards while Delilah hid in the hallway, peeking through a beaded curtain as Marcel raged, sneered, called Annie names. *Witch. Liar. Spoiled rich girl slumming it in Kitsilano with the little people . . .*

He was Delilah's least favourite of their roommates, even before then. She didn't like the stupid wine-coloured beret he wore all the time, even when he first woke up in the morning. All he talked about was jazz, and he used big words Delilah didn't understand. He had been drifting coolly through the house for days leading up to the fight and had stopped taking any interest in Delilah whatsoever. His girlfriend, Jackie, had barely come out of her room lately. Things had changed in the house. Nobody set up watercolours in the living room or sang Carole King at the piano. Annie no longer hosted parties, twirled boas around people's necks, and urged the women to wear the men's jackets as she staged elaborate photographs or cooked five-course vegetarian meals for twelve. She was spending her days curled up on the sofa, staring out at the overgrown garden, and her nights as a ball of frenetic energy, pacing the hall outside Delilah's bedroom on the phone, having whispered, urgent conversations with someone and staying up all night drawing in her room. She would emerge almost catatonic with fatigue in the mornings, a home-rolled cigarette in her mouth, to get Delilah her breakfast before school.

After Annie went to pack the night they left, Delilah had watched the dark arms of the cherry tree outside her window wave to her in the night breeze. She had raised a hand to wave back. She remembers feeling something small break inside her, scattering like the blossoms.

"DON'T GET ME WRONG," her dad says now. "I'm happy as hell to have you. I missed you both like crazy."

She nods, watching a raven dip above the rocky ledge.

"Did she . . . was everything okay when you left? I sent money for rent."

Delilah thinks carefully before she speaks. She thinks of tiptoeing through the kitchen to get her favourite owl mug the night they left, sidestepping a shattered bottle of red wine leaking blood-red pools onto the linoleum floor.

"She said maybe it was time for a change. She said maybe things were going good for you up here. And the air would be better for my asthma. They had a little going-away party for us. Jackie made a cake." She's lying. Nobody, not a single person, was there to see them off when they left that misty grey morning. Marcel and Jackie were still asleep, and nobody else even knew they were leaving.

The raven lands and hops twice, turning to stare at Delilah with its unreadable black eyes. It's huge, at least twice as big as any crow she's ever seen. She waves her finger at it.

"Well, she's right." He shifts his weight. "About all those things. It was a rough year for you. Lots of trips to Emergency. It's drier up here. Less pollen. And things are going good for me. She's right about that." He's watching the raven too. "They're smart, ravens. Did you know that? Smarter than crows. They can mimic other animals, even human voices. Sometimes, if they find a dead animal, they'll call the wolves, entice them to come so they rip it open. Then the ravens can swoop in for the leftovers."

The raven cocks its head and lifts off in a sudden rush of black.

"I kept telling her it would be better for you guys up here," he says. "But she wanted to stay. All those art school friends and her parents. We put the application in for the housing in Vancouver and everything. Jeez, she can't sit still, can she?" He laughs. "But now we're together. We're all together. Like it's supposed to be." He brushes some long hair from his face, and Delilah notices he has marks on his hands. Probably from working. They look like scars, only fresher.

"So I guess you'll start school in a few days," he says. "I can take you in, get you registered. You think you'll be okay at a new school? The kids are pretty nice here. Ones I've met, anyway."

"I guess," she says.

She has switched schools eight times in seven years. In her experience, kids are often interested in making friends with the new girl. Sometimes rival groups will even fight over her. She usually has a friend or two within a few days. Not the popular girls or the outcasts, but the ones people don't pay much attention to either way.

She wonders how the Bee Gees routine went in Vancouver. The girls would have done it last night. They must have had to get someone to fill in for her. She left without saying goodbye, and she doesn't know their addresses. She has a collection of addresses from left-behind friends. She keeps the scraps of paper in a purple envelope she decorated with glitter when she was six. She has never written to a single one. She isn't sure why. It's funny how easy it can be to let people go. Leaving isn't so hard, Annie told her once. It just takes practice.

The raven is swooping above their heads in a high, wide circle.

"Why do they do that?" she asks. "With the wolves? Why don't they eat the dead animals themselves?"

"They can't break through the skin with their beaks. Smart, like I said. The trick to life is knowing your weakness. Knowing what you're good at and what you're not, and finding ways to cover for what you can't do."

Delilah watches the bird differently now that she knows it can summon wolves. Not only summon them, but make them do what it wants without it even occurring to the wolves that they're being tricked. How can something so small be so smart? She wishes she was a raven. What would she make the wolves do when they came?

He gathers his cigarettes and lighter and stands. "You know what I think? I think you're going to love it here. I can get my friend Muddy to take us up in his plane when the ice is gone. Once you're up there, you'll think you're the luckiest kid in the world to be living here now."

She looks at the sky, the shards of disappearing sun. Feels the crisp air like clean, fresh water on her skin.

"It was a damn good decision your mother made," he says. "Bringing you here."

He wouldn't say if he disagreed. She knows that. Delilah has never heard her father say a bad word about Annie. Even when she loses her keys or money or doesn't come home when she says she will or forgets to check dinner when she's drawing and it chars to a lump of smoking coal in the oven. It's not that they don't argue—they do. But usually it's Annie telling Mac the things she doesn't like about him. Not the other way around. He never complains about Annie, even when he has a right to. It bothers Delilah sometimes. Like now, when he has so many reasons to complain . . . most of which he doesn't even know about.

He smiles at her, dying light reflecting in his beard. So far most of the men Delilah has seen up here have big beards. She isn't sure how she feels about it. All these men with their hidden faces.

✳

"Charlie! Charrrlie . . ."

Delilah startles awake. Somewhere outside the shack, a woman is calling for someone. She sounds angry. Delilah tries to pinpoint the source and decides it's coming from the rundown little white house next door.

"Charlie . . ."

Weak light filters through the small square of her bedroom window. She turns on her side, burrowing under a heavy pile of blankets on the hard couch. Her back aches from the dip in the middle. She pulls a pillow over her ear, but she can still hear the voice calling through her dreamy early-morning fog.

"Where you at, Charlie Boy?"

A dog howls a mournful response. The woman isn't angry, Delilah realizes as her eyes drift shut again. She's sad. Something she loves is gone, and she wants it to come back.

✳

ANNIE IS SINGING JONI Mitchell when Delilah wakes again. Delilah can hear her in the little kitchen with its sloping floor and the plywood counter, exposed cupboards and an old gas-burner stove that had resident mice when her dad first opened it.

Delilah's room is just big enough for the old couch and a drooping wardrobe that's missing its front doors. There are a few shelves nailed to the walls and hooks to hang her clothes. Delilah has piled the miner's belongings in the small room near the back door and lined up her books and *Archie* comics on the shelves. Under the bed is a box with her art supplies, journals, and old stuffed animals.

She yawns and turns toward the heavy wool blanket that serves as a door until her dad builds her a real one. He said this was pretty near the top of his list, right after getting her a bed, fixing a hole in the roof, and putting a door on the bathroom. Which she would prefer he did first. It's not actually a bathroom, as she had pointed out when she first saw it, because it doesn't have a toilet. Or a sink. Or a bathtub. It's a tiny, dark closet with only a hand-built wooden box with a toilet seat on it. A honey bucket, her dad had said. Most of the shacks in Old Town had them, if they were lucky. Either that or an outhouse.

"Bucket?" she had said.

"Yes, it's basically a plastic bucket with a lid on it."

"But . . . how do you flush?"

He had laughed. "You don't. There's no running water in this house. No plumbing. We get our water delivered by truck, and we use that for dishes and baths. We have a little aluminum bathtub out back. We can bring it into the living room by the fire and fill it with hot water from the stove.

I'll show you later. But mostly we'll go for showers at my friend Red's place."

Delilah was still staring at the wooden box. "But . . . if you don't flush, where does it all go?"

"We empty the bucket once a week. The City comes and collects the bags." He was grinning at her.

This was new. This was something that, in all the places she had lived, she had never experienced. They always had a toilet that flushed. It never occurred to her that it was a privilege, that she had somehow been living the high life until now.

"Gross," she'd said.

※※※

"I am on a lonely road, and I am travelling, travelling, travelling, travelling," her mother sings now. "Looking for something, what can it be?" Pans bang, water swishes.

Delilah sits up and looks out her window. All she sees is lichen-covered rock. It's the side of the pilots' monument where she climbed with her dad the night before. There is a fly buzzing angrily around the window. Her dad has warned her about the mosquitoes, like the coming of the apocalypse, but she hasn't seen one yet.

She pulls the wool blanket aside, letting in the oven warmth of the kitchen. Her mother is swinging her hips, long velvet skirt flowing, as she bangs the bottom of a rusty bread pan to loosen the freshly baked loaf.

"Do you want, do you want, do you want to dance with me, baby?" Annie sings, letting the bread pan clatter on the counter as she turns to Delilah, arms wide.

Delilah allows herself to be embraced, swayed. Annie smells like cinnamon, yeast, and rosewater. Over her shoulder, Delilah can see six loaves of bread cooling on the counter, a pan of cinnamon buns crusted with brown sugar and raisins. A tiny, familiar alarm sounds in her chest.

"Mom?"

Her mother releases her. Cups her face and peers into her eyes. Delilah looks away. Annie kisses her cheek and turns back to her work. There's another batch starting, a bulging damp cloth covering a large silver bowl.

"That's . . . a lot of bread."

Annie waves a delicate hand. "I'll freeze some. I could probably leave it outside at night. I won't need to bake for weeks." She digs a fork around a cinnamon bun and releases it, turning to offer it to Delilah. "Breakfast."

Delilah takes it. It's heavy, probably from barley flour and molasses. Delilah has seen the fluffy kind of cinnamon buns with the white icing, but she has never tasted one. She imagines they would melt like snow on her tongue.

"Thanks. Where's Dad?"

Annie shrugs her thin shoulders. "Don't know. Outside, I guess." She dumps the dough out of the bowl and starts kneading, humming to herself.

Delilah pulls on her Keds and her rainbow sweater, opens the door, and walks out into the bright morning, gnawing on the cinnamon bun. The wind chimes tremble when she closes the door, singing a hesitant song behind her.

The little hill outside their shack is a sloping dirt road that curves at the bottom and heads toward a strange building that looks like a tin can stripped of its label, cut lengthwise and then plunked cut-side down onto the ground. A sign outside by a rickety wooden porch reads WEAVER & DEVORE TRADING. There are brightly coloured shacks scattered on either side of the road like a string of mismatched beads. She can feel herself acclimatizing to her new surroundings, a strange calmness descending on her after the last few months of chaos. She likes this place.

Her dad is standing by an old yellow truck heaped with firewood, talking to a large man who's unlatching the tailgate. Delilah wanders toward them, tossing the cinnamon bun into the brush beside the road for the birds. She hugs herself to keep warm. It looks like a sunny spring day, but it has bite.

Her dad looks up as she approaches. "Hey there."

"Hey," she says, tracing her fingers along the side of the grungy truck. She feels like she's interrupting something.

Her dad points to the man. "This is Will. I told you about him. He lives down the road in Rainbow Valley."

She's seen him before. He's the man who gave them directions. He's huge, at least six inches taller than her dad. He's wearing a suede jacket with fringes and flowers made from tiny beads. There's a grey and white knitted hat on his head that's unravelling on one side. "Rainbow Valley?" She wipes her fingers on her jeans.

"Yup," he says. "Sounds like some kinda heaven or something, doesn't it?" There's a husky curled near the back wheel of the truck licking its paws.

"I met you," she says.

"You did?" he says, feigning shock. "Where'd you meet me? You been hangin' out at the Gold Range or something? How old are you? You look pretty short for nineteen, kid."

"You told us how to get to Old Town."

He laughs and starts piling wood into Mac's arms. "I see you made it here okay," he says.

"Will and I work together at Giant," Mac says. "And we're planning a little trip out to the bush."

"The bush?" Delilah thinks of the blackberry brambles that had invaded their backyard in Vancouver the previous summer, she thinks of cedar hedges, the frond-like leaves of huckleberry plants.

"Out in the wild. They call it the bush here. We head out in a few weeks. Going out to the Barrens." He walks toward the woodpile and Delilah trails behind. "We're doing some staking for a mining company. We've done it once already. It is utterly gorgeous out there, Delilah. You would not believe."

Delilah likes the sound of this word. Barrens. It sounds dangerous, somehow.

"Hey there, Mac!" her mother calls from the porch.

He turns toward the shack, his arms still full of wood. "Hey yourself!" he calls back. "What's the princess of Yellowknife doing up there in her castle?"

"Come on in here and see!" Annie does a little spin, her skirt swirling.

"She's baking a hundred loaves of bread," Delilah says.

"Ah," her dad says. "That's okay. We can always give some away. It's great she's settling in." Delilah rolls her eyes. He dumps the wood and heads to the house, calling over his shoulder to Will, "Be right back, man."

"Sure thing," Will says from beside the truck.

The wind picks up, and Delilah can hear the chimes starting.

"You know why those chimes are there, kid?" Will starts loading up his arms with firewood.

She shivers. "No."

He gestures to Delilah with his chin. "Come give me a hand, will you? Load me up. It'll go faster."

She walks to the back of the truck. He holds his arms out like he's offering her something. She picks up a chunk of wood and places it awkwardly on top of the others.

"That's right. Get as many as you can on there."

When he's fully loaded she follows him to the side of the house. She sees that the white cabin next door has a sagging porch and two broken stairs, a blanket over the window. There's a cooking pot and the cracked ribs of a broken lawn chair resting on the ground in the yard.

"Martha Shearwater's place," Will says as he dumps the load and starts stacking it on the woodpile.

"I think I heard her this morning," she says. "She was calling someone's name."

"That'd be Charlie. He goes out every morning. Walks uptown and goes for coffee. He tells her where he's going, but she forgets. Calls him, goes looking. Phones people, knocks on doors. Been doing it for years. She thinks he's run out on her. God forbid she's still in a bad mood when he comes back home."

Delilah thinks about this a minute, about waking up every morning and thinking you've been left. "That's sad."

He piles the last piece on top of the stack. "No shortage of sad things, kid."

"You know her?"

He brushes his hand on his filthy jeans and grins at her. "I know everybody."

"What about the wind chimes?"

"Right. So Josie Apple, she was an old-timer back

from the gold rush days. She claimed that wind chimes were used in ancient India and China to scare away the evil spirits. She put up as many as she could fit because she believed bad spirits are always after us, trying to make us do bad things. Trying to hurt us. She figured if she protected herself then nothing bad would happen. You believe in that kinda thing?"

"I don't know."

"Yeah," he says. "Most folks say that. Or they say it's a bunch of superstition." He points up the hill toward the shack. "But you know something funny?"

She follows his gaze to where the chimes are dancing under the eaves, playing their strange symphony of wood and bone.

"Those chimes have been there ever since she died nine years ago. Five different people have lived in that house since, and not one of them has taken them down. What do you make of that?"

She watches the chimes. "That maybe . . . people don't want to believe in those kinds of things, but they're scared they might be true?"

"Right you are, kid." He starts walking to his truck. "Okay. I'm all done here. The rest of the wood is for someone else."

She doesn't want him to go. She wants him to stay so she doesn't have to go back inside and watch her father praise Annie for all the unnecessary bread.

But she can't think of anything else to say. Will lets the husky jump into the back of the truck before he hops in the cab and slams his door shut. "I'll see you around," he calls from his open window.

She watches him drive away, mud spinning from his tires, until he disappears over the hill.

***

DELILAH SITS ON A battered couch, clutching a towel and a big bottle of discount apple-scented shampoo. She is mortified to be sitting in a stranger's house waiting to use their shower. She imagines hair in the bathtub, crumpled tissue in the garbage. But for a week she's been splashing cold water on herself every morning from a chipped basin, and she needs to wash her hair before she starts school on Monday. The last time she washed it had been the motel in Fort Providence. The lank, greasy strands are pulled back into a lumpy ponytail now. Her dad had offered to heat up buckets of hot water and drag the aluminum tub out, but there is no way she's having a bath in the living room. The stranger's shower is the lesser of the two evils.

There are cozy blankets thrown over couches and chairs, the walls covered in stained and curling nautical maps and large, abstract paintings of naked women. Mac told her the owners of this ramshackle house on Yellowknife Bay are Red and Maggie and their thirteen-year-old son, Jones. He said she would have met them already, but the family has been away visiting friends.

Mac has been having showers at Red and Maggie's ever since he moved to Yellowknife. "That's what people do here, Lila," he had said as the three of them drove the bumpy road from home. "That's why we're here. It's all about community in Old Town, people working together to survive the harsh elements. This is uncharted territory. A melting pot of folks from all over trying to make it in the big north."

Annie had smiled, trailing an arm out the window. "Well, my love," she said lazily, "if having to shower with our neighbours makes us a community, I'm all for it."

"Why?" Delilah asked, trying to change the subject. "Why don't people have their own showers?"

"Running water is a challenge, like most things are here," he said. "Things that are easy in the city, that people don't think twice about, are a lot harder here. You see what I'm saying? Sometimes even finding a carton of eggs is a challenge. That's the beauty. You know?"

"No." Delilah couldn't see how a lack of eggs was beautiful.

"Red's a fisherman," Mac said to Annie as they chugged around a corner. "Salt of the earth. Grew up on a farm in Saskatchewan. You'll like him."

He was always trying too hard, Delilah thought. It mattered too much to him that Annie liked everything he wanted her to like. Annie didn't respond, gazing out the window, her floppy suede hat pulled down over her hair. She hummed to herself softly.

Annie had been quieting down. It's what usually happened after what Mac brushed off as a "creative burst." Days of frantic activity followed by some sort of artistic episode. After two more days of baking, she had started putting shelf paper in the crooked cupboards, sweeping out dark corners, scraping black stuff from the windowsills. The day before, she had washed all their clothes in a plastic tub outside in the yard with a bar of Ivory before hanging them on a line in the back. Delilah wants to believe this means Annie will want to stay, but she knows it doesn't mean anything at all.

Once, in Toronto, Annie had spent two days waxing the floors and washing the drapes by hand before making a three-foot-high sculpture of a rose bush out of whole-wheat macaroni and Delilah's kindergarten glue. Once it was a small rock waterfall in the backyard of their Winnipeg house. Last night it had been sketches. Dozens of them, all of the vacant lot out back with the rock beside it. They were strewn across the living room floor now, abandoned by Annie when she finally fell asleep on the couch after hours of sitting and chewing her hair while she sifted through them, asking Delilah and Mac their opinions on the best one, the shading techniques, the composition.

"Maggie's an artist too," Mac said, reaching over to trace the brim of Annie's hat with his calloused finger. "She's from Montreal. Used to be a nurse until they came here."

"Mmm," Annie said. "What does she do?"

"Paints, I think. They have big canvases up all over their place. You two'll get along just fine."

In the back seat, Delilah had watched Bessie's little checked curtains flutter in the breeze and kept the hood of her red parka pulled tight around her head. She was getting used to the tickly feeling of the fur around the hood. Her mom bought it for her at Second Hand Rose, a thrift store uptown. She liked the jacket, even though it was red. She would have preferred blue, but they didn't have a blue one.

"Beggars can't be choosers, Delilah," her mom had said, inspecting a long silky dress printed with daisies.

"Are we beggars?" Delilah had asked.

Her mom had just laughed. Delilah knew they didn't have much money. She knew there were student loans and bank loans from when her dad tried to start one of his businesses. They always shopped at thrift stores, but Annie told her it was because she believed in sharing, reusing, being kind to the environment. She gave the same explanation for why they often lived with other people in co-op rental houses. Delilah's friends usually lived in houses with their parents and maybe a sibling or two. A dog, perhaps. But not other families, or lone drifters who slept on their couches, played their records and made giant communal pots of lentil stew.

Here in Yellowknife, though, the definition between what Delilah would call rich and poor wasn't as clear as in the cities. She would have thought, because the newer, fancier "regular" houses were uptown, that all the people uptown had lots of money, while the people who lived in the shacks with the knotholes in their walls would be poor. But it wasn't necessarily the case.

Her dad had told her, for instance, that Josie Apple, former resident of the green shack, had hidden jars of cash under the floor in the back bedroom for years, money she saved up from cooking out in bush camps, plus money her husband Walt made from the mines. Uptown, aside from the government workers and the mining bosses, were a lot of young families trying to get by. They didn't want to live down where the shacks were, so they had higher rent and some of them could barely make it. Lots of people had left Old Town over the years, Mac said. Lots of people came and went. He said every season a few new Yellowknifers were born, but lots of them died away.

***

RED AND MAGGIE'S IS a little shack by the water, the ghosts of fishing equipment in a heap in their front yard, a lean-to filled with wood against the house. Red, a thin man with coppery hair and a beard even longer than Mac's, had pumped Delilah's small hand in his own enthusiastically. Maggie, with her gauzy skirts and long dark curls and her French accent, reminded Delilah of a princess in second-hand clothes. There was something deeply dignified yet carefree about her. She seemed to be exactly where she wanted to be, barefoot in the cool May air. Maggie and Annie had hugged as though they were old friends.

Now her dad and Red and Maggie are laughing and drinking dandelion wine in the small kitchen while Annie showers. Delilah sits on the lumpy couch and tries to read the nautical maps, which is impossible. There are lines of tiny numbers and words she's not sure of. *Sounding line. Magnetic north. Fathom.*

She's squinting at the one nearest to her when a gangly boy bursts through the door, a shock of red hair around his freckled face, his entire body covered with dirt. Both knees of his jeans are torn and blood seeps from the jagged denim holes.

He stops short. "Who are you?"

She hugs her shampoo closer. "Mac's daughter. We're here to use your shower."

"Oh."

Dirt is encrusted in every nail; dust coats his hair and eyebrows.

"What happened to you?" she asks.

He looks past her toward the kitchen as a peal of Maggie's laughter trickles out. "It's a long story."

She wouldn't mind hearing his long story. Anything that doesn't involve politics of the north and the Berger Inquiry and gold mining operations and charcoal versus pastel.

The boy sits on the other end of the couch. His filthy sneaker taps on the orange shag carpet, and the rest of him seems to be hovering like a bee, barely touching down. Delilah has the sense that if she moves too suddenly he will fly away, not out of timidity, but out of some sense of urgency and importance. She doesn't want to accidentally remind him he should be somewhere else.

"Who are you again?" he asks.

"Delilah."

"Really?"

"Yes. Why? It's a name." *Like Jones isn't a weird name,* she thinks.

"Isn't that a Bible name?"

"Yeah."

"Wasn't she the one who shaved off that guy's hair and made him weak?"

"Yes. But I . . . they didn't name me after her. My mom just liked the name. Plus, she says that the Bible Delilah wasn't evil or anything. She was just trying to make a few bucks."

Red comes through the door from the kitchen and ruffles the boy's already messy hair.

"Hey, hey, there Jonesy. What the hell happened to you? You fall in a dumpster?"

"What happened to who?" Maggie floats out of the kitchen with a bunch of celery in her hand, Mac following behind. He heads down the hall, probably to check on Annie, who is taking forever.

"Your kid," Red says. "Take a look at him."

Maggie shakes her head. "Crazy boy. You're going to get killed out there. What were you up to?"

He shrugs.

She waves the celery at him. "Okay, Jonesy. I'll make you some soup. This is the best I can do. I relinquish control." She returns to the kitchen.

"Well, I'm gonna take off," Jones says. He's already heading for the door.

"Hold it," Red says. He points at Delilah. She tries to squirm into the couch cushion and disappear. She knows what's coming.

"What?" Jones asks.

"Take her with you. She doesn't know anyone here. Take her down to the docks or over to Weaver's or something."

"Oh, no, that's okay," Delilah says. "I'm waiting for my shower anyhow. I think we have to get going soon." She peers down the darkened hallway where her mother disappeared so long ago.

Red laughs. "Well, if you want hot water, you're gonna have to wait until after dinner. You can only take two showers here before you run out. It's a good tank, but it's not huge. This ain't the Hilton!"

After dinner? They're staying for dinner? She remembers the celery stalks Maggie had been waving around. She's making soup. And she just started. It could be hours.

"Go on," Red says on his way back to the kitchen. "Jonesy won't bite."

Jones and Delilah stare at each other. "Come on then," he says.

Delilah dumps her towel and shampoo bottle on the couch, miserable. The smell of pot wafts through the beaded curtain hanging in the doorway to the kitchen.

They head out into the afternoon sun, Delilah pulling her rainbow sweater around her. She left her parka at Red and Maggie's. Her rubber boots slog through the thick mud on the dirt road. Dogs bark from a handmade pen on the neighbour's property, about ten or twelve of them from what Delilah can see. They're beautiful silvery white huskies, and she stops a few feet from their pen.

"Can we pet them?"

They bark vigorously, but some of their tails are wagging.

Jones turns. He's been walking several feet in front of her. "Are you nuts? No. You have to know them. They would attack you without even thinking about it." She pulls her sweater tighter, trying to hide the cloud buttons. "Come on," he says. He stays closer this time.

At Weaver's, Jones buys her a Coke with the handful of change he has in his back pocket. They browse the magazines, the rows of lights above their head trapped under metal cages and humming like busy mosquitoes.

She sneaks peeks at Jones over her *Betty and Veronica Summer Digest*. His hands are still covered in grime, his mother's demand ignored. He flips through a movie magazine with *Star Wars* on the cover. A jagged cut criss-crosses the length of his left thumb. When he's flipped to the last page he closes it and puts it back on the shelf.

"Let's go."

They wander the road in silence, sipping Coke. They pass a man lying under a rusty old-fashioned truck, his unlaced boots sticking out underneath. A small child wearing only an undershirt and yellow rubber boots is running circles around the truck holding an empty beer bottle upside down and singing "Husha, husha, we all fall down!"

As they approach Jones's shack near the shore, there are crooked docks jutting out over the thin, broken ice of the quiet lake, fishing boats tied to them, men and women calling to each other and hauling gear.

Delilah closes her eyes for a second and listens. She hears the demanding singsong of the child, a man from the fishboats yelling "Lenny! The beer ain't gonna walk to you," a dog barking. She smells freshness, lake water, sunshine on warm rock.

Her toe catches on something and she stumbles, lurching forward. She looks around her feet, embarrassed. Jones assesses her again with his green eyes narrowed. "You're kinda spaced out, aren't you?"

There it is. A small rock the size of her fist.

"Yeah," she says. "I guess."

He nods. Chews his injured thumb. He walks toward the house, where a bunch of rundown vehicles have appeared in their absence. She follows his skinny frame across his front lawn, watching for rocks and sidestepping a dismantled bicycle lying in a heap. An old oil barrel sits in the dry grass, flames licking its edges. As they approach the house, Red comes out holding a big pot, carefully, like he doesn't want to spill whatever's inside.

"Heya, guys. Good timing. Jonesy, go shuck some corn. Your mother's got it inside there. Muddy brought it up on his latest trip from the big smoke. You can bring it out and chuck the husks in the fire." He sets the pot on a metal grate over the barrel.

"How much?"

"Oh, all of it, I think. City Jane and them are here too."

Jones hooks the edge of Delilah's sweater sleeve with his pinky, barely holding on before he lets go again. "C'mon."

He leads her inside where the kitchen is buzzing with laughing adults and thick with the smell of Drum tobacco. He weaves through the crowd but Delilah hangs back by the door.

Maggie is in mid-story at the stove, stirring her pot of soup and smacking away the hand of a short man with grubby work pants and a plaid shirt. "Four days in intensive care and this poor old man still can find the strength to slap my ass," she says. Her laugh is lyrical and sweet. Everyone seems riveted.

Delilah's dad is at the crowded kitchen table in his quilted work jacket with a bottle of beer. He seems to be having a serious conversation with a man with long, stringy hair and funny-looking eyes, watery and pale blue. He looks like he got something in them and hasn't had a chance to rinse them out.

Mac's voice rides the waves of the noisy crowd over to her like a radio signal she just tuned into. ". . . Have to be ready to take the risk . . . like anything else, you could win, you could lose, but . . . gold's not going anywhere, I'm just saying . . . yes, absolutely, politics are always a factor. In anything." Steady, calm, insistent.

Her dad rarely yells or even raises his voice, but sometimes Annie says things like, "Jeez, it must be nice to be right all the time, Mac. Tell us what that feels like."

Annie stands in the far corner, her hand on the shoulder of a man with his back to Delilah. Annie is looking at him intently, listening, really listening. Delilah knows that look. When Annie does it to her, it makes her feel like Annie is trying to crawl under her skin, be somehow absorbed by her.

The wafting smoke is making Delilah wheeze, and she wants to go back outside. She's jostled from behind. She turns, and there's Will in his fringed jacket, carrying a large aluminum roasting dish covered in foil.

"Sorry, kid."

Maggie yells hello from the stove, and Will raises the dish.

"Got it," he says above the voices.

"Yes!" she shouts. "Red's starting the fire. You can bring it to him, he will cook it up."

Will jiggles the dish at Delilah. "Want some?"

"What is it?"

Her dad has noticed her from across the room now and gives her a wave. The watery-eyed man downs the rest of his beer and lights a smoke.

"Caribou," Will says. His round face is pockmarked, Delilah notices. It's rough, like small chips in smooth pottery. He has a scar by his left eye that cuts through the eyebrow. "You know all these folks yet?"

She shakes her head. He shifts the dish to his hip and points with his free hand, first at the watery-eyed man.

"That's Muddy. He works the ball mill with me and your dad. That man talking to your mom, that's Bear. He works out at Con Mines." He points over to a blond woman with her hair parted straight down the centre and feathered softly around her face. She's wearing bell-bottom jeans and a thick wool sweater with holes in it, but she's easily the prettiest woman in the room, or could at least give Annie a run for her money. "City Jane. Reporter for the *Yellowknife News*."

Maggie shrieks as Red grabs her from behind and tries to waltz through the room with her. City Jane hops down from the counter and walks over to them. She smiles and her teeth are white and perfect.

"Hi Will. You need a hand with the meat?"

"Nope, thanks anyways, but I'm gonna pass it off to the big man there." He walks past her, bumping her shoulder gently on the way by, and heads outside. Delilah can see Jane watching him as he goes.

Jones appears beside Delilah, swinging a bag full of shucked corn. "Come on, space cadet," he says. He drops the corn by his mother's feet, and Delilah follows him out the door.

Outside the air is cooler now, and Delilah tries to take a deep breath and roots around in her sweater pocket for her inhaler. She wonders if she should go find her parka. The other guests are trickling out of the house, and more have come from neighbouring shacks. The yard in front of Jones's house is like an outdoor living room. There is a listing picnic table and an old kitchen table with rickety chairs that people seem to be carrying over from their houses. Red is forking hunks of dripping meat onto the grill on the rusty barrel.

Soon everyone is outside, seated around a big open fire that someone has started in a pit. Steaming platters are on the picnic table, a giant bowl of bright yellow corn, Maggie's soup and a collection of mugs to eat it out of, a stack of half-charred meat, boiled potatoes, and salads.

Delilah sits on a log by the fire and chews on a piece of the caribou. It's delicious, cooked in some kind of sweet, tangy sauce. Will comes over with a loaded plate and settles beside her on a lawn chair. There's a woman with him, plump and much shorter than him. Her hair is in long braids on either side of her face. She's wearing layers of skirts, moccasins, and a man's blue ski jacket. Will's silver dog curls at his feet.

"Good meat, eh?" he says.

Delilah nods. She's watching the dog. "Is it friendly?"

"What, Laska?" Will picks up a cob of corn. It drips salty butter onto his plate. "Laska never hurt a fly. Chased a bear out to hell and gone a few times, though."

The woman laughs and pats Laska on the head. "Good dog. She's a good dog, Laska."

Will takes a bite of corn, then wipes his mouth with the back of his hand. "This is my sister, Mary Ellen."

Delilah raises her hand. "Hello."

"Mary Ellen, this is Delilah. Mac's girl."

The woman reaches across Will for Delilah's hand. She's beaming, little crinkles around her eyes. She looks older than Will, who Delilah figures must be around thirty-five like her dad. She reaches out her hand, and Mary Ellen clasps it tightly above Will's plate of food. She doesn't say anything.

Finally Will says, "Okay, let me eat."

Mary Ellen releases Delilah. "Eat! Yes, eat, eat."

"Are you going to eat something?" Delilah asks politely. The woman doesn't have a plate of food.

But Mary Ellen is gazing off at something across the yard and doesn't respond. She rises from her chair and wanders over to where some children are playing with an old hula hoop.

Delilah feels there's something different about her. When they lived in a housing co-op in Victoria there had been a woman who always wanted to play with Delilah's dolls in the common room. She would pick them up and dress them and undress them, sing to them softly. Delilah hadn't liked it because she didn't understand why she had to share with an adult. Annie had explained that the woman looked like an adult but she was a child on the inside. She told Delilah to treat her as she would treat another little girl, respectfully and kindly. If another seven-year-old took Delilah's doll, she would have grabbed it back, but even at that age she had understood the difference.

"She doesn't say much," Will says. "She likes to take care of people. Feed them, make them things, give them jam. She lives next door to me with our brother Jethro."

He points with the corncob toward a thin, grey-haired man standing by the front porch smoking. He looks at least ten years older than Will.

Delilah takes a delicate bite of potato. She wonders where Jones is and sees that he has been pulled into his mother's lap on the other side of the fire. He looks mortified. City Jane is singing softly while someone plays a guitar. The sun slips below the hills on the bay, turning the sky a pale yellow.

Annie has been curled beside Mac in an old easy chair, but she wanders up to Delilah and Will now, a mason jar of red wine in her hand.

"Well, hello," she says, easing gracefully into the chair Mary Ellen left behind. She takes a sip of wine and runs her fingers through her long hair. "How's everyone doing over here? It's Will, right? You gave us directions when we rolled into town." She extends a pale hand to Will.

He takes it, shakes it once, and releases it. "Yup. How'd the bread turn out?"

Annie smiles, the tiny dimple showing in her left cheek. "Perfectly. Bread isn't easy. It's a skill I learned from my pioneer grandmother."

This is the first Delilah's heard of a pioneer grandmother.

"The music is great," Annie says. "Makes me want to dance." Her body moves gently from side to side. "You know the musicians?"

"I know everyone," he says.

Go away, Delilah urges her mother silently. *Don't do this.*

The drums are louder now, pounding across the yard. Annie stands. "I have to go. The beat is calling me." She reaches her hands out toward Will and Delilah and swings her hips. "Come join me?"

"No," Delilah says, panicking. No in so many ways. Don't ask me to dance. Don't ask him to dance. Don't *dance*.

Why couldn't she leave people alone? Men especially. Why couldn't she just go sit with her husband? Mac never said anything when Annie draped herself across men's laps at parties, danced next to them like a slinky cat. When Delilah would look at him to gauge his reaction, it always seemed like he was shrugging it off, putting on a show of laughing at his wild, untameable artist wife, but she could see the hurt under the surface.

Delilah's glance flickers across to where Jones is sitting eating his corn, free from his mother's embrace.

"Not much of a dancer," Will says to Annie. "Got a bit of that . . . what's the expression? Bull in a china shop thing going on."

Annie turns, swaying, her arms raised above her head. "Too bad," she calls over her shoulder.

Delilah lets out her breath slowly, her pulse racing, fire in her veins. She tracks her mother to see who she will move on to next, but Annie disappears into a group of people beside Red and Maggie's shack.

Will looks over at her. She can't tell what he's thinking. Laska is still sitting at her feet. The dog looks up at Delilah with those crystalline blue eyes. People eyes. Her ears are cocked like she's listening to something carefully. Delilah reaches out her hand tentatively so the dog can smell her. Laska leans forward and licks the remnants of the barbecue sauce from Delilah's fingers.

Delilah smiles. "She likes the meat."

"Yup." Will saws at his steak and offers a small morsel to Laska with his big fingers. She takes it gently between her teeth.

"Why is her name Laska?"

He doesn't answer right away, placing his plate on the ground by his feet, taking a small leather pouch out of his jacket pocket and rolling a cigarette. Someone offers him a beer, and he takes it, settling it between his thighs while he lights his smoke.

"Little girl named her. Name was Alaska but the kid couldn't say it."

"Whose little girl?"

Will exhales a long stream of smoke and pulls a thread of tobacco off his tongue. In the firelight his face is softened, the scars barely noticeable. He watches the sparks dance.

"Mine."

Delilah looks over to where the small gang of children is playing. A couple of them are wrestling, rolling in the dust, and two girls are playing a clapping game. Mary Ellen stands by them and claps along. "Is she here?"

"No," he says. "She's gone."

Delilah feels the sadness of this small word. It nestles in her belly like a stone. "Oh," she says. "Gone away?"

"That's right."

"Where?"

He takes a swig of beer. "Seattle, last I heard."

Delilah is confused. How can you not know where your own child is? "Is she coming back?"

"That's the plan, kid."

Delilah considers this. That it would be "the plan" that your child was coming back to you, but not a certainty. That you wouldn't know for sure.

"How long has it been since you saw her?" she asks. "How old is she?" She wonders if they could have been friends here. Or still could.

Will smiles. "You like the questions, don't you? You might wanna talk to City Jane about being a reporter."

He grinds his beer bottle into the dirt by his chair. "Been about two years now. Left here in the summertime two years back with her mom. She's eight. Birthday last week. Taurus. Stubborn as hell, just like her dad."

Delilah can feel something like pride in the way he talks about her. Something full, like he's brimming up with the thought of her. But then a hollowness because she's not there. Delilah knows about loving something—someone—that's not there. She felt it when she thought of her dad while she was in Vancouver. Wishing he'd walk in the door and surprise them like they did to him when they came to Yellowknife.

"I'm a Leo," Delilah says.

"That so?" he says, glancing at her. "Then you're stubborn as hell too."

It warms her up inside, thinking she has something in common with Will's lost girl.

Across the way the musicians are multiplying. Someone is playing a silver flute, and Muddy taps spoons on his knee. A man with wild black dreadlocks is pounding on the big wooden bongos. They play faster and faster as the sun finally sinks below the back of the house. Annie is dancing all alone by the fire, eyes closed, her long skirts flying.

June

AFTER TWO WEEKS AT Mildred Hall Elementary School, it becomes clear to Delilah that there is some sort of dividing line between Old Town and uptown, and she is on the wrong side of it.

After vague interest from several groups of girls on the first day, they seem to all have decided she is boring. She isn't good at sports, she's quiet, she doesn't have stylish clothes, and she isn't from anywhere interesting like Irish Jimmy.

Sometimes when she is weaving through unfamiliar children, she feels as though she isn't there at all. As though if someone reached out a hand, it would go right through her. This sense of invisibility has always made her panic. It makes her want to do something ridiculous so people see her. A handstand in the crowded hallway. A spontaneous performance of the national anthem.

Delilah always hated playing hide-and-seek for this exact reason. When she was little it terrified her, or at least once she had finally figured out how to play. She used to stand in the middle of the room while her mother counted. *One, two, three, four, five, six . . . ready or not, here I come!* And there Delilah would be, standing not five feet from Annie, her hands over her own eyes. She still remembers believing that nobody could see her if she couldn't see them. Believing that she was safe as long as she didn't look.

Annie would play along, saying, "Where could that Delilah be . . . where on earth could she be? Is she under the couch? No. Is she on the bookshelf? No . . ."

Delilah would stand like a tiny volcano ready to erupt with glee until finally she would open her eyes and shout, "I'm here! I'm right here!"

But Annie would continue the game. Pretend she couldn't see her. "I still don't see that silly girl," she would say, looking over Delilah's head. The glee would vanish, and terror would take its place. How could her mother not see her if she was standing right in front of her?

Later, when she would play with whatever tie-dyed, long-haired children they lived with, Delilah would only hide places that were obvious. She would hide behind a chair but stick her foot out where it could be seen, or hide in a closet and cough when the seeker ran by. They would tease her and tell her how terrible she was at the game, but Delilah couldn't explain to them that she had no interest in being lost. The only part of the game she liked was when they finally found her.

Today she is approached on the field at the end of lunch hour as her classmates gather for gym. Jones is nowhere to be seen. He is in her class, thank God, but most lunch hours he disappears behind the school to the woods. He seems to be considered weird and untouchable. He isn't bullied exactly but, like her, is utterly and completely ignored. That he chooses to disappear at every opportunity is no surprise to Delilah.

Three uptown girls walk over to her, all children of Giant Mine executives, one of them a horsey girl named Misty, the other two chubby, pink-cheeked, and named Tammy and Heather. She feels a rush of hope that maybe they have decided to give her a chance. Maybe they're going to invite her to Mr. Mike's for fries after school.

Misty looks Delilah up and down. "Delores, right?"

Delilah looks down at her blue cotton dress, her thick wool tights, her heavy rubber boots.

"No," she says. "Delilah."

She steels herself, looking beyond the girls and their long, wavy hair, their tube tops and short skirts under winter jackets, scanning the field for an ally or even a teacher.

"Nice tights," Heather says. "Do you always wear your long johns to school?"

Delilah says nothing, a red flush creeping up from her chest, the blood in her own body betraying her. She knows now there will be no Mr. Mike's invitation.

"Did you hear her, *Delores*?" Misty says, aggressive now.

The bell rings, and the gym teacher starts putting out the bases for a softball game. More kids are milling in groups, but no one comes near them.

"I'm sorry, I can't hear you, little mousie. Can you hear her, Heather?"

Misty grabs Delilah's thin wrist and comes close, leans in to whisper something savage in Delilah's ear. Her silver hoop earring grazes Delilah's cheek and suddenly Jones is there and grabbing Misty's wrist, the hand holding Delilah's, and twisting it until she lets go.

She gives an outraged shriek. "You little penis," she shouts, breaking free. "You can't do that. You can't hit a girl."

"I didn't hit you."

"It's practically the same thing, you retard!"

The teacher has heard them. She strides toward them, her giant thigh muscles working under her gym shorts, a stack of orange cones in her hands. "Hey! What's going on over here?"

Jones, with his mussed hair and the rumpled Atari shirt he has been wearing for four days, says, "Nothing."

A torrent of accusations come from Misty's frosted lips. They are all sent to the office, where Delilah says nothing and Jones admits freely to twisting Misty's wrist. Misty bursts into tears, cradling her hand as though it were a fragile broken bird. Jones receives detention; the girls are all released back to class. On the way down the hall Misty closes in on Delilah. "You and your dirty little weirdo boyfriend are so dead," she hisses before joining the other two girls.

Delilah lingers in the hall on the shiny polished floors, listening to the low and steady hum of teachers in the classrooms. Her skin feels translucent, like rice paper. It could crack and split open at any moment. She holds her own sore wrist, touches the place that was pressed into. Feels that small knot of pain.

✳✳✳

DESPITE MISTY, DELILAH DOESN'T miss Vancouver. Sometimes she would miss places when they left, like Toronto with the wood floors she could glide on with her socks, twirling like a figure skater down the long hall. And the butterfly stained glass taking flight above the doorway. Or Winnipeg with the teacher who let the kids call him Andrew and played Rolling Stones tapes in the classroom and gave them Smarties if they got good marks on their Friday spelling tests. They had lived in a house there with a single mother and her two daughters. One of them had been the same age as Delilah, the other a year younger. Franny and Alice. They had all shared a room and called themselves triplets. At night, by flashlight under their blanket forts, they made pinky swears to live in that creaky old house together for the rest of their lives. Delilah and her parents were there for five months before they moved again, Delilah crying all the way to the airport.

But Vancouver had meant her dad was gone away to work in Yellowknife, and it meant being left alone for hours on weekends and evenings while Annie was at art school. Vancouver was Annie and the roommates drinking and debating in the kitchen with candles stuck in wine bottles till all hours, smoking pot and spilling their drinks on Delilah's homework. Vancouver, worst of all, was Marcel. It was Annie slowly spiralling and nobody for Delilah to talk to about it.

Once, before it got really bad, Annie took Delilah out late on a Tuesday night to a little underground café with wine served in coffee mugs and plants hanging from the roof. Marcel and Jackie came with them, and Delilah remembers Marcel complaining to the waitress about their wine list. A woman came out and stood on the stage in a simple dress that looked like the one Alice wore on *The Brady Bunch*, with a little scalloped apron. She looked like she was about to cook a roast beef dinner, except she had bare feet and her hair hung loose around her face. But after everyone waited for what seemed like forever to Delilah, the woman opened her pretty mouth and screamed. For a long, long time without stopping.

At first, horrified, Delilah had watched, thinking that surely it would end soon, that the woman was pretending to see something that scared her, and the play would carry on from there. But soon she realized this *was* the play. There was nothing but the screaming.

Delilah had covered her ears and pressed her forehead to the table, but the sound bounced off every hard surface, every tabletop and coffee mug, every plate and fork that people casually continued eating with, taking bites of brownie, homemade apple crisp. When it was over, Delilah looked up and the woman was smiling pleasantly, as though she had just taken the perfect roast out of the oven and was so glad she could share it with everyone.

People murmured and applauded, and the adults at Delilah's table said things like, "Wow, man. Yeah." Marcel clapped, too loud and somehow offbeat. Jackie was whistling her approval.

Annie was looking off into space and nodding. Then she patted Delilah's hand. "You'll understand that someday, little bird. You'll be glad you saw that. Art is not always comfortable."

But now women who wore black dresses with black tights and chain-smoked Indian cigarettes and used words like *chiaroscuro* have been replaced with women who wear coveralls and thick sweaters and have long, shining hair and bright eyes. They run dog teams, chop their own wood, butcher caribou in their front yards in Old Town, the bowls of dripping meat scattered across makeshift plywood tables.

Here the evenings are filled with big dinners with the Old Towners and trips out in Red's fishing boat to see the islands. Here she has Jones, and on weekends, they walk uptown and wander around the drugstore, buy takeout eggrolls from the Gold Range, and drink Cokes at Mr. Mike's, avoiding the other kids.

This is the first time in a long time she hasn't wished she was somewhere else.

DELILAH HAS PICKED UP some sort of undercurrent she doesn't understand since she and Annie settled into the shack. She sensed it first in Annie's almost aggressive takeover of the house, the way she started rearranging things the minute they moved in. She pronounced the sagging living room sofa "mangy" and the next day found a couple of strong guys to haul it out to the side of the road, where it disappeared within hours. She hung batik on the walls, unpacked her art and photography books onto the one long shelf in the cramped living room, and transferred flour and oats into large glass jars that she displayed on the listing kitchen counter.

Annie walks through Old Town taking photos and then drops the film off to be developed. When she gets the photos back, she leaves them spread across the coffee table, on the kitchen table, on the floor. There are photos of fireweed, shrubs, a whole series of the grey rock taken behind their house at the pilots' monument. She flips through them absently, a cigarette in her mouth, mugs of thick black coffee beside her. She flips and flips, as though she's looking for something she can't find.

At breakfast one morning, Delilah watches her mother play with a camera lens, cleaning it, taking it apart, cleaning it again. Mac is leafing through a geology book. Delilah eats her blackened toast, cooked on a wire camping toaster that sits over the element and never toasts evenly. She spreads more marmalade over the cold margarine.

Annie looks through the lens at Delilah, takes it down, blows on it delicately, and wipes it again. "I think I'll go get a job today," Annie says, setting her lens on the table.

Mac looks up, his finger holding the place in his book. "A job? Why?"

"I want to." Annie rubs her temples, then folds her hands together on the table. "I'm bored."

Delilah puts down her toast, leaving it with the singed crusts on her plate. Bored isn't good. Bored is what happens right before Annie starts making crazy plans. Getting a job might make her settle in, but what job can she get? Flower photographer? Lake sketcher? Delilah knew they had lived on student loans and art grants from the government the whole time they were in Vancouver, plus whatever her dad could send them. Mac has always been the one with the jobs.

Mac laughs, but nervously, Delilah notes. "Bored already?"

"It's a big change from the city, James, you have to admit." She sweeps her arm around the room, past the snowshoes mounted on the wall, the milk crate bookshelves, the rickety tin airtight stove with a half-rusted pipe.

"True enough," Mac concedes. "Where do you want to work?"

Annie shrugs. "Anywhere." She brushes a stray strand of hair off her face and takes a sip of coffee.

Mac's hand is still resting on a page of his book that features photographs of rock samples. Delilah wonders how that could possibly be interesting to him. There's so much rock here in Yellowknife, every step you take it's underneath you. Their shack is built right into it.

"All right," Mac says with a tinge of wariness that doesn't go unnoticed by Delilah. "But you don't have to. We're doing okay. I'm working more shifts. I don't want you to think you have to. And I'm going away in a few weeks, remember?"

He is working more. Heading off to the mine at all different times of the day and night. He told them he's saving up. For what, she's not sure.

"So?" Annie takes another sip of coffee, then turns the mug to inspect it. She wipes something from the rim with her sleeve.

"So . . . Delilah. That's all I was thinking."

"She'll be fine. She's almost thirteen. I'm not going to take a night job as a janitor."

"Right, I just thought . . . you said *anything*."

"Anything within reason." Annie stands and dumps her cup in the sink. She clicks a fingernail on the counter as she looks out the small, grubby window. "How long are you gone?"

Mac closes the book. "Three, four days tops."

He's excited. All he does, practically since they got there, is talk about that trip when he's not at work. He hasn't replaced Delilah's bed yet. And there is still just a curtain for privacy in their honey-bucket room. It's mostly Barrens this and Barrens that, especially when Will comes over. Mac is always showing Delilah rocks, explaining how they take samples for the company and some for themselves and then send them off to the labs when they get back. Cross their fingers and hope for the best. He said finding a mine is like finding a needle in a haystack. A gold vein in a million acres of rock. But still. It happens.

It's curious to Delilah why her mother doesn't seem to want Mac to go on this trip. Annie's irritation with Mac's plans is nothing new, but her sullenness confuses Delilah.

"Why can't I come?" she asks her dad, hoping to lighten the mood. She's already asked twice and been turned down because he doesn't want her to miss school.

"Still no," he tells her.

"I want to see the Barrens too. It sounds pretty."

"It is pretty," he says. "It's beyond pretty. Takes your breath away. But we're going to be working and—"

"Just take her," Annie says. "What's the big deal?" She pours some water from a jug into her cup and rinses it roughly. "One of us should be getting some adventure."

"Well, you can come too," Mac says. "There's room in the plane. We could all go. I can ask Muddy . . ."

"No," Annie says. She walks over and takes Delilah's face in her hands, cradles it. Delilah can smell Sunlight soap. Annie kisses her on the cheek. "Just take the little bird."

She leaves the room. Her camera is on the table, lenses lined up as though they're waiting for something important to happen. Annie's restlessness waves like a small red flag in the back of Delilah's mind.

※※※

DELILAH IS CHOPPING VEGETABLES with Will at Jethro and Mary Ellen's. Jethro and Mac are outside by the lake looking at Jethro's canoe. He made it himself, so Mac wanted to see it. He said he wanted to make his own one day, which was news to Delilah. Mary Ellen is showing Annie her small garden plots in front of the house, still withered and dead from the summer before. She had led Annie out of the house by the hand like a child.

Delilah likes it here. It's a cozy three-room shack, filled with what her mom would call junk. Piles of fishing rods and tackle boxes by the door. Cardboard boxes stacked on either side of the sagging plaid couch for end tables. A collection of stuffed animals and old dolls spilling off a shelf above an old TV. A cotton sheet hung clumsily in the window for a curtain.

Delilah transfers the carrots she's been chopping to a large green plastic bowl and picks up a plump cucumber. "Slices or chunks?" she asks Will, who is rooting around in the refrigerator.

"All goes to the same place. Don't think it matters, kid."

She turns back to her cutting board, considering. Slices, she decides. She cuts thin pieces and carefully layers them over the carrots. It's a rainy, cool day, and the cabin is filled with a warm earthy smell coming from the oven. Will opens it to check on dinner. She glances over and sees a big roast with root vegetables simmering in rich gravy.

"What kind of meat is that?" she asks.

"Moose," he says, testing the roast with a charred wooden spoon. He slides the rack back into the oven and closes the door. "How's that salad coming along? Never knew you were a vegetable artist. You got an exhibit coming up?"

She smiles and keeps slicing. Moose. She doesn't know if she can eat a moose. But she doesn't want to be rude. Would it make her gag? The thought of it makes her gag. It smells so good, though . . .

Will rinses a bunch of radishes in the plastic basin sink and then plunks them in front of Delilah. "You can make those into flowers or something."

"I'm not *that* good," she says.

"Practice makes perfect." He leans against the plywood counter and takes a swig of beer, looking out over the lake through the window across the room.

"Hey, Will?"

"Yeah?" He's still watching something. Delilah turns and sees it's Jethro and her dad talking by the shore.

"What kind of feathers are those?" She points to a bunch of feathers, at least twenty of them, held together with ribbon and hanging in the corner above the front door.

"Duck," he says.

"Duck?" This seems strange to her. Duck feathers don't seem special enough to hang by your door. Eagles, maybe. Hawks. "Why are they there?"

"Clem collected them."

"Who's Clem?" She has started on the radishes, thicker slices so they crunch when you bite them, and they are so small they require concentration.

"My kid. Clementine."

The radish slips from Delilah's finger.

"Oh." Clementine. She's never heard her name. She likes it. It's old-fashioned and sweet. "She likes feathers?"

"Yeah." He sits at the rickety card table Jethro and Mary Ellen use as a kitchen table with his beer and picks up his tobacco. "Clem, she went through this phase once when she was two. Thought she was a duck. 'Put your shoes on,' I'd say, and she'd say, 'Quack.' 'Don't run in the kitchen,' Sarah'd say, and Clem'd quack as she ran by. Went on for a week. 'Your fault,' Sarah told me. 'Always taking her to see the ducks.'" He laughs and then pauses to lick the rolling paper and seal his cigarette. His Zippo flashes as he lights his smoke. Delilah is watching him, radishes forgotten.

"Lots of ducks at Frame Lake that spring. She watched them for hours, sitting still and quiet when they came peeping up from the water. She knew to be quiet. Seemed strange to me. Only two and she knew to be quiet." He looks at Delilah as though he wants her to agree, to understand how special it was that she knew this. "Clem watched the mom and dad ducks flap their wings and send up a spray when another group of ducks came by. 'Clem,' I told her. 'That mom and dad is just like your mom and dad. Keeping their babies safe.' Kid didn't say a thing until she got home and Sarah says, 'What do you want for lunch? Macaroni?' And Clem looks up and says, 'Quack.'" Will laughs, a deep belly laugh. Then he shakes his head. Takes a drag as he looks out toward the lake. "She had this runny nose and these giant black eyes always looking somewhere else. Looking at you and then behind you. Beside you. Wants to see it all at once. Trying to figure it all out. She collected those feathers. Made us keep every one. Gave a bunch to Mary Ellen."

Delilah is suddenly sad for Will and this big-eyed little girl. She wants to meet her. "When will you see her again?"

He stubs out his cigarette. "That is the million-dollar question, kid," he says, his tone harder. "Been two years. Sarah keeps saying she'll send her up for a visit, but then the plan always changes."

"Can't you go there?"

He stands. Takes another long sip of beer. "It's complicated. You about done with those vegetable flowers or what?"

She knows this means he's done talking about it now. She picks up a new radish and tries slicing tiny petals into its bright skin.

✻

DELILAH IS READING *Carrie* by the bright evening June sun coming through the living room window in the green shack. She is curled in the easy chair by the cold wood stove, Etta James on the battery-powered record player, and Annie is absently strumming Mac's battered old guitar, her back propped on a pillow against the arm of the couch, her bare feet in Mac's lap. Mac is giving her a foot massage, something she sometimes demands. "Be a love," she says in a bad English accent as she presses her feet into their laps.

Annie worked the dinner shift at the Wildcat Café in her platform velour boots, so her feet hurt. She brought home whitefish dinners and strawberry rhubarb pie wrapped in foil for their dinner. She seems happier now that she's working, and she takes as many shifts as possible.

"I know a good one," Annie says.

"A good what?" Mac asks. Delilah turns the page. It's the part at the farm with the pig and the bucket and the spurting blood. Her stomach, full of lemony fish and sweet pie, lurches.

"Thunder Bay," Annie says, strumming gently on the guitar. She can't play. Not any real songs, at least. Delilah has never seen her try to play a real song.

"What about it?" Mac asks.

"That night at the Chinese restaurant."

Delilah senses tension and watches out of the corner of her eye as Mac releases Annie's foot. It just sits there in his lap, pale and pretty, a thin silver chain looped daintily on her ankle. This is the most affectionate she has seen her parents since she and Annie arrived. She can't think of the last time they were all there together. If her mom is home, Mac is usually working, and vice versa.

"Come on, Annie," he says, like he's trying to keep things light. *Come on, Annie, let's all get along.*

"No, I'm just saying. You wanted an example, and that's a good one. You said, 'Give me some evidence that I make irresponsible decisions that affect the family.'" She's mocking him, but her tone is mild. Delilah turns another page and pretends to read.

"It was not an irresponsible decision." He sounds wounded. "It was a shitty situation, but I wasn't trying to be irresponsible."

Annie laughs, pulls her feet from his lap and sits up straight, setting the guitar against the arm of the couch. "Nobody tries to be irresponsible. It's not something people set out to do when they wake up in the morning. Delilah, do you remember that night in the Chinese restaurant?"

"Annie, come on," Mac says.

Delilah rolls her eyes behind her book. She doesn't want to be involved. Annie won't back down until she wins, and she always tries to drag Delilah in as a witness.

"No, I'm just wondering," Annie says. "She was three, so she might remember. I'm not persecuting you here, Mac, I'm just trying to give you some evidence. That's what you were asking for. Delilah? Do you remember?"

Delilah sets her book down, a flicker of anger twitching in her belly. She isn't sure how to answer. Saying no might help her dad, which she would rather do, if she has to choose. Saying yes might too, if she actually remembered and could say it wasn't bad, whatever it was. But she could easily be caught in the lie. "No," she says.

Annie tucks her long legs under her, her white cotton skirt flowing to the grubby shag carpet on the floor. "No? Well, it wasn't the end of the world. But I thought you might remember."

Mac lights a smoke and leans back, looking weary.

"So we were living in Thunder Bay, and it was winter and you were three. Your dad had this truck. An old Ford truck from the forties. He loved that truck. Didn't you love that truck?"

Mac doesn't answer, taking a long drag and looking out at the slowly sinking sun. It's around ten-thirty. Delilah wants to go to bed, but she feels cornered.

"He loved that truck. But it broke down all the time. Almost every time he went to start it, he had to go jiggle the battery cables and run back and forth until it started. We didn't go out much, you and me, Delilah, because we didn't know anyone there, and it was winter and it was viciously, unrelentingly cold. Your dad would go to work with this man, Gord, building a new Burger King or something downtown, and we didn't go out much. But this one night we had to do laundry, and your dad had to go help Gord move. Because his wife kicked him out. Is that right?"

"That's right," Mac says. He's resigned, Delilah can tell, because he knows she will tell the story whether he wants her to or not.

"So he says, 'I'll take you to the laundromat, and you can do the laundry while I help Gord.' There was a Chinese restaurant beside the laundromat, and I thought it would be fun for you and me to go have some sweet-and-sour chicken balls while we waited. As a treat."

A memory trickles into Delilah—a street light with snow falling around it, swirling down as she looked up, the flakes touching down delicately on her eyes as she blinked them away. A plate of sticky sweet chicken balls, her mother licking sauce from Delilah's pinky finger like a cat, both of them giggling.

"So we do the laundry, we have our chicken balls, but your dad doesn't come."

"Annie. Things happen. Cars break down."

"We wait with our big garbage bag of folded clothes in the restaurant, and the staff is getting antsy because they are supposed to close. It's nine, and he was supposed to be there at seven-thirty. And we don't have any money for a cab because we spent all our quarters at the laundromat. And there's a blizzard outside. A snowstorm. We live three miles away."

Delilah remembers being cold, remembers looking down at her pink snowsuit under that street light, watching the snow settle on it in tiny gentle drifts. She doesn't know if this was before or after the chicken balls. She doesn't even know if it was that night. She doesn't remember being worried or scared or upset that her dad had forgotten them.

"There was nothing I could do," Mac says. "It was ten years ago. I apologized. Profusely. I felt terrible." He stabs his cigarette out in the ashtray on the steamer trunk they use as a coffee table. "You got home safely. Nobody died, Annie. This isn't some story that proves I make terrible decisions designed to somehow hurt you and ruin your life. I love you. Everything I do is for you and Del—"

"Who said anything about ruining my life?" Annie says. "I'm capable of making sure my life isn't ruined by you or anyone else. No, you asked for an example of irresponsible behaviour because you don't seem to think that spending all your free time on some wild goose chase with Will looking for gold in the Barrens is irresponsible. Or the fishing boat you wanted to buy in Vancouver. Or the barge you wanted to build on the Great Lakes."

Delilah has heard this list of wrongs her dad has committed before. That's nothing new. But being stranded in Thunder Bay in a snowstorm . . . this is new. "Wait, what happened to us that night?" Delilah asks.

They both turn to her.

"What happened?" Annie says. "We borrowed tip money from the waitress and took a cab."

One Good Thing

Mac shakes his head. "I was frantic," he says to Delilah. "I was going out of my mind. I could not get that goddamned truck to start, and I was going out of my mind. The cab took half an hour to get to me because of the storm, and by the time I got to the restaurant you were gone."

"I told you to get it fixed. Four times," Annie says.

"You were safe," he says to Delilah. "You were okay."

She nods, slowly, trying to understand. Trying to remember. *Was* she upset? Did she even know?

"I will always be safe and okay," Annie says, her voice rising, the pleasantness gone.

He was talking to me, Delilah thinks.

"But you go from one thing to the next blindly, one town to the next, always with a different agenda, and it always fails. You don't think about consequences."

"Me?" he says, and Delilah inwardly rejoices that he is finally angry. "Was it my decision to leave Regina because the art scene was better in Winnipeg when I had a good paying union job? Was it my decision to leave Winnipeg for Toronto because they had a fucking vegetarian co-op housing project you wanted to live in?"

"Yes, because our quality of life is what matters to me," Annie says. "*How* we live, not whatever shitty job you manage to get to pay the bills. I don't want to live in some isolated apartment in a high-rise because you have a union job and can afford to go out and buy fancy new shoes for Delilah or take us to the Four Seasons for dinner. I had that life. I grew up with that life. I was given diamond earrings for my twelfth birthday when what I wanted, what I really needed, was some recognition. To be seen. Do you understand that? Do you get it? I don't want that kind of life. Meaning well doesn't make you a good person. Doing good things makes you a good person. It's a lot harder to do good things."

Doing good things? Delilah thinks. *Being a good person? Is she for real?* Marcel's final words to Annie flood back into her mind. *Witch . . . liar . . .*

"What, so now I'm not a good person?" Mac sounds stunned, injured.

"I don't want to be here," Annie says, frustrated now. "This is not my home. I keep trying to tell you I don't fit in here, and you keep telling me to give it time, but time isn't going to change how I feel."

What? Annie wants to leave? This is the first Delilah has heard of this, and her heart sinks like a cold stone. Unlike any other time she has been told they might be moving, this time she feels something close to panic.

"I'm not leaving," she says, surprising herself, her book shaking in her hand. Annie and her father look over, startled. "I'm staying here."

"Of course not, little bird," her mother says. "We're not leaving right now. But this was never a permanent move. That was never the plan. And I'm just trying to express myself, that's all. I have a right to express myself."

"Why can't it be a permanent move?" Mac asks. "We could buy a house here. I know you don't like it now, but you haven't been here long. Give it a chance. I don't understand why you give up on places so quickly."

Delilah is frozen in place. She wants to leave the room, but she doesn't want to miss anything.

"The fact that you don't know that is the problem, Mac. The fact that you don't know what makes a home."

"But we keep trying to create them, and you keep wanting to leave them."

Annie leans forward, her features tightening with gathering rage. "You left me alone in Vancouver with our child. I had to do everything. Make all the decisions, do all the work, and all while I was trying to go to school. Do you know how hard that is? How many sleepless nights I had from worry and exhaustion?"

Delilah almost laughs in disbelief. *Alone?* She finally gets up and walks out because if she has to listen to one more word, she will hurl her book across the room. She goes into her bedroom and pulls the blanket across her door frame, wishing she had a door so she could slam it.

THE NEXT DAY WHEN Delilah walks into the living room after school, she hears a moan of protest from the pile of blankets on the sofa. The room is dark, the sun blocked out by the heavy green drapes, the kind that rich people hang in their dining rooms, corded and swirled with shiny patterns. Annie bought them at the thrift store and nailed them above the windows in an effort to keep out the relentless light.

The tiny alarm goes off in Delilah's chest when she sees her mother under the blankets on the couch. "Sorry, Mom."

Her mother tosses a cushion to the floor as she stirs, burying her face under a pillow. The cushion just misses Delilah as she goes by.

"Do you need something?" Delilah whispers.

"No," her mother mumbles. "Just let me rest."

Delilah knows that once Annie goes down like this, she could stay down for at least another week or so. She saw it coming, long before last night's fight. Annie's wave of lit-up happiness always crashes eventually.

There is an untouched plate of bacon and eggs on the chest that Mac had made her mother that morning, the fork and knife lying neatly beside it on a paper towel. Delilah considers going to her room and crawling into her own bed with a book, but she's hungry. She wants macaroni and cheese, but she can't clatter around in the kitchen, so she heads to the door and backs out, closing it silently.

She sits on the crooked porch, wondering how long until Mac comes home from work. At least if he cooks he'll be the one who has to deal with Annie yelling that he's being too loud. She considers heading down to Jones's, but he might think that's weird since she was just with him at school. She checks her shorts' pocket for change, thinking maybe she could get a bag of chips at Weaver's. Sixteen cents.

Her stomach shrieks at her. *Shut up*, she tells it. She could go in and make some macaroni. Her mother wouldn't kill her. But instead she walks to the top of the road and looks down the hill toward Latham Island. A dog is wandering the brush beside Martha's shack. The Van der Meers' five-year-old twin girls are climbing, shirtless, on the old washing machine in the vacant lot. The lake is shining, and the breeze lifts Delilah's hair from her eyes. The chimes sing behind her.

She starts down the hill, something breaking free in her as she walks away from her house. She walks faster, liking the slap slap slap of her sandals on the road. By the time she reaches the bottom, she's running, hurtling down at top speed, legs flying, her arms open wide to catch the wind.

She slows when she reaches the little bridge to Latham Island and walks down the quiet road along the shore until she gets to Rainbow Valley. She passes the colourful shacks, groups of children staring at her curiously, three men bent over a truck engine who don't notice her go by. At the end of the street is Will's pink shack. His truck is parked beside it. There's a canoe lying across two sawhorses with old rusty cans of paint or varnish and a stained canvas beneath it.

Jethro's dogs bark at her from their pen next door, and Laska comes trotting out of Will's open door and runs toward her. The dog licks her hand and sits on its haunches, looking up at Delilah as though to say, *What are you doing here?*

Will ambles out of his shack, a cigarette tucked in his mouth. He sees Delilah and stops. He has paintbrushes and some other tool in his hand and he sets them down on the canvas. He takes a drag and squints at her. "What's up, kid?"

"Hi," she says.

"You just in the neighbourhood or what?"

Laska licks her hand again. Delilah pets her bristly head. "I guess."

He points at the canoe. "You wanna give me a hand? This is important work I'm doing here. Time sensitive, as they say. Gotta get this thing in the water while the pike are biting."

"Sure."

He shows her the hairline fracture on the bottom of the fibreglass canoe. "See that? We need to patch it up. It's a slow leak, but those will catch up with you, and soon the water's up to your knees."

He gets her scrubbing down the canoe with a bristled brush while he mixes some sort of sealant. She can feel herself relax as she scours the winter grime off, back and forth, back and forth. The sun sizzles down on her forehead, and before she knows it she's sweating. He shows her how to lay the strip of fabric across the fracture and paint on a coat of sealant.

"You hot?" he asks after a while.

"Yeah," she says, stepping away from the canoe. She feels dizzy and then she remembers how hungry she was. She looks up the hazy road toward home, wondering if she'll make it back without collapsing.

"Come on," he says. He puts his brushes in a tin can and walks to the house. She follows, Laska at her heels. Will leaves the door open wide, probably to let in the breeze off the lake.

Inside it is dark and cool, the windows facing the lake covered in thick canvas. It's one big room with a stove, a rough counter, a fridge, and a table with two chairs. His bed is built high and into the wall. Across from his bed is a cubbyhole of a room with no door. Delilah sees a pile of wood on the floor and a half-built frame of some sort taking up the whole space.

He points to the table. "Have a seat."

"What are you building?" she asks, sitting down. She's been in here before, briefly, while her dad picked something up, but she's never stayed before. Will doesn't host dinners at his house. The gatherings are always next door at Jethro's.

He's rummaging in a cupboard and setting things on the counter. He turns, a tub of margarine in his hand. Glances over at the frame and smiles. "Bed for Clem. She's coming in July. Used to be a woodshed but I knocked out the wall and framed it in a few years back."

"She's coming? For how long?"

"A month, maybe," he says, returning to his task. "Her mom is going to fly her up."

"You haven't seen her for a long time, right?"

"That's right," he says, pulling a butter knife out of an old mug where he keeps his cutlery. "But a month is a good long time to get reacquainted. She's gonna love you. Used to love the big girls. Followed them around like a puppy."

Delilah imagines playing with her, giving her piggybacks along the shore, hunting for pretty stones.

There's a large piece of paper tacked to the wall beside the table, tiny dots and lines scattered across it. There are staple marks where he must have pulled it from a magazine. She peers closer and realizes the dots are constellations. *Andromeda. Canis Minor.*

"What is this?" she asks.

He sets a Mountain Dew in front of her, then returns to the fridge where he rustles around. "Star atlas," he says.

She pushes down the round tab of her drink and takes a long sip. Nothing has ever tasted so good and so sweet. Her head is throbbing from the sun and the lack of food. There is a bowl of apples on the table, but she's too shy to ask for one.

She surveys the star atlas. There are a few photos stuck to the edge with tape. There's one of a red-haired, delicate woman holding a baby wrapped in blankets in a canoe with the rocks and trees of the shore behind them. She's beautiful and pale, somehow out of place in the wild landscape. In another there's a little girl in a tiny parka on

Will's shoulders, maybe about three, her mouth wide with laughter, her dark eyes shining. Will is all teeth, grinning wide, wearing his fringed jacket and his grey wool cap.

"Is that Clementine?" Delilah asks, although she knows it is. Outside, the dogs at Jethro's start barking.

"Yup," he says. She watches him pull bread from a plastic bag, assembling a sandwich on his dirty counter. The table is dusty, and Delilah traces a star on the surface with her finger.

"And that was your wife?"

Will is silent as he pulls a plate from the basin of dirty dishes. Delilah has a thousand questions about that child in the tiny parka, but she doesn't ask them. He pours water from a jug onto the plate and rubs it roughly with a paper towel. He puts the sandwich on it and plunks the plate down in front of Delilah.

"Eat up." He sits across from her and lights a cigarette.

She looks down at the sandwich. It's bologna and mustard on white bread with a slice of processed cheese. She has never eaten a bologna sandwich in her life. She picks it up and takes a bite. It's tangy and salty and delicious. She closes her eyes as she chews.

"Good?" Will asks.

She nods and takes another bite.

"That's Sarah," he says, pointing his chin at the red-haired woman. "She wasn't my wife. She's Clementine's mother."

"Why did she leave?" Delilah asks.

She knows she's maybe being rude, but she can't help herself. In one of the photos, the red-haired woman is laughing, her hair drifting around her face in the breeze, as she sits beside Will at a picnic table, Clementine between them eating a banana, cheeks bulging. Will looks younger in the photo, but it probably wasn't too long ago. They were a family. *What happened?* Delilah wonders.

"Why did she take Clementine?"

Will just takes a drag of his smoke and points to Delilah's plate. "Eat up," he says.

Delilah picks up the second half of her sandwich, knowing to stop asking questions now.

"You were hungry," he says.

Delilah nods. Her mouth is full.

"Why'd you come down here?" He doesn't say it meanly. He flicks his ashes into an empty creamed corn can.

Delilah thinks carefully before she speaks. "I don't know. My mom wasn't feeling well."

"What's wrong with her?"

She shrugs. "She gets . . . I don't know. Bored, maybe. Doesn't get out of bed sometimes."

"Ah," Will says, and it makes her think maybe this isn't such a strange thing, to have a mother who doesn't get out of bed.

There's a long silence as Will watches her calmly, maybe waiting for her to say more. She looks over at the wall to escape his gaze.

"Why do you have a star atlas?" she asks.

"When I was growing up I wanted to work for NASA."

"Really?"

"Yeah, really." He takes a drag of his smoke. "When I was a teenager, they launched that Russian satellite into space. First one to go up there. Sent a dog up with it, but the dog didn't make it. Space is no place for a dog, isn't that right, Laska?" She is curled on the floor by his feet and her ear perks when she hears her name.

Delilah finishes the last of her sandwich and wonders if it would be rude to ask for more. She licks mustard from her finger. "So why didn't you?"

"Turns out you need to be good at science." He laughs. "Hadn't thought that through. By then I was almost out of school. It was . . . how do you say that? . . . out of my skill set. Mostly I was good at skipping school and drinking hooch behind the bar with my friends. Then my parents died, and Jethro was looking after us. Had to work."

"Oh." Delilah thinks about this. About Will's parents dying and him and Jethro and Mary Ellen being on their own. She thinks about how, if that happened to her, she would be completely alone because she has no brothers or sisters. It strikes her suddenly, how alone she would be.

"Too bad," she says. "You could have been the first man on the moon."

"I could have been a lot of things." He puts out his smoke in the can. "Anyway, doesn't matter. I learned about it all later. Still learning. Hey, I got a riddle for you."

"Okay."

"In 1908 an explosion hits a remote part of Siberia. Flattens some eighty million trees over eight hundred square miles."

"Eighty million? Really?"

"Really. But not a single person is killed because it happens so far from the nearest city. What do you figure it was?"

Delilah thinks for a second. "I was going to say it was a bomb. But why would they set it off so far away from people?"

He shakes his head. "This was no bomb. The energy of the explosion was about a thousand times more powerful than the atomic bomb they dropped on Hiroshima. They don't make bombs that big."

"So it was like an asteroid or a meteor or something? Did it leave a big hole?"

He smiles and sits back in his chair. "You're getting warm. But no, it left nothing. No crater whatsoever. Just the flattened trees." He makes a motion with his hand, flattening the trees with it.

"What? That makes no sense."

"No? Take a wild guess."

"I don't know. What is it?"

"You give up already? You sure?"

She takes a sip of her pop. "A bomb is the only thing I can think of."

Will seems like he's enjoying this. "Ever heard that thing about how killing someone with an icicle is the perfect crime?"

"Like stabbing them with it? Why?"

"Think about it, kid. You stab someone with an icicle, then the weapon melts. No evidence."

"Does that happen a lot in Yellowknife?" She has been warned of the cold more times than she can count. Her father tells her icicles hang three, four feet long from the eaves of the shacks, as thick as elephant trunks.

He laughs. "Nah. But think of this thing in Siberia. You got a major impact . . ." The heel of his big hand hits the table and rattles her pop can against her plate. "But you got no crater. So what could do that?"

"Ice? What kind of ice? From where?"

"What's a comet made of?"

"Ice. But space dirt and rock and stuff, too." They had done comets at school last year. She had made one out of papier-mâché and got a B-plus on it.

"Ice."

"So it was a comet?"

He shrugs, his eyes twinkling. "Who knows? Still a mystery. Thousands of scientists and nobody's been able to prove anything."

"Wait, you don't know? You don't know the answer?" She feels tricked.

"Nobody knows for sure. Some say comet, some say a meteor hit the atmosphere and exploded on impact, made debris so small it's unnoticeable."

"Does that happen, though? Do meteors and stuff land on earth?"

"Oh, yeah. All the time. Most of 'em are tiny, just particles of rock and iron. But some are bigger. They've recovered thousands over the years. People go looking for them."

"Go looking for them? Why?"

"Valuable. Those pieces can make you a small fortune if you find them." He's all lit up now, talking about those hunks of rock.

She thinks she understands why. "Not just the money, though."

"How's that?"

"Like, it's a piece of space. Right? Something that's not from Earth. That's pretty cool."

"It sure as hell is, kid."

"But they don't know for sure what happened in Siberia? Doesn't it bug you that they don't know?"

"Does it bug you?"

"Yeah." It does. It makes her feel unsafe, like the sky could fall on them at any time. How can all those scientists not know what caused something so destructive?

"What's life without a bit of mystery?" He points to her empty plate. "You still hungry?"

"A little."

He gets up. "I'll make you another one. Then you better get out there and help me finish up that canoe. You gotta earn your keep if you're gonna eat all my food."

"Will?"

He's rustling in the fridge again. "Yeah?"

"I just like to know why things happen. Don't you?"

He sets the cheese on the counter and turns to her. "Not always, kid," he says. "What happened is what happened. Knowing why doesn't change a thing."

✳✳✳

SUNDAY MORNING DELILAH TRAILS Jones down a path to the edge of Yellowknife Bay where his family's canoe is tied to a rock. He has piled some lumber by the shore, mostly broken sheets of plywood and two-by-fours. He overturns the canoe and starts loading the wood into it. She helps him, careful to not catch the old nails on her pink peasant blouse. The sun is hot, but there's a cool wind off the water that flutters the thin fabric near her waist.

He throws the canvas over the mound of tools and wood in the canoe and pushes it off the sand. "Hop in," he says over his shoulder.

She does, wobbling as the boat tilts under her weight. Jones tells her to move to the front and she sits facing away from land. She feels Jones shove off and then scramble into the boat. He sits at the back and starts paddling. Delilah can see small fish swimming in the dappled shallows, an old tin can, a length of rusted chain, and then it's too deep to see the bottom.

They glide across the rippled surface, Delilah's eyes almost drifting shut with the rhythmic movement of the canoe.

She likes the feeling of freedom out here on the water. Only five more days of school and then they can do this every day if they want to. She and Jones haven't discussed the Misty situation, but there isn't much to discuss. When Delilah passes her and Tammy and Heather in the hallways they call out "Delorrres" and laugh when she flinches and keeps walking, head down. But aside from that, there have been no further attacks. Soon they will get bored and move on to someone else. Delilah has seen it happen before.

When the rocky edge of Joliffe Island is ten feet from the boat, Jones turns the canoe to the right and edges along sideways until they come to a small beach. He hops out and drags the rope to a pine tree near the shore to tie it. Delilah gets out.

"We gotta walk a bit with the stuff," Jones says.

"Where's the cabin?" she asks.

He has started stacking the lumber and the gear on the beach. "Just up through the trees a little."

"Who lives there?" she asks, pointing to a strange structure just off the shore to their left. It's a home of some sort, made of what looks like aluminum siding and a patchwork of old wood. There are plastic lawn chairs and piles of rusty machinery scattered across the rock around it.

"Old Tom. He's okay. Kinda weird. He talks about the army a lot. Doesn't go over to the other side very much. He won't bug us."

Across the lake, Delilah can see Willow Flats, Jones's house, and the long tail of Rainbow Valley. She can see the road that leads uptown. From here it all looks like a child's Lego village. She could crush it with her hand or step on it with her shoe. She likes being so far away, separated by water from everything else.

It takes them four trips to bring everything to the old cabin site. It's halfway across the island, but only five minutes of easy walking over the rocks. In the centre of the trees is a rickety platform with three walls and some rafters. Wood lies in scattered piles around it, crunching beneath their feet as they walk to the edge of the platform and deposit their goods on the ground.

When they have all their gear, Jones stands back and looks at the cabin. Delilah scratches a mosquito bite on her arm. The cabin is small, maybe eight feet by eight feet. The remains of an ancient wood stove lie in a heap in one corner, and what might have been a table but is now missing legs leans against one of the walls. The plywood floor looks like it could cave in if a mouse ran across it.

"Doesn't it belong to somebody?" she asks. "Won't they get mad?"

He's flipping through the wood he brought, his thin back to her. "No. Belongs to some guy who lives in an old folks' home now. He was a miner like a hundred years ago. His family lives out east somewhere. My dad told me. Nobody will care."

"How can you fix it up with just this stuff? Is it enough?"

"There's wood here too." He turns to her. "We're not only doing it today. We have all summer. Today I want to put the tarp up. Like a roof. And we can use the canvas for the wall. And maybe fill in some of the holes."

She realizes she might be offending him. He had been excited to bring her there, and she might sound like she's complaining, like she doesn't think it's good enough. It's basically just going to be a fort. And as far as forts go, it's pretty cool. The structure is there, it's just been sitting too long not being used. In her mind, she sees the plywood bits Jones brought stitching together for the walls and the roof. Shingles recovered from the surrounding brush around their feet and nailed back up where they belong. New windows, maybe, from the junk shop by Weaver's. She can see sunflowers blooming around the edges of the cabin. Daisies sprouting along a path made of lake stones. She wonders if she will be in Yellowknife long enough to finish the job before her parents make her leave.

TWO HOURS LATER THEY are sweating despite the breeze. Delilah is sitting by a pile of wood scraps she salvaged from around the cabin site and is pulling out rusty nails and placing them in a pile on the lichen beside her. Her shorts are filthy, streaked with the rich black earth the bones of the old house rest on. Her knees are covered in two circles of muck from kneeling by the floor and holding the side of the canvas while Jones stretched it across to the other wall and nailed it to the corner beam.

They have eaten all the food they packed—the entire box of cookies, both apples, and the Thermos of juice. Delilah is still starving, daydreaming about bread and butter and a giant chunk of cheddar cheese, but she doesn't want to go yet. She looks up at what they've accomplished so far. Jones is inside, and she can't see him because of the canvas stretched the length of the missing wall, almost to the height of where the roof should be, but she can hear him hammering something.

She pulls the last nail from a shingle with her grimy finger and tosses it aside. She stands and brushes the twigs and dirt from the back of her shorts. Lifting the corner of the canvas left loose for a door, she ducks under. Jones is patching a hole by the floor under an old countertop.

"You think it's safe for me to come in too?"

Jones stops hammering. He inspects the uneven floor, warped with time and decades of deep snow. There is a smear of mud across one freckled cheek, a dead leaf caught in the hair above his left ear. "Should be."

She steps over the ledge. The floor seems solid enough. She takes another step, pulls herself up, and lets the canvas drop behind her.

"We need a door," she says.

"Yeah, I know." He's watching her walk, watching the way the floor gives a little under her sneakers. When she makes it halfway across, he turns back to his hammering.

Standing in the centre, Delilah turns slowly in place. It almost looks like a real house, if you forget the sunlight is streaming in overhead and slanting across the floor by her feet. The counter is the only thing left standing, but Delilah sees Jones has gathered the pieces of the old table and put them in a pile to work on later. There's room for a couple of chairs. Maybe they can find some at the junkyard and bring them in the canoe. And blankets. She could bring the giant fuzzy pink pillow she won at the PNE in Vancouver. There are a lot of things they could bring.

Delilah sits cross-legged in the middle of the floor. Above her are the dark rafters and the tops of trees outlined black against the sky. She can hear birds singing to each other out there, insistent and loud.

"Jones?"

"Yeah?" He finishes hammering and sits down with his back against the wall, facing her. He sweeps his arm across his damp forehead.

"Do you think we could stay out here ever? Like, for more than a few hours?"

"Overnight?" His green eyes catch hers and flicker away to study his hand. "Yeah, sure. Why not? It's no different than camping. And we'll have the roof on today."

Overnight. That wasn't what she meant.

"Oh," she says. "I was just thinking . . ."

Jones turns pink and bites the nail on his thumb. "Well, yeah. I know. But I was planning on staying out here sometimes. By myself. I was going to build a bed and bring out some old blankets for the mattress. Over there." He points across to the canvas wall. "Right against there."

"You would stay out here by yourself?"

He shrugs. "Why not?"

Delilah thinks about this. She thinks about getting away from her house, from the fighting. From Annie.

"I could stay out here too."

"Sure. There's room."

They're silent for a moment, looking up through the roof that isn't there. Dust swirls around them, lit up like tiny fireflies.

* * *

"SMASH IT, DELILAH. LIKE this." Esther grabs a head of iceberg lettuce from the box and slams it core side down on the wooden butcher's block in the kitchen of the Wildcat. She pulls the loosened leaves apart, tosses the core into the giant garbage can, and then wipes her hands on her round white chest.

Delilah chooses the biggest lettuce out of the box. She slams it, hard, on the wood. The leaves fall apart in her hands. She looks to Esther for confirmation that she has done it right, but the cook, a large woman with unruly curls and little round John Lennon glasses, has already turned back to her gas range with the simmering pots. Delilah plucks the leaves methodically, drops them into the plastic bin with the others.

She stops to scratch a blackfly bite behind her ear. It's a big one. She had been riding out to the dump with Jones in the back of his dad's truck. They were leaning against the old refrigerator Red was hauling out for some lady who lived uptown and didn't have any family to do her dump runs for her. She had given Delilah and Jones a pop each, one of those generic colas that comes in the round little bottles. Red hit a bump and they both spilled some on the front of their T-shirts, which they thought was hilarious until Red stopped the truck and they were swarmed by an army of giant, bloodsucking flies.

It wasn't until she got home to the green shack and she was absently picking at her ear while she poured some fruit punch that she realized the damage. Her fingers caught on a scab the size of a dime and came back bloody. Blackflies aren't polite like mosquitoes, Will had told her. They don't just take a taste. They rip off a chunk and save some for later.

Annie glides into the back of the café with a tray of loaded dishes. "They're gone. Thank God for that. Friggin' tourists. All wearing matching sweaters, and the blonde has a California tan and they're carrying subarctic parkas. It's June. There's no snow. So sorry to tell you. They must be sweating like pigs out there." She dumps her tray by the double sink. "Better wash your hands, Delilah," she says over her shoulder. "Esther doesn't want your scabs showing up in their moose burgers." She starts running hot water.

Annie is happy again, no trace of the heaviness that lingered on her for days and kept her buried under blankets. Delilah feels something frenetic about her mother today, buzzing, like she is a crackling spark about to ignite. At least she hasn't said anything else about leaving.

Annie wipes her hands on the dishtowel lying on the counter. "Delilah! Wake up! Did you hear me?" Delilah is still holding a piece of lettuce in one hand, scratching her ear absently with the other.

Esther turns from her pot with a grin. "What the hell. Extra protein, hey?" She is seasoning the pots on the gas stove. The smell of caribou stew, sharp and meaty and wild, fills the small kitchen. The back door is open, letting in cool fresh air off the bay.

Delilah drops the lettuce and walks over to the sink, dips her hands in the soapy water and then rinses them under the cold tap. Her mother takes the last plate from her tray and slides it into the water.

"You gonna waitress one day too, Delilah?" Esther carries a giant pot dripping tomato sauce remnants over to the sink. "Can't keep a pretty girl like you hidden away in the kitchen."

Delilah glances out at the big rustic dining room that had been full of laughter and cigarette smoke and clanking dishes before the group of tourists left. She likes being in the kitchen where she can watch her mother glide from table to table, effortlessly charming, a hand on a shoulder, a smile while she tucks her hair behind her ear. Delilah knows she could never do that, that she would drop plates and forget orders, spill stew in someone's lap. She picks up her broken lettuce head, starts separating the waxy leaves again.

"Sure, yeah. Maybe someday."

Annie walks over, grabs a head of lettuce and bangs it roughly on the counter. "Like this," she says. Delilah doesn't like the dress her mother is wearing. The royal purple swirls and hot magenta paisleys are angry, almost violent.

Esther returns to the stove with a clean pot full of water. "You know your mother makes more tips than any waitress I've ever had here? It's no small feat to get those tight-fisted old-timers to cough up. But your mama has the golden touch."

Annie laughs and smashes another head of lettuce, her fingers flying as she separates the leaves. Delilah picks her own lettuce apart slowly. She sometimes feels like if she stays utterly calm she will somehow balance out her mother's intensity. Neutralize it. Annie is spinning into her upward spiral.

"I should get back out there," Annie says. "My public is calling me. Gotta feed those hungry mouths. I'm saving up for my retirement in Mexico." She tosses the last leaf into the bin and walks to the sink to scrub her hands.

"You got a few years left before retirement, my dear," Esther snorts, shaking a box of macaroni into the pot. "As for mine, you're looking at it."

"Oh, I plan to retire early," Annie says, drying her hands vigorously on a clean dishtowel. "Not going to be a working drone for the rest of my good years. No no no. Art on the beach, music by the fire. Fresh papayas every morning. That's the life for me." She winks at Delilah.

"Dream on, dreamer," Esther says, stirring the macaroni.

The bell rings as a new customer enters the restaurant. Annie walks past and gives Delilah a nudge in the ribs. "Hard work, isn't it?" Annie whispers to her, loud enough for Esther to hear. "That Esther, she's an old battle-axe. Make sure she doesn't rip you off at the end of the day."

Esther whoops from her pots. "Oh, I ain't paying her! She's a volunteer. Just doing it out of the goodness of her heart. Ain't that right, Delilah?"

Delilah turns, but sees only Esther's broad back, her arm stirring, stirring the macaroni. "Umm . . ." she says. Two dollars an hour. That was the deal. Two hours a day whenever her mom has shifts. She's saving for a pair of bell-bottom jeans.

Her mom presses a long finger to the bridge of Delilah's nose and gives it a gentle little stroke. Her finger shakes slightly, the faintest tremor in the tip. "She's only messing with you," Annie says. She picks up her tray and leans in to kiss Delilah's cheek. It's so faint she can hardly feel it.

* * *

ON FRIDAY AFTERNOON AFTER the last day at school, Delilah and Jones buy pepperoni sticks and ripple chips at Weaver's and head up on the rocks at the edge of Back Bay, climbing to the top and wandering around the low brush. They eat their picnic on the clifftop about twenty feet above the lake near a clearing sprouting with tiny blue wildflowers. Delilah finds a white bone nestled in the moss that Jones tells her is fox. The sun warms their bare arms, and Delilah can feel the prickle of a sunburn across her nose as they lie in the rough, lacy lichen studying the clouds. They are barefoot, their shoes in a pile by their food. She feels a lazy, joyful relief that this will be her life for the next two months. Outside with Jones, she is the calmest and most at ease she's felt in years.

"What's asthma feel like?" Jones asks, out of the blue.

Delilah considers this question. In a way, she is surprised he noticed she has asthma at all. She has tried to hide it from him like she does with everyone, but her surreptitious puffs from her inhaler when they've been running or after gym class aren't always easy to hide. That's nothing, though. Not compared to Vancouver with the hospital stays, the trips to ER. Here she can breathe better than she ever could. It's the dryness, her mother said. Not as many types of pollen swirling around in the damp air like in Vancouver.

"Sometimes it feels like you're holding your breath underwater," she says.

He looks over. "Yeah?"

"Yeah. Like when you go under and you hold your breath for a super long time until your lungs feel like they're blowing up like balloons and you know if you take a breath you might drown. It kind of feels like that."

Jones looks intrigued. "Why is it any different than holding your breath?"

"It's . . . I don't know. The pressure or something. Like you're being squeezed by something outside yourself. You don't get that when you just hold your breath."

He nods. "I know that feeling."

"You do?"

He sits up. "Yeah."

He's looking out toward the water. Something seems to be troubling him, but she can't guess what. She sits up as he walks over to the edge of the rock and looks down. He whips off his T-shirt, takes a few steps back, and then runs to the edge and jumps high in the air.

"Hey!" she calls, standing to watch him, laughing at his spontaneous leap.

He hits the surface of the lake in a lazy cannonball, all folded skinny arms and legs, and disappears below. She watches the water for what feels like a long time, and a trickle of fear runs through her. Where is he? There are jagged rocks along the shore, she knows. Just under the surface. Maybe he didn't jump far enough out?

She climbs down the rock to the narrow beach beside the cliff, scraping her bare knee when she slips. Along the sand there is a trail of sandpiper tracks, like someone has pressed a broken fork onto the beach. She walks closer to the water until her sneakered toes are touching it.

No bubbles. Nothing.

A terrible feeling grows in her as she watches the passive lake, and she tries to talk herself out of it. Jones is a strong swimmer. He'll be back up. There is no reason for this rush of panic. But still. *Come back,* she thinks.

Seconds later there is a ripple and a splash and he flails his way to the shore. She steps back. Folds her arms across her tripping heart.

At first, he's gasping, and he can't get his words out. He flops to the sand, and Delilah sits beside him, noting the bumps of gooseflesh on his thin white arms, his heaving chest.

When he finally speaks, he says, "I held my breath until it hurt and I thought I was gonna die. Is that what it feels like?"

She tries to keep her voice steady. "Yes. That's what it feels like. Only difference is you just had to swim up for air when you needed it."

Jones shakes himself like a dog, sending lake water shooting out around him. "I guess. But it's not all bad, right? You get to miss school."

Delilah thinks about this. About the hospital stays in Vancouver where her mother brought her lasagna from the Greek restaurant so she didn't have to eat the disgusting food, or how in Regina her dad once brought her a silver balloon and tied it to her bed rail, saying it was her silver cloud, which was even better than a cloud with a silver lining.

"No," she says. "It's not all bad."

If she wasn't worried about hurting his feelings she would tell him that holding his breath in the lake doesn't come close to what it's like in real life. How sometimes it feels like someone is stealing her breath away from her, someone mean and cold and angry. She wishes she could explain that it's hard not to take it personally.

JULY

SKYNYRD'S "FREE BIRD" BLASTS from the eight-track deck in the front of the de Havilland Beaver as the plane dips lower over the tundra, gliding like a graceful duck to settle on the surface of the ruffled lake. Delilah knows the song well because her dad tried to learn it on the guitar. It sounded thin and sad when he sang it. He finally gave up, claiming it wasn't the same on an acoustic. Muddy has been playing the song on repeat since they took off from Back Bay at the Old Town float plane base an hour earlier.

Before they left, Annie had gone to work cheery and bright-eyed, a piece of buttered toast in her mouth as she pulled the screen door shut behind her after kissing them both on the head.

Delilah, perched in her window seat now, can't get over how the land changes so completely from one place to the next up north. Mac had tried to explain the Barrens to her before they left. He told her that when you're flying over them you feel like no one has ever been there before. You're the first ones, nestled in that small buzzing plane, about to embark on an adventure somewhere nobody has ever bothered with before.

"Amazing," he said in the truck on their way to the base. "You think, 'How could we have missed this?' But that's not the case. Far from it. Dene have been hunting there for thousands of years, living off it. It's just . . . it's the endlessness. The flatness. It looks like nothing special until you see the exploding oranges and yellows and reds of the low brush, the sand eskers that look like moonscape. You think, 'How can anything live out here?' And then you see the caribou grazing and lifting their heads to the sound of the plane. Incredible. I never thought I could feel so at home somewhere so far away from anything familiar."

Now, between the music and Muddy singing along and the noise of the plane they can't speak unless they shout, so most of their communication consists of Mac tapping her shoulder, pointing below to a fox skirting the perimeter of a small stand of stunted trees. *There*, he shouts, and she sees a caribou and her calf resting on the lichen. *There*, he shouts again, and she sees an abandoned trapper cabin rotting into the rock it was built on.

They land, and Muddy cuts the engine as they drift toward shore. He pulls off his headphones and turns to them, his wide grin gaping from the missing front tooth. "Gentlemen, welcome back to paradise. And you too, of course, milady." He tips his fingers in a royal salute to Delilah, then reaches down by his feet and extracts a bottle of Jack Daniels. "Care for some champagne before we begin?" He reaches the bottle toward Will, who is organizing his notes into a canvas bag that holds glass jars and a strange wooden box Mac had told Delilah was for mineral samples.

Will shakes his head, but Mac takes the bottle and has a swig before handing it back. Muddy opens the door, and a glacial chill carries in off the lake. Delilah shivers. It smells strange, like clean laundry flapping on a line and ancient layers of silt and grit.

"Why do you fly with bare feet?" Delilah asks as Muddy takes a long slug from the black-labelled bottle.

Muddy laughs and twists the cap back on. "Sure you don't want some?" he calls over to Will, who is beside Delilah, still going through papers.

"Nah," Will says without looking up. "One of us better stay sober to protect your sorry drunk ass from the grizzly bears."

Grizzly bears? Delilah looks over at her dad, but he just smiles, shaking his head. *Don't worry.*

Muddy is peering out the door at the calm lake. "Like to feel the metal vibrating beneath my feet," he says. "Helps remind me how fragile it all is—those two inches of steel that mean the difference between soaring through the sky on wings and a fiery death." He fixes his strange blue eyes on her. "I know," he says. "Lost countless buddies." He glances over at the other men. "As many men get hurt or die in the mines, ten times more lose their lives in bush planes."

She isn't sure what she thinks about what Muddy said. But to Delilah, the bare feet seem like a rebellion, like he's saying screw off to the danger. Despite her mild distaste for Muddy, she was never once afraid they would crash while they were in the air. Somehow, he seems both reckless and capable.

Muddy hops out and stands on the left float, a wooden oar in one hand and the end of a rope in the other. His cotton shirt is only buttoned at the bottom, leaving it rippling around him as he balances there in his bare feet. His long stringy brown hair plays in the wind, and to Delilah, he looks a little like Jesus, only a dirtier version.

He sits on the float and rows with the oar, then jumps ashore onto a tiny sandy beach with the rope in his hand and indicates for Mac to do the same off the opposite float. Rope in hand, Mac aims himself toward the brush-covered shore and makes it by an inch, his right foot slipping into the frigid water before he can pull it out. He trails the rope to the right until he finds a boulder about twenty feet along and ties the rope around it. Muddy has done the same in the opposite direction. Still sitting in the plane, Delilah feels like a spider in a web, anchored on both sides.

Will manoeuvres the gear from the floats to shore, tossing the tents and duffel bag of food toward land. The sun is high in the blue sky, and Delilah knows it will not be going anywhere for a long time. The night before, she got up to get a drink of water just before midnight and the kitchen was as bright as morning.

Delilah shoulders her backpack filled with books and extra shorts, a sweater and her bathing suit—although her dad has warned her the lake is cold. After a short hike over lichen and wildflowers, they set up camp in a small valley between two high esker ridges. Nobody has been saying much, Will whistling to himself, and Muddy taking swigs from the bottle. They set up the testing and gear tent and then a large sleeping tent. Delilah had been worried about sharing the tent, but when she sees the size of it, she doesn't mind.

Muddy takes the far side, and Mac motions for Delilah to take the other side. He sets up his bedroll beside hers, and Will drops his sleeping bag next to him. Even with all their beds and gear, there is still at least three feet between each of them. Delilah takes out her books and stacks them neatly, leaving her extra clothes protected in the backpack from rogue insects. "See you're roughing it," her dad says as he pulls a small pillow out of a stuff sack.

"Yes," she says. "I only brought three."

"I was teasing. You won't get bored out here, don't worry."

"Are you going to make me work?"

"You know it. Camp life isn't for the faint of heart."

Outside, Will starts a fire from some dry willow twigs he found near the shore. They heat cans of Libby's beans on the coals and eat them straight out of the can with tin forks.

"Nectar of the gods," Muddy says, mopping the sides of his can with a slice of Will's Wonder Bread. Delilah is ravenous. She has never tasted anything so delicious in her life.

"Slow down there, kid," Will says, laughing at her. He hands her another slice of bread. "You're gonna choke."

She takes the bread, embarrassed.

"It's the air," he says, setting aside his tin can and wiping his hands on his jeans. "Don't get much fresher than this."

"Beats Annie's seed bread, eh?" Mac says.

Delilah nods, her mouth full of the delicious paste that is Wonder Bread.

Will tosses his empty can into the ashes of the fire.

"You ready?" Mac asks him.

"Yup," he says, getting to his feet.

Delilah has one more bite of beans and tosses her can at the fire but misses. It rolls near Muddy's grimy foot. He grins and kicks it toward the fire. "Nice shot," he says. "You folks go on ahead, I'll catch up." He licks sauce from his thumb. "I'll put out the fire."

Mac heads toward the side of the tent, and Delilah trails him, shaking dried lichen out of her sneakers.

"First things first," he says. He picks up a stack of wooden stakes he had laid against the tent earlier and hands them to her. "Can you handle these? It's quite a walk."

She nods and accepts the load. Will emerges from the gear tent with the small wooden boxes and a canvas bag. "All set," he says.

For a second nobody moves. Mac is just standing there, looking over at Will in his frayed jeans and his fringed suede jacket. They look at each other for what seems like a long time and Delilah knows they are having a conversation she can't hear. Finally, Will nods once, and then Mac starts walking. She follows them through the low brush, the smell of the fire and the charred remnants of beans behind them.

They dip into a little valley spread out in a brilliant carpet of red brush, just like her dad had talked about. She stops to take it in.

"Not bad, eh?" Will says, taking a swig of water from a skin bag. He has set his box and bag beside him. Mac is still walking ahead of them.

"Did you . . ." Delilah says. "Dad says you used to live out here sometimes."

"That's right," Will says. "Hey, Speedy Gonzales!" he shouts at her father. "You worried we're gonna run out of light, or what?"

Mac stops and turns, squinting at them in the relentless sun. He pulls his own water out and takes a sip.

"Spent the autumns out here with the family when I was a kid," Will says, replacing his water in the bag. "We picked wild cranberries for my grandmother. Pity the kid who didn't pick his share. My grandma wasn't one for excuses." He laughs. "Hunted wolf and fox with my uncle and Jethro. Scraped caribou hides and left them in the sun to dry." There is a nostalgia in his voice. She hears it sometimes when her dad talks about fishing on the St. Lawrence with his dad or the oak trees in front of the brick house he grew up in scattering its leaves so they settled on the cars. She doesn't feel wistful about any of the places she's lived. At least not yet.

"Did you come here every fall?" she asks.

"Pretty much."

They start walking again, and Delilah pictures a little Will running through this strange vastness, hunting with his brother, sliding down those rocky hills. She imagines herself there too, a small child running wild and happy.

"You always live in cities, kid?" he asks.

She nods. "Yeah. I think because . . . like, my mom always likes to be around artists."

"Ah." Will slows his pace a bit so Delilah can keep up. "Artists. I see. So what do you like to be around?"

She thinks about his question. Nobody has ever asked her that before. She steps carefully to avoid treading on the delicate, lace-like brush beneath her and looks around at the rippling land peppered with sprinkles of tiny flowers, the blue sky cloudless and enormous above them.

"This," she says.

***

LATER THAT NIGHT, DELILAH lies in the tent in the faded glow of nighttime sun listening to the men talk by the fire. They have all had their fair share of the Jack Daniels, possibly even started on a new bottle by now. Delilah can hardly keep her eyes open, exhausted from pounding stakes and hiking for what seemed like miles. They returned with some rock scrapings in the sample bottles and she helped Will catch trout for their dinner from the shore of the lake. Muddy fried them in a cast iron pan over the stove, adding a dash from the whiskey bottle to the sizzling pan every once in a while.

She can hear every word they're saying out by the fire. The canvas does nothing to dull the noise. They are talking about what they found that day, speculating on the mineral samples. But as she starts to drift, she is startled awake by her father saying, "What if it all goes wrong? What if we're blowing our money and taking these risks for nothing?"

Another voice, Muddy's, says, "Jesus, have another fucking drink. Whose fucking idea was this? It's a no-brainer. We're being good fucking businessmen."

There is a crash that makes Delilah jump, but she soon realizes it's probably an empty liquor bottle hitting the fire.

"What the hell," Mac says after a while. "What the hell. You gotta go forward sometimes or else there's nothing to do but go back." To that, the only response is the crackling of the fire. Will hasn't said a word.

Delilah drifts off again as Muddy starts singing "Sweet Home Alabama," and wakes up only when the men crawl into the big tent, their boots banging on the hard earth beneath the tarp. Her eyes flutter open and through the tent doorway she sees that the sun has finally disappeared as her dad and Will sprawl on their sleeping bags still wearing all their clothes. The sky is a faded, hazy blue. The thick canvas tent makes it so she can't see much but the rough outlines of their bodies.

Within minutes Muddy is snoring in a reeking cloud of booze.

"Need one of them pine tree air fresheners in here," Will says quietly.

Delilah smiles.

"No doubt," Mac mumbles. "That guy can knock it back."

There's silence for a few minutes and Mac whispers, "He okay, you figure? Muddy?"

Delilah's ears perk. They don't know she's awake.

Will doesn't answer right away, but then he says quietly, "Don't know. Ain't the sharpest tool in the shed."

"You trust him?"

"Much as I trust anyone."

"How much is that?"

"Not much."

Delilah feels a strange pounding in her chest, a worry she can't put her finger on. What are they up to? It all seemed clear before today when her dad explained it: they discovered a promising patch that could mean gold, they're staking and taking samples. So why all the whispering? Why does it matter so much that Muddy is trustworthy?

Mac starts to say something but there is a sudden, loud howling outside and he stops short. It sounds like a man wailing, an intimate, grieving sound.

Delilah sits up. "Dad?"

"It's okay," Mac says, but he sounds tense.

It's not far off, maybe even just above them on top of the esker. Delilah squints toward the door of the tent and makes sure she can see the sharp outline of the rifles. They're there, resting against someone's pack.

"Wolf," Will says. "Lie down, kid. It won't hurt you."

"We have the guns if we need them, Lila," Mac says.

Delilah can't lie down. Her skin feels alive, every hair an antenna.

The wolf howls again and again, long and low, each time ending in a wavering shudder. She thinks of the ravens, how they call to the wolves to come rip open the dead animals. Has this one been summoned, tricked here by the birds?

"Why do they howl like that?" she whispers. She doesn't know why she says it. She knows, she read about it in *National Geographic* at the doctor's office. They do it to communicate, to rally the troops. But why *that* sound, is what she means. Why that long, heartsick song when it could be just a bark or a yip?

"He's calling for the ones he lost," Will says through the dark. "Telling them to come on home."

***

THEY AREN'T SURE WHEN Annie left, only that she is gone when they come home from the Barrens. They return to the shack from the float plane base, sunburned and punch-drunk on three days of fresh air and glacial lake swims. They see that Bessie isn't parked by the woodpile but think nothing of it, figuring Annie has a shift at the Wildcat.

But they figure it out pretty soon. The first thing Delilah sees when they walk in are the wilting flowers. She and Mac sit on the couch staring at them, Mac still in his work pants, his dusty steel-toed boots, Annie's note in his hands, both of them struck dumb. Annie left the note on the steamer trunk, a small vase of wild daisies placed beside it, a plate of homemade oatmeal cookies with a red dishcloth covering it. Mac reaches out to touch a cookie, as though to see if it's still warm, if they somehow just missed her, if there is time to run after her and change her mind, but Delilah had already done the same. They're cold. Baked hours ago, or worse, days ago.

"She'll come back," Mac says shakily. "She'll be back."

Did Annie leave the minute their plane took off? Delilah wonders. Watch it from the bridge, even, until she knew it was safe to go? Delilah gets up from the couch and walks to her parents' bedroom. Annie's clothes are gone from the shelves, her jackets and sweaters missing from the hooks on the walls. Mac's jackets have been moved over to cover the spaces as though they had never been there at all. Delilah sinks to the bed. Annie is gone. Gone gone gone. There is no air left in Delilah's body. She needs her inhaler, but her legs suddenly feel too thin and useless to carry her out to the living room.

That night, her dad drinks eleven of the twelve beer he bought at Weaver's on their way home from the float plane base. He doesn't touch the toasted cheese and lettuce sandwich she gives him for supper. When she goes to bed, she hears him through the knotholed walls, crying as he wanders through the house like he's looking for something.

She's gone! Delilah wants to scream. *She left us and went to California!* But she lies there silent and still until he finally settles on the couch.

Delilah knows Annie will be back. She said in the note that she'd be back. But it isn't the being gone that bothers her. Her dad was gone for months when he moved up here, and she missed him, but she could still sleep at night. So it isn't that.

It's the leaving. The leaving is a cut, a sudden unexpected gash, violent and quick, and it leaks out, bleeds a little. She will have to wait for it to scab over like a scraped knee or a blackfly bite.

SINCE ANNIE LEFT, MAC spends his days either at the mines working or silently absorbed by small, trivial jobs around the house. Nailing up shelves in Delilah's room, moving the couch to a different position. He prepares small, simple meals for them in silence, macaroni noodles with shredded cheese, Lipton soup, fried hamburger patties. She hasn't eaten a vegetable since her mother left. They leave the dishes piled in the sink. Before, this would have made her happy. Just her and her dad, eating whatever they want, doing whatever they want. A break from Annie's moods, her intensity, her searing criticism. But everything Mac does now scrapes against Delilah, needles at her. It bothers her how silent he is, how sad, how lost inside himself he has become. He doesn't know the things Annie does. He doesn't know how outrageous it is for her to cause him this pain on top of the other betrayals. Delilah keeps quiet, quiet as a mouse, because if she opens her mouth, it will all come spilling out—Marcel. The others.

She spends her evenings reading while he sits at the table and flips through mineral reference books, rubs his hands through his hair, stares out the kitchen window at the bright night sky.

She watches him like a hawk, waiting for the day he says they have to follow Annie to California.

***

SIX DAYS LATER DELILAH is washing dishes when Mac comes home from Red's with his hair wet at the tips, his face scrubbed and pink. He has finally had a shower. This is a good sign. He smells like the lavender soap Annie left behind, the kind with the tiny seeds Delilah hates because they scratch her skin.

Mac sits her down and pours her a glass of Tang from the plastic pitcher. She had never in her life tried Tang until he bought it that week, though she asked Santa for it the Christmas she was seven. On Christmas morning Annie told her Santa must have loved her too much to bring her Tang, which was full of chemicals and processed sugar.

Mac takes two Oreo cookies out of a crinkly package

and puts them down on the table in front of her. She picks one up and takes a bite. The sugar might kill her, if he keeps this up. It's jangling her nervous system like the whine of a chainsaw. He rubs a hand over the top of his head, back, forth, and back again. He reaches for one of her hands and she offers it, tentatively.

"I have to work nights," he says, gripping her sticky fingers and holding her gaze for the first time in days. "A few of them overnight. I have to work, and that's what they're offering. I can't say no. See, what I'm thinking, Lila, is I just need to save as much money as possible. Save up for a house. For all of us."

"Here?" she asks hopefully.

He looks away.

"I don't want to go to California." She licks the sugary white icing from the fingers of her free hand.

"Well, sure, maybe. I mean, if we have a better house here, with running water. A little studio space for her. I mean, she might love that . . ." He sounds shaky, a little desperate, which turns Delilah's stomach. She is only half listening, watching a fly do a drunken dance by the back door, trapped on the inside by the heavy screen.

He tells her two nights a week she will stay overnight at Red and Maggie's. Two nights a week, she can go to Will's or Jethro and Mary Ellen's until eleven, and he will pick her up after he gets off.

"Sorry," he says. "Just for now, though. I mean, there are some other things in the works, Delilah, that might turn out to be pretty interesting if we just . . . just hang in there." He suddenly seems so thin and dried out. She wants to shake him, shake some life back into him.

The fly lands on the inside of the screen. It's like he's looking out to the overgrown lawn, wondering why he can see it but can't quite get to it.

"I'll be fine," she says.

* * *

AT WILL'S, THE BOWL of apples is still on the table from two weeks before, though now there are only two, and the dented Mountain Dew cans with the circles popped out of the tops are still there too, except now they are dusted with cigarette ashes. She's sitting in the same old rickety chair.

It's seven, and she and Will have just returned to his shack after having dinner at Jethro and Mary Ellen's. Her father is working the night shift, and she is supposed to stay at Will's until eleven. Outside, Will is loading up the truck with scrap lumber for the lean-to Mac has been working on back home.

Will comes in and turns on his two-burner stove. "All loaded up," he says as he fills the enamel coffee pot with water from a jug and pours in some coffee grounds from a large can on the counter. "I can bring it up there later and drop it off for your dad."

"Okay," she says. "Maybe I'll go too. I'm not feeling good." All evening, during Mary Ellen's rabbit stew and the card game afterward, she had felt quiet and subdued. There's a familiar tightness in her chest, a faint wheezing with each breath that is making her tired. She had to excuse herself twice to go take a surreptitious puff of her inhaler during dinner. She wants to go home and crawl into bed with a book.

Will glances at her. "Sure thing. Any time. You gonna live or what?"

She nods. "I'm fine. You can make your coffee first."

She sees that Will has wiped the table free of dust, except where she traced the star with her finger last week. But now there are two stars traced in the dust. She's puzzled. She's sure she only drew one.

"Will?"

"Yeah?" He takes a cup from the shelf above the counter. The fresh evening air coming in the window smells cool and clean, like melting ice.

"Is that your star?"

He turns around, cup in hand. "Huh?"

She points to the two dust stars, close together by the inner edge of the table.

"Oh. Yeah." He sets the cup down carefully. "I guess I was thinking about binary stars when I did that."

"Binary stars?"

Will comes over, drags the other chair out and sits. He leans forward, his big forearms resting on the table. He points to the stars. "Binary stars. They go in pairs. Most stars like to go in pairs, or at least some of 'em do."

Delilah didn't know this. She always thought of stars as lonely things, up so high and far away and spread out. She knows that what looks close together from Earth can be millions of light years apart up there.

"The one star . . ." He points to hers. "The one star, it's pulled toward the other star and they spin. Orbit each other." His hands show her the orbit. "It's like they can't go anywhere else. You know? They can't pull apart. They don't want to."

"Oh."

His orbiting hands are resting on the table now, folded peacefully. "Yeah. But once in a while, every once in a while, one of 'em gets sucked down. And then it's all over."

"Sucked down by what?"

He shrugs. "Darkness."

She's skeptical. What do stars know about darkness?

"You don't believe me?"

She shakes her head.

He picks up two wrinkled apples, which leaves the brown bowl empty in the middle of the table. "Okay. This star here . . ." He holds one out. "And this star here . . ." And he holds out the other. "Are going like this . . ." He circles them around each other, crossing his hands in front of him. "That there," he says, indicating the bowl with his chin, "is a black hole. You know what a black hole is?"

She starts to say yes and then realizes she doesn't. She's heard of one, of course, but she doesn't actually know what it is.

"It's a star that died. Exploded in on itself. It creates a darkness so heavy that no light can escape it. Okay? So this star here starts to get pulled in by the black hole. Pretty soon it starts falling, losing energy, getting all sucked away by the darkness. Now you understand?"

She nods. One wrinkled apple is wobbly now, orbiting the edge of the bowl instead of the other apple, which Will holds still in his left hand. "Then . . ." Thud. The apple lands in the bowl.

"Oh. The star . . . dies?"

"Kinda. Yeah, it kinda does. But what happens is that the other star, because it was exchanging equal energy with that star, when the one star loses all its energy, the other gets this big rush of it. So much it goes flying." He pulls back his arm like a big-league pitcher and tosses the apple across the room.

She follows the apple's flight path. It bounces off the coat hanger antenna of his TV and lands in his wood box.

She laughs. "It does not!"

"Oh, yes it does. Right out of the galaxy. See, they think they can't live without each other. It makes 'em go right off course. That other star was their one good thing. They don't want anything else. That's the problem. That is the problem right there."

Behind him the pot is boiling like crazy, the smell of thick, burnt coffee tickling the back of Delilah's throat. Will's watching her, but she's still looking at that one apple in the bowl. He stands and turns the coffee off, putting it aside to let the grounds settle.

Delilah gets up and walks to the wood box. Despite her fear of spiders, which she knows for sure are lurking under the cut pine, she feels around in the dark bottom until she finds the soft, sunken apple. She looks at it carefully, its little dimples and puckers, the wrinkled yellow skin. She smells it, but it's lost most of its fresh apple smell. It smells like tangy cider now, like something old and about to turn rotten. She presses it briefly to her cheek before putting it safely in the pocket of her sweater.

She turns and sees he is watching her from the counter. "I'm ready to go now," she says.

**

BACK HOME LATER THAT night, Delilah wakes up drowning, her lungs filling with water, lead, useless scraps of thin paper. She sits up gasping and leans forward on her rumpled blankets to try to pull in more air. She reaches for her inhaler, knocking a cup and a pile of books off the crate beside her bed as she scrambles for it. She takes a puff, sucks the metallic spray deep into her chest, then takes another. She sits back against the wall waiting for it to ease, for the relief to spread though her chest, the hand to loosen its dark grip. But the inhaler does nothing. Every breath is a long, rasping wheeze. The air reaches the back of her throat but refuses to go farther.

She gets up and stumbles to the living room, checking the clock above the stove as she goes by. Nine-fifteen. Her dad won't be off for almost two hours. Will's number is scrawled on a piece of paper tacked to the wall for emergencies, Maggie and Red's beneath it. She picks up the phone and dials.

When Will bursts through the door to the shack, she is on the floor trying to pull her shoes on, but the effort is too much for her. He slips them on her feet and pulls her up from the floor, scooping her up in his arms like a child and carrying her to the truck.

"Don't talk," he orders, settling her in her seat and slamming her door shut before running around the front of the truck to the driver's side.

The drive to Emergency feels like it takes hours, though Will drives like a Formula One racer. No, it takes 102 breaths. She follows his order and doesn't say a word, only breathes, in, out, in, out, counting, her chest heaving. The window is open and she leans her head out, trying to gasp any extra oxygen she can into her lungs.

Will drives hunched over the wheel, watching the road with razor focus. She feels like she is floating away, barely there. She thinks of Annie, who would always breathe with Delilah when she was having an attack, holding both her hands, making her look at her. *In, out.*

Delilah melts back in her seat, light-headed. She feels Will shake her shoulder roughly, and she knows he's scared. He says words she doesn't hear. She is disappearing, she is nothing but her useless lungs refusing to expand.

In Emergency, amidst the white lights and noise and flashes of nurses in blue and green, they give her a shot of adrenaline and hook her up to the nebulizer before they lay her back against the raised hospital bed, murmuring to her as she watches them over the soft plastic mask. *In, out, in, out.*

Will talks to them at her bedside, but she doesn't hear what he's saying. Someone sticks her with an IV needle, and she doesn't flinch. A doctor comes back to check on her, his head huge above her, and listens to her chest. He shouts an order at a nurse. Someone takes blood from her thin white arm. Mac's face appears above her at one point and she realizes Will must have called him. The drugs have hit her system, and her hands shake, her heart races under her flannel pyjama top.

She still wheezes with every breath. She feels a detached amazement at her body's stubbornness. Nothing they do can make her breathe.

Hours later she is in a dim, twilit room on the ward in an oxygen tent, finally stabilized. Mac told her before he left that the doctor said it had been close. That if they hadn't got to the hospital when they did, he isn't sure what would have happened. Something about blood oxygen levels. Mac was shaky, pale. He wanted to stay in her room, but the nurses convinced him it was okay to go.

There had been talk of putting her on a plane to Edmonton before the drugs finally kicked in. They have pumped her full of adrenaline and cortisone and she has had two more nebulizer treatments. There is only a tiny rattle now when she inhales. She has at least a few hours before it all wears off and she has to have another mask.

Pale moonlight shines through the clear plastic tent surrounding her bed. There's a blue jug of water sweating on the rolling side table beside her and a Styrofoam cup of cranberry juice she had two sips of to placate the sunny nurse. There are two little old ladies sleeping in the other beds. One of them looks so old and fragile that Delilah isn't convinced she's still alive.

She walks her fingers up the inside of her crinkled plastic tent, following a glimmering line of light. When she was little and had to stay in the hospital, she used to lie in the tent at night and play games with her fingers to keep herself amused. She would name them. Gwendolyn and Annabelle. Clarice and Chantelle. They would have conversations about their little dogs or the dress they had bought that day.

"Jeez, kid," she hears from the entrance to her room. "You scared me there."

She lets her hand drop to her lap and turns on her side. Will is standing in the doorway. She hadn't seen him after her dad arrived. She assumed he had left.

"Sorry," she says. "I'm okay now."

He comes closer to her bed and looks at the tent around her, reaches out to touch the plastic. "You like that boy who lived in the bubble, or what?"

She smiles. She had seen that movie about the boy who could never leave his plastic bubble the year before on TV in Vancouver. "I guess. Except I get to come out in a couple of days."

"Well . . . I just wanted to say good night. Hope you can sleep okay." He lowers his voice. His face is distorted through the plastic. "Those old ladies might keep you up with their partying."

She laughs. "Good night," she says.

He looks like he wants to say something else, but he turns to go.

"Will?"

He turns back. "Yeah?"

"Thank you for taking me to the hospital."

"No problem, kid. Thanks for not dying on my watch."

She settles back on her pillows and feels her body relax, the tight muscles around her ribs and chest letting go. She's so tired. Since she was young, whenever she was sick, she was afraid to go to sleep in case she stopped breathing in the night. It was only when she was in the hospital, surrounded by people who could save her, that she would finally feel safe enough to close her eyes.

JULY 13, 1977
SEASCAPE ARTIST'S COLONY, CARMEL, CALIFORNIA

> *Delilah, I know you don't understand. But people are meant for certain things, little bird. It's hard for you*

to get that now because you don't know yet what you were meant for. But listen: There's what we think we are, what other people want us to be, and then there's what's real. What we're destined for.

I'm an artist, Delilah. I can't apologize for that. I am an artist who hasn't been doing art. I lost my muse up north, I couldn't find her anywhere. She doesn't like that bare, dead landscape.

Try to understand that a part of me was dying there. It's not unlike being a mother who can't find her child but knows she exists, knows she's out there somewhere wandering alone. I was feeling lost and empty until I came to the colony and met these people.

I wish I hadn't left the way I did. I wish I could take that back, but I just couldn't fight, Delilah, I couldn't stand the thought of arguing with your dad about what was best for me and best for you. I know what's best. So many women artists went mad because they felt constrained . . . look at Camille Claudel. What other incredible things could she have created if she wasn't so oppressed?

I want to be a good example for you. I want to show you what a woman should do for herself. Ursula Le Guin has a quote: "I want young girls to explode like volcanoes." I want that for you. But how can I model it if I'm dormant myself?

It's only three months. It's not an eternity. If I had the money, I would have taken you with me, but as

I said in the note it wasn't possible. You need to settle in there, make some friends. Have some adventures. And then maybe we can talk about the best place for all of us to be together. You will forgive me someday. I know you will.

All my love,

Annie

✱✱✱

ONCE SHE HAS RECOVERED from her three-day stay at the hospital, Delilah and Jones spend every day they can out at Joliffe hauling old chairs, blankets, and crates for shelves to the old cabin. For the most part, the adults leave them alone. On nights that Mac works, Delilah eats dinner at Jones's or with Will and Jethro and Mary Ellen. Often half of Willow Flats or Rainbow Valley is at one of those houses cooking chicken or whitefish or caribou steaks over the fire.

Old Town never seems to rest; it's like everyone knows to use up every moment of the daylight before the winter comes back. Delilah can't imagine it, this cold darkness she hears about. Now, there is no darkness at all. Some nights she wanders home at midnight alone from Jones's, the sun barely set and the entire southern horizon awash in smouldering light as she sinks into her bed.

Mac is drifting farther and farther away, unmoored from her world now by working all the time, turned in on himself when he's home. Delilah tries not to think of Annie because she doesn't like the confusion that wells up when she does. She won't speak to her when she calls, shaking her head silently at her dad when he tries to hand her the phone. She isn't sure why. It's a strange thing, she thinks, to wish someone hadn't left and to wish they would never come back at the same time. The hurt, when she probes it, is so vast it spreads out around her, touches the edges of things. In certain moments, she never wants to see her mother again. In certain moments, she wishes Annie would disappear for good, imagines her driving away down the dusty dirt road outside their shack until she becomes a tiny speck on the horizon, no bigger than an ant.

※※※

ALTHOUGH WILL HAD LONG ago finished Clementine's little nook in his former woodshed, she doesn't come in July after all. When Delilah asks him about it, all he says is, "Not sure, kid. Guess her mom had a change of plans." He doesn't mention it again, and Delilah doesn't press it though she can feel his disappointment. Mac tells her it's because of Sarah's parents.

"What's wrong with them?" she asks. "Why won't they let her see him?"

"It's complicated," he says. He won't elaborate.

Delilah is so tired of adults thinking she can't handle the truth.

※

ONE EVENING IN LATE July Jones bangs on the door while Delilah's on her couch reading. Her dad is working the evening shift. "Hey, Will's taking us to *Star Wars*," Jones calls from the porch.

She sits up. "Really?" *Star Wars* is all Jones has been talking about for the past week. He's furious that Yellowknife got the movie months after the rest of the world has already seen it.

"Yeah," Jones says through the screen. "Hurry up, it starts in ten minutes. Will's in the truck."

Delilah scrambles to find her sandals and runs out of the house. Will is in the driver's seat, his arm resting on the edge, a cigarette dangling from his fingers. "Hey, kid. Hop in back there, you two. You can catch the breeze." Laska is beside him on the seat. Delilah and Jones climb up and Will takes off up the hill, honking at Bear as they pass a group of people in front of Weaver's. Delilah thinks briefly of Clem, imagines her snuggled next to her in the back of the truck while her dad drives them up the hill, as she would have been if she had come to visit when she was supposed to. Delilah knows it's silly, but still. She imagines a squirmy, giggling child laughing beside her as the breeze whips their hair. A little phantom sister.

They have to wait in the long line that trails down Franklin Avenue, and Jones is so nervous about not getting in that Delilah thinks he might bolt to the front, but he contains himself. Will buys them popcorn and red licorice and they find seats.

"All right, Jonesy," Will says, settling his big body back in his seat. "Now we get to see what you been shooting your mouth off about all this time."

Jones sets his popcorn on his lap. "This is going to be the best movie you have ever seen," he says.

Will laughs and chews his licorice. "That so?"

After the movie Jones is on fire. He babbles non-stop about dark forces and battleships and dying planets. Delilah tries to keep up as he reconstructs the entire movie while they walk to Nettie's for food. Will humours Jones with good-natured teasing, and they settle into a booth at the packed restaurant. Apparently, everyone else has had the same idea.

"Other worlds . . ." Jones is saying after they order their orange pop and cheese perogies and Will orders his Labatt's and bratwurst and onions. "Like, his imagination with all these worlds and the creatures. It's genius."

"Genius?" Will says. "You think so?"

"Well, yeah," Jones says. "It's all make-believe. It all came from his imagination. He didn't base it on anything he knew or had ever experienced before."

"Ah," Will says, and thanks the waitress when she comes over with their drinks.

She nods at Will. "This one causing you trouble, kids?" She's grey-haired and soft, like a sassy grandma.

They laugh.

"He's a charmer, but he's a troublemaker." She winks.

Will takes a swig of the beer and winks back. "Must have me confused with someone else," he says.

"Oh, I don't think so." She smiles and walks off to another table.

"So," Will says. "You don't think there are other worlds

out there? Other people living their little lives, just like us?"

Jones stares at him. "What, like aliens?"

Will shrugs one shoulder. "Maybe like aliens."

"That's nuts," Delilah says.

"Yeah?"

"Yeah."

Jones slaps a hand down on the table. "Wait. You believe in aliens? For real? Like, aliens with weird faces and green skin?"

Will nods solemnly, then his face breaks out in a wide grin. "Nah! Just pulling your chain."

He sits back and surveys the busy room. "Tell you what, though. It's a great big universe. If we think we know everything that's out there, we're in for a big surprise."

"Do you think there are other planets like Earth?" Delilah says.

Will waves at someone across the room. "I do."

"With people on them?" Jones asks.

"Why not?" Will says. "You know how many planets in a galaxy? Billions. You know how many galaxies in the universe? Billions. You know how many stars are out there? You know how long humans have been living on this earth and having their children and working at their jobs and loving who they love and hating what they hate? Two hundred thousand years. Think about it."

Jones sits back.

"Make you feel small?" Will says.

Jones nods.

"Good," Will says as the food arrives. "It's supposed to."

He thanks the waitress and then leans across their plates of perogies and sausage. "Any time you start feeling like maybe you have some big problems nobody else ever had before, walk outside and look up. Then you'll see how big you are. How big those problems are. Look up and you see where we came from. Where every single thing you look at and play with and love and hate and wonder about and think about came from. It's all from up there. And that's where we go back to when we're gone. We are small. We are very, very small. You never forget that, and you'll be okay." He smiles at them. "Eat up."

***

DELILAH SITS ON THE bow of the *Aurora*, leaning against the cabin, her face turned to the late-evening sun. The light dances off the bow wave as it slices the water. There is noise to the stern, someone singing, someone yelling. She has left Jones at the crib tournament in the cabin below battling Will for first place.

By tonight they will be at a small island off Lonesome Point. It's a six-hour trip, after touring around the North Arm for a while, and the fishing boat is packed with Old Town residents. City Jane had arrived at the docks with Will and an expensive-looking backpack. Louise, a waitress from the Wildcat, and her four-year-old son Dusty came with their gear stuffed in garbage bags.

"This seat taken?" Mac settles beside her. He's wearing a pair of worn cut-offs, and he's sweaty and already sunburned.

"Nope." Delilah's skirt ruffles in the breeze.

Mac takes a sip of his gin and tonic, the ice cubes rattling in the cup. He's had more than he usually would. She doesn't mind, though. This is the most relaxed, the happiest he has looked since Annie left. Earlier Delilah and Jones had been making drinks for the adults, taking orders like waiters and throwing extra shots of gin in before handing them over innocently. The counter inside the boat is strewn with lemon carcasses and spilled tonic.

"Beautiful, isn't it?"

She nods. There is nothing out here but water. Once in a while they pass a small unpopulated island of rock and trees, but otherwise, nothing. It's hard for her to grasp that this is just a lake. It feels like you could go for days and never see another person.

"First time you'll be camping since you were five," Mac says, tossing the ice from his cup into the lake. "Aside from the Barrens trip."

"Yeah."

They were in Saskatchewan when she was five. Delilah remembers dust and heat. She remembers walking from their tent to the lake, how she just wanted to drink it. She sat in the water with her pink bucket, filling it and dumping it on her head over and over.

"Dad?"

He looks over at her, his hand shielding his eyes from the sun.

"Are you and Will having a fight about something?" She has noticed they haven't spoken since everyone got on the boat. Not once. No good-natured ribbing, no whispered conversations away from the crowd like usual. Nothing. They avoided each other, sitting at opposite ends of the boat. It's unsettling for her. Mac puts his hand down and sits back. Closes his eyes.

"No. We're not fighting."

"But you're not talking to each other."

He smiles sleepily. "Not talking doesn't mean you're fighting, Lila. Just means you have nothing to say."

"Okay."

He takes a swig of his drink. "So listen, Lila . . ."

She feels a tug at her belly.

"I've been talking to your mom . . . and the thing is, you know, it's just too hard on everyone for us to be apart."

She is watching Mac, every squint, every breath he is taking, the rise and fall of his sunburned chest. Suddenly it comes to her.

"We're going to California," she says flatly.

He takes another sip of his drink and sets the empty cup down. "I'm sorry, kiddo. I know you like it here. But she says she won't come back. So I'm thinking . . . you know, we head down there and surprise her."

"Are you crazy?"

He is taken aback. "What?"

"I . . . no, I am not going to California. I'm going to school here in September. Grade 8. I already picked my classes in June. I'm taking sewing . . ."

"Kiddo, I know it isn't ideal, but it's not like it's the middle of the school year or anything."

"No. No. I'm not." She knows she sounds like a toddler, but she can't help it. Her mind is racing. She thinks of Jones playing cards downstairs. She thinks of Will. Of Maggie, making everyone avocado sandwiches in the galley. Red, driving the boat wearing some old navy captain hat over his scraggly hair. She feels desperate and latches on to the one thing she thinks might buy her time.

"She was with Marcel." She can't bring herself to say "slept with" or worse, "had sex with." She wants to crawl out of her own skin, but she knows she must do this.

The wind has picked up off the lake, and her hair is blowing wildly around her. She tries to tame it with shaking hands. Her father is staring at her.

"*With* him?" he says numbly.

She nods, miserable.

"How . . . how do you know that? You could have misunderstood . . ."

"I heard them! So many times. They were in the room next door to me. Mom always thought I was sleeping, but I never was." She is almost yelling. The indignity of having him question her when having to even say the words is like pulling off her own fingernails. Having to remember. Marcel's stupid deep voice whispering things to Annie . . . disgusting things, Delilah is sure.

Mac looks like he has been punched in the guts. He lets his breath out in a sudden rush, as though he had been holding it a long time. He looks out across the water. "I see," he says.

"Yes. So . . . so you shouldn't go down there. Because that's what she did. And . . . and not just with Marcel." Delilah is blinking back tears, either from her whipping hair or from the sting of hurting him, she isn't sure.

Someone shouts from the door to the cabin, calling for Mac. He stands, a little unsteadily.

"Dad?"

"I should do down," he says. He isn't looking at her. "See what they want."

"Dad . . ."

"See you later, Lila."

And he's gone. She's hurt him. Even though it wasn't her that did the terrible things, she still hurt him. She wonders if telling him was the right thing to do after all.

***

DELILAH AND JONES SPRAWL on the bunk in the wheelhouse, high above the chaos and drinking below on the decks and in the cabin. She has put her book aside, a battered mystery she found in a box of odds and ends under the bunk when she was looking for her sandal. Jones is twisting the dials on a transistor radio trying to get something besides the static and white noise. They are too far from anything, he had said, but he keeps trying.

The boat sways and rocks them, keeps steadily on, and Delilah feels relaxed, the worries that gnawed at her since her talk with her dad finally quieting for the day. He was laughing and playing backgammon the last time she saw him. Maybe he will be okay. Maybe he just needs to think about it for a bit until he realizes that he and Delilah should stay in Yellowknife and let Annie do whatever she wants. The pillow under her head smells of must and oil and faintly of old fish, which is strangely soothing. Red has gone to get a drink, but he will come up and check his course again in a minute. He has been sitting at his captain's chair quietly, letting them lie there in peace. Delilah's eyes drift shut as she focusses on the drone of the engine, the laughter below, the lightness all around her.

***

THE ISLAND IS A chunk of rock with small stands of trees, surrounded by nothing but water as far as the eye can see. They manoeuvre into a spot by the jumbles of boats moored offshore. Delilah and Jones are standing on the deck as they come to a full stop. The party is in full swing. There are tents scattered all along the beach, but a large space has been left clear for a giant bonfire, which is roaring and sending sparks flying. Children are running and screaming in the shallow water, and the adults are dancing and laughing. Delilah has seen photos of Woodstock, and this looks like a mini version. The sun still shines on as the adults take trip after trip in the dinghy to bring the gear to the island.

Delilah points to the boats moored near them. "Look at them all," she says to Jones.

He yawns. "I know. My dad said there would be like a couple hundred people here. Some Giant guy might even come by helicopter."

"Helicopter? Where would it land?"

"Don't know. I think there's a clearing on the back of the island somewhere. It's just rock."

They watch Louise carry a sleeping Dusty onto the beach. Maggie guides them to the dinghy when it's their turn, and they join the throngs on the island. There are bongos going, and with this strange tribal soundtrack, Delilah feels like she's just landed in the Amazon. She scans the crowd for Will and spots him farther down the beach with City Jane, smoking, Laska by his side.

She tells Jones she'll see him in a bit and goes to look for her dad. She finds him putting up his small bush tent by a grove of trees. She dumps her pack on the rocky ground. "Need some help?"

He pounds a peg into the dirt and wipes his forehead. "All done. You tired? You can go to bed any time." He doesn't seem angry with her. Just a little distant. He hasn't mentioned what she told him. Hasn't asked her any questions, which she finds confusing. Why wouldn't he want to know?

"I'm not tired," she says. There's too much excitement to sleep. She helps him drag in the foamies and sleeping bags and sets up her bed.

Float planes come in and people stream from them. Muddy's plane appears around midnight, just as the sun is starting to fade. He buzzes the beach before landing what seems to Delilah too close to the shore, then dives off the float and swims in with the rope in his teeth. The crowd applauds him as he rises shirtless from the lake, his long hair and beard dripping down his chest, his eyes wild.

The music goes on for hours, adults dancing on the beach, singing at the top of their lungs. Will plays a Scottish drinking song on the guitar that has them all roaring with laughter. Jones and Delilah eat charred hot dogs, corn from a barrel of boiling lake water. They drink Coke after Coke and wander through the crowds. They are chasing the twins and Dusty in the shallows when the helicopter with the Giant official appears overhead, whirling and roaring, and the children run after it as it hovers over the far end of the island before touching down. She keeps an eye on her dad, and he seems committed to having a good time, drinking and dancing and singing along wildly to the music.

Later that night, Delilah goes into the deep bush to pee, and when she comes back, she finds her dad and Will and Muddy by the dinghy on the shore, talking intently. They aren't shouting, exactly, but their posture is tense. It's mostly her dad and Muddy speaking, gesturing while Muddy sways on his bare feet, a bottle in his hand. Delilah can hear *knew it was a risk, give it a chance.* Muddy says *ever heard the word "traitor?"* Will responds so quietly Delilah can't catch a word. He looks up and sees her standing by the trees, and she holds his gaze for a minute before turning away and heading back to the crowd. This is it. Whatever has created the silence between her father and Will, this is it. She stumbles along the beach, splashing ankle-high in the sun-warmed water. It must be about the mine, she thinks. The Barrens, maybe. But what? She spots Jones by the bonfire and goes to join him.

By two in the morning Delilah is exhausted, lake mud dried on her feet and ankles, her hair tangled and damp, the Coke churning in her stomach. She crawls into her tent and falls into an instant deep sleep, the sound of the bongos still echoing in her ears.

She wakes up to a raven cawing outside the tent. He is insistent, low and throaty. She waits for him to fly off so she can sleep in peace, but he doesn't stop. She rolls over and covers her ears with her wadded-up sweatshirt, but still all she can hear is the raven. Finally she crawls past her snoring father and unzips the tent.

Outside, the offending bird is sitting on a small stump, a half-gnawed ear of corn by his feet.

"Thanks for waking me up," she whispers.

He croaks in return and pokes at the corn.

She wanders through the tents in the early-morning light. They are set up at awkward angles, like they were put together by drunk people, which they were. There are clothes scattered on the lichen, beer bottles everywhere and paper plates being picked at by birds. The lake is still and smooth, morning sun reflecting in the blue black. The boats bob peacefully offshore, their owners probably fast asleep on board. She wonders how the argument between her dad and Muddy and Will ended the night before.

Delilah walks to the end of the beach, imagining she is the only survivor after a nuclear meltdown, kind of like *The Chrysalids* meets *On the Beach*. Her days are numbered. But then she can hear a baby crying, a mother shushing it. There is a small green tent at the farthest tip of the beach, and just as Delilah gets close, the front rustles and a woman comes out. It's City Jane. She's wearing cut-offs and a thin camisole, and when she sees Delilah she crosses her arms across her chest. Her hair is a mess.

"Hi, Delilah," she whispers and clears her throat.

"Hi," Delilah says, her eyes flickering back to the green tent. There are heavy mine boots outside it, and a pair of work socks. They look like Will's boots. Did Jane sleep in his tent with him, or did he sleep somewhere else?

City Jane stands there a second in her bare feet, hugging herself. "I have to pee," she whispers. "See you later."

"See you." Delilah's nuclear aftermath imaginings dissolve, and she's transported back to reality. She slept in there with him. Delilah can tell from Jane's embarrassment. She rolls this over in her mind. Does this mean they're together now? Dating? Behind her, one of the boat engines starts up. She can smell woodsmoke from a breakfast fire. Children have started trickling to the beach behind her.

There's still not a sound from inside that green tent, but those are definitely Will's boots.

* * *

"SO THEY'RE DOING IT?" Jones doesn't sound surprised. More intrigued than anything.

"I guess," she says, slapping at a mosquito on her thigh. She still hasn't told Jones that she saw the three men arguing near the dinghy. She isn't sure why, but it worries her, and she wants to keep it to herself. She did want to tell him about City Jane being in Will's tent, though.

They're perched at the bow of the *Aurora* in the late evening. Delilah isn't sure what time it is. It could be anywhere between seven and midnight. Their feet dangle into thin air below, far from the deep water. The lake drops off to an endless pit about forty feet from shore, but if they want to go back for some reason, they can take the dinghy or jump in and swim there.

That morning, after a breakfast of fire-cooked bannock and jam and coffee made by Maggie and Louise and Esther for the crowd, Delilah and Jones had explored the island, taking Laska with them as they wandered across the rock picking wild raspberries, swimming in the small warm bay they found on the north side of the island.

They've been on the boat for hours, leaving the adults lolling on the beaches, sunning themselves, and dozing off while the kids napped. They made themselves ham sandwiches down below for dinner. Things are just getting started on the beach.

"Do you think she likes him?" Jones's arm is so close to Delilah's she can feel the heat of the day radiating off him. They are still in their swimsuits after diving off the boat an hour or so before. They each have a glass of tonic with a splash of gin and three lemon wedges. It's warm, and Delilah couldn't stand the taste, but she added two spoonfuls of white sugar to hers, and it's a little better.

"I think so," she says, and takes a small sip. Jones taps the side of the boat absently with his heel, the muscle in his leg shifting with each tap. Delilah has a strange, sudden urge to place her hand on his thigh, run it down the cord of muscle. She takes another sip. "I don't know if he likes her, though."

"But they're doing it," Jones says, as though this were proof that he does. He's looking at her, his eyes seaweed green.

"Yeah. But still. I don't know."

"I think he likes her," he says.

"How can you tell?"

He shrugs his thin shoulders. "She's pretty. For an old person. Why wouldn't he?"

Delilah rolls this over in her mind. "Is pretty all that matters?" she asks.

She knows it isn't. She knows lots of couples where the woman isn't the prettiest person in the world. But she also knows it helps. A lot. She's not sure where that leaves her when it comes to things like this.

"No," Jones says. "But you have to think the person's pretty. Like, even ugly people usually have someone who thinks they're pretty."

Delilah knocks back the rest of her drink and sets the cup on the deck. "Jones?"

He taps his foot again, lost in thought. "Yeah?"

"Do you think I'm pretty?"

He stops tapping. She holds her breath until her lungs ache, heart tripping under her ribs.

"Yeah, I guess," he says, looking down at his drink.

A smile spreads through her. She doesn't say anything. Jones resumes his tapping. They sit there, "Bobby McGee" drifting over the water toward them from the fire, the adults joining in on the chorus as she and Jones rock gently on the deck in the starless twilight.

august

SEASCAPE ARTIST'S COLONY
AUGUST 12, 1977

Little bird. Still not a peep from you.

The colony here is so wonderful I can hardly even put it into words. I hope one day you will find your people the way I have found mine. I just want to hug them all. I paint every day here. I'm surrounded by rolling fields, streams, mountains . . . how could I not be inspired?

I guess you received my birthday package. I'm sure it must have arrived by now. Don't open the wrapped gift until your birthday, but there's a T-shirt in there for you too. I hope you like it. It's a silkscreen of a painting I did of the most incredible redwood I saw while walking in the forest with a dear friend. We stopped beneath the most towering, majestic tree I have ever seen. So humbling to feel so small, so insignificant, so young in the face of something so rooted and ancient. I wish you could have seen it. My friend said it was the biggest one he's ever seen by far.

I wish you would call me, Delilah. Just to say hello. Think about it. I hope your breathing is okay since your hospital stay. Your dad says you're doing better now.

All my love, Annie

✱✱✱

"Esther?" Delilah calls, standing at the back door of the Wildcat.

Esther turns from the counter where she is elbow-deep in a plastic bin of marinade, turning chunks of red meat with her hands.

"Delilah? How are you doing, kiddo? Come on in." She shakes her hands, spraying marinade into the bin, then walks to the sink.

Delilah steps up over the crooked last step and into the small kitchen. She can see Louise chatting with a group of tourists in the front room, a pen jammed into her ponytail and a jangle of silver earrings hanging from her ears.

"What can I do you for?" Esther asks, her plump face soft and kind. She comes over and rubs Delilah's arm. "Everything okay?"

"Yeah. Yes. I just was thinking. You know how my mom left?"

"Yes, honey. I heard she's gone for a bit."

"Well—"

Gary, a boy from school, walks in from the front with a handful of dishes and plunks them in the sink. He nods at Delilah and she raises a hand in acknowledgement. Esther already has a dishwasher, she thinks. Now what?

"I . . . uh . . . I was wondering if you still needed any help at all. Like when I came and helped before."

Esther looks at her thoughtfully. "Ah. Gary, let that one soak," she calls over Delilah's shoulder. "That egg won't come off unless you let it soak. Well," she says, wiping her hands on her apron. "Let's see here. How old are you? Twelve?"

"Thirteen in a week."

"Thirteen in a week. That's a bit young, to be honest, Delilah. For a real job, you know. Gary here is my nephew, so he's helping out like you were before."

"I know it's young. I just thought . . . I can help out too. Like, not wait tables or anything, but I can chop things and wash dishes maybe." She can't keep the pleading out of her voice. She wants this job, she needs this job.

Louise comes to the counter, peels an order from her pad and slaps it down, hollering out, "Whitefish special times four, Esther. Please. Oh hey, Delilah."

"Hey," Delilah says.

"How's it going? You and your dad okay? Thanks for helping out with Dusty at the Point. You ever want to babysit, just let me know."

"Sure." Delilah doesn't want to babysit Dusty. She knows Louise is trying to get closer to her dad. She had noticed her making eyes at him on the boat.

Louise is wearing blue eyeshadow, and to Delilah it makes her look like a Muppet.

"Okay, well, you tell Mac, if he needs anything, I can help out. I can drop off a meal or what have you."

"We're fine. I can cook."

"Of course you can, hon. What was I thinking? Well then, anything else. Tell him I said so." Louise smiles, her lips pink and glossy as a teenager's, and turns back to the dining room.

Esther watches Louise walk away and then turns to a bin of marinating fish fillets and places them on the hot grill.

"Tell you what. How about you come in a couple hours a day for prep. You can do the cucumbers and the carrots and peel the potatoes. Maybe help bake the bread. Come in around nine in the morning before the lunch rush. Okay?"

Relief swells through Delilah. "Yes. Thank you."

Esther turns to look at Delilah. "You can start tomorrow. You saving up for something?"

Delilah nods.

"What, some makeup? New clothes for school?"

Delilah is saving up because it has occurred to her that despite the information she gave her father, he might still decide to leave. She wants to save money in case this happens. She isn't sure what she would even do, what she *could* do, but she wants to be as prepared as she can.

"Yeah, I guess," she says to Esther.

Within three days, Esther is trusting Delilah to add the spices to the moose meat chili and plate the whitefish with the little lemon spiral and the sprinkle of parsley flakes. Delilah feels like she has a real job, like she is grown up now.

She wakes up alone most mornings, Mac long gone to the mines. He is working every shift he can get his hands on. He hasn't mentioned leaving again, and school starts in a week. She has her breakfast, usually Rice Krispies and a glass of fruit punch, and then walks down the short hill and around the corner from Weaver's to the Wildcat. She is making two dollars an hour and working three hours a day. In a month, she will have over a hundred dollars.

***

ON HER THIRTEENTH BIRTHDAY, Delilah wakes up craving bacon. She must have been dreaming of it, or maybe a neighbour is cooking it. She sits up, a slow excitement creeping through her.

Thirteen. Finally.

She gets out of bed and pulls on her shorts and the glittery kitten T-shirt she ordered from a *Tiger Beat* magazine back in Vancouver. The house is quiet. Mac must have left for work. At dinner the night before, he hadn't mentioned anything about it being her birthday today, but she knows he's bluffing. For all Annie's nonchalance about gifts, he loves giving them. In Toronto, he had pretended to forget her birthday once, and she had been almost in tears until he asked her to go out to the garage for a box of light bulbs. The lavender banana-seat bike she had wanted from the Sears catalogue was sitting there by the car. Annie told her that her dad had spent half the night assembling it.

Delilah pads through the empty house but finds no note or presents, no birthday cup of cocoa waiting for her, no cinnamon bun from the bakery uptown, her favourite treat now that Annie's gone. She steps outside the front door, brushing the chimes aside as she walks to the edge of the porch and sits, her bare feet trailing in the dust.

Martha is sitting on a lawn chair in front of her own house, her round face turned to the sun, her cotton dress hitched up, and a beer bottle wedged between her thick legs. Charlie is pounding a board into their broken front step.

Delilah has no idea how old Martha is. Fifty? Sixty? Charlie seems old, shrunken. His shoulders cave in and the hair at his temples is grey. He wears little round glasses and stoops when he walks by with Martha on their way to Weaver's. But Martha is a small mountain, a volcano, every part of her swollen and huge, vibrating.

There's activity down by the waterfront. Delilah can see a few small boats on Back Bay setting out to fish. Jones is with Red on the boat, but he has said he'll come by in the evening and they can go to Weaver's for an ice cream sandwich.

The realization that her dad has forgotten her birthday dawns on her. Instead of feeling hurt and betrayed, she just feels tired. The weariness of having to tell him, having to deal with his horror when he remembers. All of it. He will race around the shack in his filthy work clothes trying to whip up some sad little Hamburger Helper birthday dinner while she sits there telling him it's okay.

She wishes the Wildcat was open today so she had something to do. She could go see what Will and Jethro and Mary Ellen are up to, but she hasn't seen Will since

Lonesome Point. When Delilah thinks too much about her dad and Will, she feels a churning in her stomach that she doesn't like, and her mind starts racing. She misses Will, is all. And she isn't quite sure who this serious, distracted, angry version of her father is.

She plays in the dirt with her big toe now, making swirling patterns.

"Hey, girl!" Martha calls from her lawn chair.

Delilah waves, still running her toe through the soft earth.

"You got any of them *Archie* comics?"

Martha never returns her comics, but what can Delilah do? Say no? Not likely.

"Sure."

She stands and heads into the shack, letting the screen door slam shut behind her. She gathers a couple of old *Betty and Veronica*s from under her bed and returns to the front yard. She hands them to Martha, who takes them and scrutinizes them carefully. Her arms are round and doughy, and one of them has little white circular scars scattered over her dark skin like shiny stars.

"That it? You don't have more?"

"Can't find any more right now. Those are good ones, though. They go on a camping trip in one and the other one has a Cheryl Blossom story in it."

Martha turns them over and inspects the backs. "Stupid girls." She shakes her head, but Delilah can hear the fondness Martha has for them. "Fightin' over that boy." She points a tobacco-stained finger at Delilah. "Boys don't respect you if you fight over them. You know that?"

"No. I didn't know that."

Martha watches her warily, takes a sip of beer. Her dress is wrinkled but pretty, small yellow flowers stitched along the round collar. "You got no boy?"

Delilah shakes her head. The sun is starting to bake down on her bare legs. It must be closing in on noon. Her stomach growls ferociously.

"No?" Martha slaps the comics down on her lap. "That red-haired boy comes around here."

Delilah flushes down to her toes. "That's just Jones."

"Mmm," Martha says, cackling. "That's just Jones." She opens a comic and starts to read, squinting in the sunlight.

Delilah feels she has been dismissed, so she goes back into the cool shack. She walks into her messy bedroom, the dark shapes of clothing and books scattered all over the floor. She reaches under her bed to feel for the small package from her mother. She had almost thrown it out when her dad gave it to her, but something made her keep it. As if she had known it would be her only gift.

She sits with her back against the bed and opens the plain brown wrapping. There's a letter and a T-shirt, both of which she shoves back under her bed. She unwraps the small present and finds something pink and ruffly. She shakes it out and a scented sachet with a tiny ribbon falls from the folds. It's a sundress, dusty rose, with a tiered skirt. The top is elastic. It stretches when she pulls on it and there are two thin straps. She looks at it for a moment. Turns it over in her hands. Then she puts it aside and walks to the kitchen and opens the fridge.

There is a full pack of bacon on the shelf, plus half a tomato and a few limp leaves of lettuce. She'll make herself a BLT. She starts to lay slices of bacon in the cast iron pan.

Four would be enough, but she keeps laying them out, peeling them off and arranging them in the pan. She adds more and more, crossing them over each other in a lattice until she has used them all and they start to writhe and spit. A tear runs down her nose, skittering into the pan below. She wipes her face with the back of her hand.

When the bacon is crisp, with no bits of rubbery fat left on it, she drains it on a piece of old newspaper and places it on a plate. All twenty pieces. She doesn't bother with the tomato or lettuce or even the bread. She sits at that table and eats it, piece by piece, until it's gone.

She spends most of the day reading, except when she walks to Weaver's for a bag of Popcorn Twists and a Mars bar. Martha is out front most of the day, watching Charlie and hollering for him to bring her things. They sit out there having a picnic of white bread sandwiches and beer while Tammy Wynette croons from their record player inside. When Delilah comes back from Weaver's, she notices that Martha has tossed her comics in the dirt by her chair.

In the late afternoon, she lies on the couch, her dad's copy of *Coma* beside her. The bacon and Popcorn Twists and Mars bar are churning in her stomach, and she feels almost comatose herself as she lies there in the heat, waving blackflies away.

She's dozing when her dad comes in, ore dust covering his work clothes, his hair crammed under a Northern Air hat.

"Get up," he says, dumping his gear by the door. "Come on, get up." He sounds frantic, like there's a fire or an earthquake. She sits up blearily, scratching a welt on her leg. A fly must have got her when she was asleep. "What's the matter?"

He strides across the room and kneels in front of her.

"I'm so sorry." His face is a sheet of crumpled misery. "I was so distracted. So busy. I just . . . all the extra work I'm doing. I knew . . . last week, I knew, and then I just had a million things on my mind . . ."

This is exactly what she was worried about. She leans over and hugs him, inhales a day of mine sweat and grit. His neck is sticky from the heat.

"It's okay," she says.

He clings to her for a second and then releases her.

"Get up," he says, pulling her up by her hands. "Let's go."

"Where are we going?"

He's already in his room, banging drawers. "Birthday dinner! You don't turn thirteen every day, kiddo. We are going out for a special dinner. And then tomorrow we are going to go buy you that ABBA record you want. And whatever else. Jeans, a book, whatever else."

Delilah looks down at her shiny gym shorts and too-small T-shirt. She walks to her room and surveys the pink dress sitting in a rumpled pile on the floor. Will it mean she forgives Annie if she wears it? She isn't sure, but she doesn't think so. It will be more like taking something from Annie, something she deserves. Besides, how would Annie ever know?

She strips out of her clothes and pulls on the sundress. It drifts around her knees and smells faintly like roses. Delilah goes back to the front room and slips on her white clogs. Her dad comes out wearing a clean T-shirt and cords. "Wow! You look beautiful. Where'd you get that dress?"

She shrugs, hugging her arms across her chest.

"Have I seen it before? You look so grown up." He's shaking his head like he can't quite come to terms with that dress.

"No," she says. "I don't think so."

"Where do you want to go? Wildcat?"

"It's closed," she says.

"You want the Explorer? You can get a nice steak, one of those virgin margaritas."

"No," she says. "Just Nettie's."

They get in the truck, and she expects him to drive straight up the hill but he swerves at Willow Flats and stops at Red's. He parks and tells her to give him a minute and then goes and bangs on the door. Delilah watches a canoe glide past the southern tip of Joliffe, disappearing into a white wash of sunlight.

Mac returns with Jones trailing behind him looking recently scrubbed, his hair still wet from a shower. "Look who I found, about to eat a plate of Kraft Dinner. Hop in, Jonesy."

Jones is wearing his Atari T-shirt and cut-offs, his knobby knees protruding. His sneakers are filthy. "Happy birthday. I was gonna come see you after dinner." He thrusts two Mars bars and a small brown bag at her through the open window. "These are for you."

Delilah takes them, surprised. She opens the bag and takes out a silver mood ring like they have at the pharmacy uptown. They had been there one day after school, and she had tried one on and inspected the stone. She asked Jones what black meant. He had looked at the small chart on the box and said, "Angry," and they had both laughed.

She feels a warmth in her chest thinking of him going back there and getting it later, of making any effort for her at all. "Thanks," she says.

Her dad is in the driver's seat, but instead of shifting over so Jones can get in she asks if they can ride in the back. Mac shrugs.

"Sure. And Red and Maggie are coming up to meet us as soon as Red showers off the fish smell. Short day on the lake, eh, Jones?"

"Yeah. The motor was acting up, so we came back in."

Delilah climbs out. Clambering over the back of the truck with her dress and her clogs isn't exactly ladylike. She perches on the wheel well, gathering her skirt underneath her so it doesn't blow up in the wind. This dressing like a girl is more work than she thought it would be.

Jones sits across from her. As her dad navigates the bumps heading out of the Flats, Delilah twists Jones's mood ring back and forth on her finger and thinks about a big plate of perogies swimming in butter and fried onions and sour cream.

She can feel the wind blowing off the disappointment of the morning as they fly up the hill. Yellowknife is a blur of colour around them, and Mac is going so fast she starts to laugh, and then Jones does too as they hold on to the side of that truck for dear life.

september

ON THE FIRST DAY of high school, Delilah and Jones manoeuvre through Farrah Fawcett-haired seniors with real breasts and combs in the back pockets of their jeans, young men with beards and long hair and army jackets who look like they should be teaching instead of carrying books to biology.

Nobody notices them. If anything, Delilah would guess that nobody here cares about them at all. They pass some former classmates from Mildred Hall, a group of boys, and Jones tenses, his jaw tightening. But no words are exchanged. It's as though the summer has neutralized them somehow. The students are all spread out, dispersed in the classes, making the clique combinations less potent.

Delilah has saved $120 working with Esther and can still work on the weekends until the Wildcat closes in the winter for a few months. Even though she knows she shouldn't have, she used half of the money and bought herself two pairs of bell-bottom jeans, a blouse with tiny bluebells stitched around the neck, and tennis socks with different-coloured balls at the heels. She also bought mascara for the first time, and a five-pack of Bonne Bell Lip Smackers. The rest of the money is shoved in a sock under her mattress.

Mac has been working almost every day and retreats to prospecting books in the evenings. Delilah spends some evenings with Will, Jethro, and Mary Ellen or over at Jones's, but she is starting to stay home alone many nights too. She's old enough now, after all. Annie still calls on Sundays, and inexplicably, Mac answers, often looking away from Delilah when he does, as if he's ashamed. He tells Annie about work and their trip to the Point and how Red and Maggie are doing while Delilah pretends she isn't listening. Mac doesn't talk about them going down and meeting Annie in California—or at least, not when Delilah is there.

At lunch, Jones finds Delilah by her locker, and they venture out to the yard to eat their sandwiches. He doesn't seem to feel the need to escape the yard like he did at Mildred Hall. She's glad for the company. Some new girls have chatted with her already today, and Sammy, a girl from Old Town, waved at her in the hall. She can see the possibility of friends in the future.

Misty is in her science class, along with a couple of her sidekicks. When Delilah walks by them to the back of the class, Misty looks her up and down and smirks. Delilah is wearing her peasant blouse and her new jeans. "Goody-two-shoes much?" Misty says.

Delilah lets it go, the words sliding off her instead of penetrating through her skin and shrivelling her like some toxic poison. It's like she suddenly has an invisible shield, a barrier between her and everything ugly around her. She doesn't know where it came from.

She sits in the back row and takes out her root beer Lip Smacker and applies it, licking the sweetness from her lips as she watches the leaves dance in the light outside the window. She relaxes into a strange peace; visions of the cabin on Joliffe, swimming in the lake, and sitting on the bow of Red's boat drift through her mind. The teacher, Mr. Grady, outlines what they will be learning that year. The elements. Cell division. Genes.

Just before the end of class, he settles into his chair, leans back, and asks them, "Can anyone tell me what carbon is?" He scans the class, his eyes landing on Delilah.

"You. What's your name?"

"Delilah," she says.

"Delilah. Any guesses on the carbon question?"

"It's an element."

"Yes, an element. Correct, although not what I was looking for. I think we've established that we are, indeed, studying the elements."

Misty snickers.

"Any other revelations to share with us?"

Delilah shakes her head.

"Anyone? No? Carbon, children, is present in all life forms. All of them. It is the chemical basis of all known life."

Delilah shifts her gaze back to the window. There is a small bird hopping outside. It stops and looks at her.

"Is anyone here wearing a diamond?"

"Me," Misty says, and everyone turns to look at her. Delilah watches the bird. It hops once more, then flies away.

Mr. Grady walks down the aisle and stops by Misty. "May I?" He returns to the front of the class and holds up a delicate gold chain with a small pendant. "Anyone know what this diamond is made of?"

George, an oversized boy with a red face and huge feet, calls out "Rock?"

"Rock, George? Hmm." Mr. Grady swings the chain. "I'm looking for an element here. Let's all try to focus. Put our thinking caps on, as they say in preschool."

"Uhh . . . carbon?" George looks around at his friends and they grin and snicker.

Mr. Grady points at him. "Correct! Carbon it is. This diamond this young lady has so graciously lent me to illustrate my point is indeed made of carbon. Does anyone here know anything about how diamonds are formed?"

Delilah does. Will told her everything about how diamonds are formed one afternoon in July when she and Jones had gone to his cabin. He was going to take them out in his canoe to fish for trout, but they got distracted and sat with their cans of pop on his back porch instead. He showed them his mother's wedding ring, the small perfect stone glinting in the light off the lake. It had been hot, no breeze to cool them. Delilah's shorts stuck to the inside of her legs, her T-shirt was damp where her back touched the nylon lawn chair.

"Anyone? Come on now, you children of miners! Show your parents proud."

Delilah remembers Will's big, scarred hand holding that tiny gold ring, the band so delicate it looked like it could snap in his fingers.

"Yes, Misty?"

"Um, are they, like, compressed a lot? Like, the carbon?"

"Correct! Yes, they are, like, compressed a lot indeed. Diamonds are formed at incredibly high temperatures and pressures deep in the earth's mantle. Does anyone know how long it takes for them to grow?"

Billions of years, Delilah thinks.

"A long time!" George calls out.

"A long time. That is very true, George, though not as specific as I'd hoped for." Mr. Grady sets the necklace on his desk and turns to the board. He picks up chalk and scrawls *one to three billion years*.

"Why do you think they're so precious?" Will had said when Delilah laughed at him. She didn't believe they took so long to grow. "Why do you think people go crazy trying to find them?"

Mr. Grady walks down the aisle and returns the necklace to Misty. "So now you can all go home and impress your parents with your extensive, sweeping diamond knowledge. Time for one more question, then I want you to gather your things. Please read chapter one in your text by Thursday so we can attempt an intelligent conversation next class."

He sits at his desk and smooths his hair over his balding head. "Can anyone tell me what the word 'diamond' means? I'll give you a hint. It comes from the Greek word *adámas*."

There is a shuffling of papers and the snap of binders closing as everyone prepares to go. "Anyone?"

Delilah can't believe Mr. Grady left out the best part. She wants to stand and tell him, to tell everyone the best part.

"Diamonds can be formed where meteorites land," Will had said, lighting a smoke and shading his eyes from the sun. Jones was sitting on the small porch with his back to them, facing the lake and swinging his bare legs. Laska was at Delilah's feet, gnawing on a caribou bone Will had given her.

"Some meteorites have star dust in 'em from dying stars," he said. "That dust sometimes has diamond crystals in it. Meteor makes its way to Earth, crashes down, and there you go. Couple of billion years later, you got your diamond ring."

Delilah thought about the diamond studs Annie had been given by her own mother when she was a kid. Those diamonds her mother hated and thought stood for everything that was bad in the world. How could she be so stupid?

"We have the same stuff in us that's in diamonds too, right?" Jones asked.

"That's right," Will said. "It comes from the same place. We all got star dust in us." He grinned. "Want me to play that song for you again?"

"No!" they had both shouted.

"Nobody knows what the word diamond means?" Mr. Grady asks now, sounding tired. "Anyone want to take a wild stab in the dark, at least?"

Delilah won't get up and tell everyone what she knows. About the meteors and how they are all, every single one of them, the jerks like Misty and the good ones like Jones, made up of remnants of stars that had fallen to Earth billions of years ago. But still. She raises her hand.

"Delilah! Care to venture a guess?"

Heads swing. She ignores them, stares straight ahead at Mr. Grady. He nods encouragement.

"Unbreakable," she says.

***

THE TEMPERATURE OUTSIDE THE shack is almost at freezing, the little bird thermometer dipping below ten degrees for the first time in months. Delilah is at home rereading *To Kill a Mockingbird* for English. She's wearing her dad's quilted plaid work jacket, too lazy to build a fire. As she reads, she is trying to formulate a subject for the required book report due Monday morning, but her mind is wandering. She's thinking about winter. She can feel it, like a sudden shake or a slap. Her asthma has been worse with the change of season, and she has had to get a steroid inhaler to take with the regular one to help get it under control.

Will hasn't been coming by the house much, and she hasn't been going for dinner there, but when she'd seen him at Red's the other night, he had talked about taking her and Jones out with Jethro's dog team after the lake freezes.

By nine it is dark, and Delilah has to light all the lamps in the house. She is in the kitchen refilling her fruit punch from the can when she hears the truck pull up. Her dad stumbles in the front door as she's returning to the living room, her punch and a small stack of Oreos in hand. She stops when she sees him. He doesn't say a word, just walks past her to the kitchen. He's wearing his mine clothes and has his head tipped back, a bloody cloth held to his nose.

"Dad?" She follows him into the kitchen where he's pouring water into the basin. "What happened?"

He swishes a clean dishcloth in the water. "Had an accident. Nothing to worry about."

Acshident.

She puts her punch and cookies on the kitchen table. "Are you drunk? Where were you?"

He holds the wet cloth to his nose and looks at her sideways. He shakes his head awkwardly.

"Yes, you are. Let me see." She tries to take the soaking wet cloth but he shrugs her away. "Dad. Let me see. You're bleeding all over your shirt."

He relents and lets her lead him to the table where he sits heavily in a chair.

She peels the cloth back. His nose is red and swollen, leaking blood from both nostrils.

"Did you fall?"

She imagines him stumbling around outside the Yellowknife Inn and falling into the street. Is he the town drunk now? She has never seen him like this, clumsy and reeking of beer.

"No, the fucker punched me. Punched me in the face."

Fashe.

Delilah tosses the bloody dishcloth onto the counter and takes a dry one off the shelf. She holds it to her dad's nose and he lets her. His head feels warm, like a child with a temperature, burning up under his skin.

"Who punched you?"

Mac shakes his head and closes his eyes. "Ow!" He flinches as she presses harder.

Delilah puts his own hand on the cloth. "You do it then." She sits across from him. "Who punched you?"

She has never known her dad to be in a fight. In fact, when they lived in Vancouver he was going through a Gandhi phase, and for a few weeks, he made her read to him from Gandhi's teachings on non-violence every night before she went to sleep. It just made sense, he had told her. "An eye for an eye only ends up making the whole world blind."

He shrugs, holds the cloth clumsily.

"You don't know?"

What should she do? Yell? Comfort him? What should she do?

He looks at her sadly with his bloodshot eyes. "We're so close, Lila," he says, muffled by the cloth hanging over his mouth. "So close. He just won't listen to me. He's on fucking . . . radio silence or something. Won't listen. So close. Why don't people ever do the right fucking things?"

"Dad. Who punched you?"

"Fucking Will. That's who."

"Will?" Her heart thuds to her feet and the room tilts. "Will did this?" She tries to imagine Will punching him, punching anyone, but she can't.

He doesn't answer, just leans his head back again.

"Why did he punch you?"

He pulls off the cloth. "I'm there having a beer at the Gold Range after work, and I try to talk to the guy, and he won't say a fucking word to me. I just wanna buy a guy a beer, that's all. And he won't say a word to me. Like a fucking . . . kid or something. A sulky kid. So he's ignoring me, and I give him a little shove, whatever, no big deal, and then this." He stares down at the bloody cloth in his hand.

Delilah stands. He shoved Will? For ignoring him? It makes no sense. She can feel the lie simmering under his words.

"You not talking to me now either?" Mac sounds plaintive.

She can't think of a good reason why Will would have wanted to punch her father, even if Mac had shoved him, which means there are other things going on that she doesn't know. Things that would make him and Muddy and Will argue out on the rocks at Lonesome Point. Things that would make Will not want to drop by anymore.

Mac starts weeping quietly.

"I miss her, Lila," he whispers, and it takes a moment for her mind to switch gears and realize he is talking about Annie. "I miss her so much."

He uses his bloody cloth to wipe his eyes and Delilah picks up her punch and cookies, her heart a hard throbbing pulse in her throat.

"Go to bed," she tells her father.

She collects her book from the living room and heads to her room. Mac is still sitting in the kitchen, blood leaking onto his chest, staring off into space like there might be an answer out there.

OCTOBER

ON THE SHORE OF the bay the cold is almost unbearable, the faint dusting of snow crunching beneath Delilah's boots like crushed glass.

"There," Will says.

She follows his finger up to the white-hot stars. The ghostly green of the northern lights flickers across the sky, as though she had blinked slowly, blurring her vision for a split second. Delilah watches as the luminescent lights grow stronger, forming and falling in long, sweeping lines above them, dripping down from the sky like a child's painting that has suddenly become electric.

Will drops his hand to his side and puts his glove back on. The flicker grows into a wide, shifting arc above them, its edges bleeding down, a paintbrush dripping paint. It snaps and bucks, spreading over the sky.

She is breathless. They watch for what seems like an hour, just standing there. She has had bad luck since it got dark enough for the lights to appear, often going to bed before they show up or looking for them on cloudy nights. Mac told her she should never work for the little tour company that takes tourists out to see the lights. They would go out of business with her around.

Her toes burn, her cheeks are numb. She can no longer feel her nose. She looks back toward the houses. Woodsmoke curls from Will's chimney, and light shines warmth from the windows of the Rainbow Valley cabins. She can see Mary Ellen sitting at the table in the kitchen of the shack she shares with Jethro. They're probably drinking Ovaltine now, settling into another game of cards. The milk had been on the stove when Will went out for a smoke and Delilah followed him onto the lake. She is so glad to be back with them, so grateful for the quiet comfort she feels with Mary Ellen fussing over her, making her wear extra socks, smoothing her hair, clucking over her like a mother hen.

Will has been quiet, he and Jethro playing their cards without the usual ribbing and bad jokes: Hey Delilah, what do you call a man with no arms and no legs in the water? (I don't know, what?) Bob.

"See Venus?" Will says now.

She sees it instantly, twice as bright as any other star up there. "Yes. There."

"That's right. Big Dipper?"

"There."

"Yes."

"Cassiopeia?"

This one is trickier. She points toward Willow Flats. "There?"

"Nope."

She studies the sky. She should know it. He showed it to her a few weeks ago. She can't find it in the tangle of stars.

"She's right there. See that W shape? That's her."

"Oh. I see it now."

Delilah flexes her fingers inside her mittens to make sure they are still working. It hurts, the cold. It's been a shock to her system after the long sunny days. But Will doesn't seem cold. She imagines his blood a different temperature than hers. In the winter hers is thin, has a sheen of ice on the surface, and is always dangerously close to freezing over completely into a solid, useless block. His is thick, like syrup when you heat it. It rolls along like a warm lazy river.

The aurora has disappeared again, faded into nothing.

"My dad says you punched him." She says it just how she had rehearsed on her way there earlier that evening. She says it matter-of-factly. Not a question, not a judgment. Just a fact.

Will scans the sky. His breath is a cloud of white. He takes his tobacco out of his pocket, pulls one glove off, then the other, and rolls a smoke. Delilah's teeth are chattering so hard she's afraid they will shatter in her mouth. She waits an impossibly long time for him to respond.

"Yes," he finally says, then takes a long drag. "Yes, I did."

"Why?"

He doesn't answer. Instead, he points and she follows his finger to five glinting stars, a jagged crooked line above them. "She was a vain one, Cassiopeia. Sacrificed her girl, left her to die. That's why she's up there, tied up there forever for what she did to her own girl. You know that story?"

"You told me," Delilah says. He had. When he first showed her the constellation. She remembers thinking, *What kind of mother would give up her daughter?*

"That Perseus guy got there just in time. He saved Andromeda, he killed the sea monster, and he married the girl." Will pauses to take another drag. The end of his smoke burns like a small red planet. "But she's just stuck up there now. Can't ever get away."

"Will?"

"I didn't mean to hurt him," he says.

"Then why did—"

"It's between us. Me and him. It's not your business."

"He's my dad," she says, flaring like a lit match.

Will looks down at her. "I know. But it's not your business."

"He came home all bloody," she says, accusingly, angry, not that he punched Mac but that he won't tell her why. That she has to live every day not knowing why anyone in her life is doing what they're doing. Not knowing why her mother left, not knowing why her father works a million hours a week and they somehow still don't have money for new running shoes for gym class.

"I know," he says.

"And you did that. You made him bloody."

He just looks at her.

"Why don't you say sorry?" she says, embarrassingly close to tears. "Just say sorry."

"I'm not," he says quietly.

"You punched him! In the face! How can you not be sorry? Any normal person would be sorry."

He puts a hand on her shoulder. "Kid. What happens between me and your dad, that's between him and me. That's adult stuff. Has not a thing in the world to do with you. I'm not sorry. Only thing I'm sorry for is you're upset by it."

She goes limp under his hand, her legs like jelly, the anger drained out of her through her cold toes and into the snow and ice below her.

"I don't want you to be fighting."

He squeezes her shoulder and lets her go. "I know," he says. "Wish I could say we had some control over what people do and don't do, but if I was gonna tell you one thing, kid, it's that you can't change a person. You are what you are. Good or bad."

"No. People change," Delilah says. "I think people change."

"If you say so. Let me ask you something now."

There is ice forming on his knitted hat, clinging to the unravelling wool. Will had told her once that it had been his father's hat. Will's mother had knitted it for him. Will said Mary Ellen kept trying to fix it, but he wouldn't let her. He even rescued it once from her sewing basket before she could get to work on it.

"Okay," she says, still thinking about that hat.

"Your mom coming back to see you soon?"

Delilah flinches. "What?"

"You heard me."

"I don't know," she says.

"Thought I heard she wanted to come see you."

"She said only if I start speaking to her first."

"Ah," Will says. He starts to roll another smoke. "When is that going to be?"

It hurts to breathe, tiny ice crystals sticking to the side of her throat with every breath. She doesn't like that Will has changed the subject, that he is making her think of Annie, of that tiny vase of wilting flowers. The empty hooks where her clothes had been. All the lies and then the leaving. Her dad bloody and crying like a lost child without her.

"Never," she says.

november

DELILAH CAN SEE HER breath as she walks out into the colourless morning. If summer in Yellowknife was a thousand shades of blue and green, November is more shades of white than she knew existed. It won't be fully light for another fifteen minutes, but she can see the sky is heavy with cloud, the stairs in front of her and the road down to Weaver's dusted with a fine sheen of frost.

She walks down Old Stope with careful steps, boots sliding on the surface of an opaque icy slick frozen overnight from the melting snow of yesterday afternoon. To her right there is a rim of ice around Back Bay ten feet wide, following the curve of shore where there had been nothing but open water the day before.

Through the dusky morning, Jones ambles toward her from Willow Flats. He waves and hitches his pack up higher on his shoulder as she reaches the bottom of the hill.

"Nice mittens," she says, teeth chattering. She has forgotten her scarf, still not used to the ritual of dressing that has to happen before she leaves the house. She misses bare legs and arms, even with the price of mosquito bites. She misses pulling on her Keds and just running off, slamming the door behind her.

Now she has to hunt for matching socks in the dark every morning, wash her face by candlelight over the plastic basin in the kitchen, brush her hair while she shivers by the wood stove. Find long underwear and somehow pull her jeans over them without them riding up, wear two shirts under her sweater, tie boots, zip up her parka, pull on a hat. She feels like she's putting on armour before a battle.

Jones inspects his left mitten. A thin red string hangs from the thumb. "My mom's started knitting again. She knits in the winter. I think she wants everyone to be warm. She'll probably make you some too, so watch out."

Delilah points over his shoulder at the government dock. There is a narrow circle of ice there as well, shining under the street light, and a thin ridge of it around the rocky shore of Joliffe. "The lake is freezing."

"Yup. Freeze-up."

"Freeze-up?"

"Yeah. That's what they call it. Breakup in the spring, freeze-up in the winter."

They start walking toward Franklin. "I thought it would do it all at once," she says.

He laughs. "What, like you wake up one morning and it's all frozen solid?"

She feels stupid. "Kinda."

He shakes his head. "No, it takes a while. A week, maybe, sometimes more before the whole lake freezes."

As they pass the dock, Delilah watches the ice. It seems thicker close to shore, becoming nothing more than a thin film farther out. The lake lies open, rippling black in the slight wind. There are still a few large fishboats moored near the dock, some tilted at odd angles as the ice has frozen them in place.

After school, she walks alone to the edge of the government dock, Jones stranded in the principal's office for skipping PE to go read magazines at the pharmacy. The ice has retreated back toward land during the mild afternoon, only two feet of crust left there now instead of ten. She thinks about the effort it takes, how it starts off with those tangling crystals forming where they can hold on to something before slowly weaving together into something massive and strong that covers the entire lake.

The next morning, she points out at the grey water to a thin sheen of ice that has broken free from the shore of Back Bay and drifted off. "Look," she says.

"Yeah," Jones says, munching on an apple he has dug out of the bottom of his bag. "It'll melt. The water out there is warmer."

"It keeps freezing and melting." It bothers her somehow. She can't put her finger on why. It bothers her that every morning when she leaves the shack the lake is different.

She sits in the frozen reeds after school every day that week, watching the progress, listening to the gurgling water trapped under the creamy, rippled ice close to shore. Sometimes she puts her head close until she hears a faint tinkling, the small crystals singing as they form and the ebb and flow of the lake's currents brushing against them.

One morning, after a night of violent wind rattling the heavy plastic Mac has nailed to the windows to keep out the drafts, Delilah sees a mosaic of broken pieces that had been swept out into open water only to return when the temperature dropped. They are frozen into the smooth surface of the lake like scattered puzzle pieces, hard and jagged and unmoving.

Finally, five days later, Jones and Delilah stop on the dock on their way to school. The ice reaches all the way to Joliffe now, creeping around to the far side before thinning out again farther out in the bay. Overnight a bridge has formed.

"A few more days and we can walk on it," Jones says.

"How do you know it's safe?" Since Delilah arrived she has heard countless stories of men falling through, dogs falling through, trucks falling through. Some made it, some were never recovered.

He shrugs. "You just do. We can take the canoe the first time."

She looks at him like he's nuts. "What?"

He smiles. "You'll see."

***

SATURDAY MORNING, THEY ARE gliding clumsily toward Joliffe, each with one foot in the blue canoe, the other on the frozen lake. They slide the canoe beside them awkwardly with every step and every time Jones yells "Push!" Delilah laughs, her parka unzipped and flapping around her, hair sweaty under her yellow wool hat, mittens long ago thrown into the canoe with the sandwiches and Thermos of Maggie's ginger tea.

"We look crazy!" she yells ahead to Jones, whose foot slips inside the canoe, sending him lurching forward until he rights himself.

"Push!" he says over his shoulder in response.

In the sunshine, closer to the shore, there are people out on the snow-covered bay, some skating, some walking with dogs. Kids have cleared a patch near the government dock for hockey.

Jones has explained to her how people use canoes to travel across to Joliffe in that brief, delicate time between seasons when they can't trust the ice yet. If the ice cracks, all they have to do is jump in the canoe and they'll be floating. Keeping one foot on something solid makes perfect sense to Delilah.

CHRISTMAS EVE, 1977

IT'S FOUR-THIRTY IN THE afternoon, and Delilah is making her way down Old Stope in the dark. The street lights show only a world of white in front of her. Snow settles on her hair, drifts in graceful slow motion around her as she crunches through the shin-deep drifts in the middle of the road.

She suggested to Mac that they borrow the sugar they need from Martha since she's right next door, but he shook his head as he stirred the huge canning pot full of boiling potatoes. "Nope. City Jane's. Who knows what shape Martha's in on Christmas Eve."

Delilah hears sad, twangy country music coming from inside Martha's shack as she passes the front porch. There's a yellow-haired cloth angel hanging in the window between two tattered curtains. Delilah wonders what Martha and Charlie are doing inside. If they have a tree. A turkey. Or if they're just sitting there drinking and smoking cigarettes,

Martha humming along with the music as she flips through Delilah's comic books. Maybe Charlie is tinkering with a wobbly bookshelf, pulling a loose nail in the floor.

Jones told her they had kids at one point, but they were taken away. He told her that once, years later, Martha stormed the social worker's office demanding they give her babies back, although by then they would have been full grown. She trashed the office, threw staplers, cleared desks with one sweep of her arm, howling for her long-lost children.

Delilah passes Weaver's, closed now, and rounds the corner. Back Bay is a long expanse of snow-covered ice as far as she can see. Giant Mine glitters like Christmas lights off in the distance.

She's tired from a long day of helping Mac get ready for the party. It started early when he shook her awake and took her out on the snowmobile to find a tree. Mac had to use a headlamp and it felt like it took hours for him to saw down the straggly pine with his handsaw while Delilah stood in the dark, shivering and yawning, knee-deep in snow. Finally, they dragged it home on the sled, and she decorated it with tinsel and popcorn strands while Mac made them scrambled eggs. They didn't know where the proper Christmas decorations were, the expensive hand-me-downs from Annie's parents. They figured Annie must have left them in Vancouver.

As it was getting light around ten o'clock, they set up a plywood table on sawhorses in the living room. It stretched almost all the way from the wood stove to the front door, leaving only a few feet for people to get in. Every chair they could scrounge from neighbours was set around the table, including Ernie Gall's outdoor weight bench. Delilah covered the table with Mac's spare king-sized bed sheet. Even though it was blue and yellow plaid and made of flannel, it was the only thing big enough to cover it. She had laid out the plastic plates and knives and forks and the plastic cups. She had folded the red paper Christmas napkins with the silver bells on them and placed them above each plate. There were tall red candles stuck to saucers in the centre of the table. They hadn't talked much, she and Mac, but he had played his Beatles records and some Patti Smith, and they sang along to "Gloria" while he baked a rum cake and swore about the uneven temperature of the oven.

Delilah doesn't understand why he wants them to have the dinner, but she can see that, somehow, it's important to him. Maggie had offered to have it, which would have made way more sense since she has a normal-sized house with a normal kitchen and a proper stove with more than two burners. But no, he wanted to have the whole thing himself, host Red and Maggie and Jones, Jethro and Mary Ellen, City Jane, Louise, Bear, Chris and the twins, and whoever else happened to come by. It wouldn't be Christmas without friends, he said. Will said maybe he would come too. He's come around a couple of times to talk to her dad, hushed conversations on the back porch, and he stayed true to his promise of taking Delilah and Jones out with the dogs the week before.

"Your dad's overcompensating," Jones had said as they walked the aisles of the Super Mart the day before. They were searching for stuffing ingredients while Mac tried to find a turkey big enough to feed them all.

"He's what?" Delilah stuck a large bunch of celery in a plastic bag.

"Like, because your mom's not here. He's trying to show he can do it all anyway. That's what my mom said. She said holidays are hard when you lose someone you love." Jones stole a grape and chewed it slowly.

Delilah felt something squeeze her heart, pressing it like a sponge and then releasing it. She took a deep breath and tossed the bag in the cart. "We need onions," she said, and steered the cart away.

Now she's on her way to get sugar because Mac used it all to make the rum cake, and he's worried someone will want it in their coffee after dinner. Delilah has seen the two cases of beer and the box of red wine and the bottles of gin and Jack Daniels by the back door. She doubts anyone will be drinking coffee.

City Jane lives around the corner by the Wildcat. Delilah passes her house when she walks to work. It's a little peach-coloured dollhouse with peeling white trim and the empty shell of a pickup in the front yard. If Delilah could live in any house in Old Town, it would be this one. It looks like one of the little houses on the east coast she imagines from the Anne books, but smaller. She wades through the drifting snow to the front door and knocks. The door is covered in stickers that say things like "Arms are for hugging" and "Nuke the gay whales for Christ." A crazy hippie used to live there before Jane, or that's what Will had told her. A couple of years ago, the man would stand in the middle of Franklin holding signs protesting the Vietnam War even though it was over. Nobody knows where he is now.

City Jane is wearing tight bell-bottoms and a big grey men's sweater. Her hair is feathered and soft around her face.

She looks like Stevie Nicks on the cover of the Fleetwood Mac album. Maggie says City Jane came from Boston where she had a fancy job in a big newsroom. She used to wear dresses and heels every day. Delilah can imagine it. Lipstick, too.

"Hi, sweetie," Jane says. "Here for your sugar? I told your dad I might swing by later. You didn't have to walk all the way down here in the cold."

Delilah comes in and closes the door behind her. "Dad said you might not come, and he wanted to make sure he had it. He thinks people might want coffee."

There are books stacked in the corners, on the ceiling-high bookshelves, spilling off the side tables. There are even some piled on the overstuffed green sofa. "Wow. You read a lot."

Jane is in the small kitchen rustling around. "Yes, I guess so. That's mostly all I do." She laughs. "Read and write."

She comes back to Delilah and holds out a plastic sandwich bag full of white sugar. "This enough?"

Delilah nods. An image comes back to her from the summer as she takes the bag with her mittened hand. City Jane crawling out of Will's tent that pink dawn at Lonesome Point. The look she had given Delilah, that sad look. How she had crossed her arms across her chest while she said good morning.

"Are you coming later for sure?" Delilah asks.

"Not for sure. I have some work to do."

"On Christmas?"

"I can always find work to do. But I might come by, we'll see. I already had dinner." She points toward her small table against the wall by the bookshelf.

Delilah can see a plate with what looks like the remnants of Kraft Dinner and toast. There's an open can of pineapple sitting by a stack of papers. "Lots of people will be there," Delilah says. "Red and Maggie and Bear and Chris and the twins and Jethro and Mary Ellen. And Will."

She's hoping for something, a smile or a glimmer in Jane's eyes, but Jane looks past her to the door. "You should probably get back before your dad starts to worry."

"Okay. But . . . are you . . . are you and Will . . . like, is he your boyfriend?" Delilah says it before she can stop herself. She has been wondering for months. They don't act like they're together when they're out at dinners and parties, but she has seen them whispering to each other in corners and sometimes they leave together.

City Jane seems frozen for a second and then says, "No. No. We're just . . . special friends. Good friends," she corrects herself. She seems uncomfortable.

"Don't you like him that way?"

City Jane laughs and hugs herself as though she's suddenly cold. "Delilah, sometimes adults have . . . strange relationships. Sometimes people have been hurt and that makes things . . . complicated."

Delilah nods. She knows this. She can tell Jane doesn't want to talk about it anymore. "Thanks for the sugar."

"Any time."

"Maybe I'll see you later." Delilah opens the door to the front porch.

"Maybe, sweetie. You have a good night."

Delilah hears the door close behind her as she steps carefully down the snowy stairs and back out into the blackness.

❋❋❋

"EVERY FUCKING TIME!" BEAR howls, slapping his cards on the plywood table with his meaty hand. The table shudders and slides on the sawhorses like it's done the last five times he did it.

Jones and Delilah look at each other. There is a rowdy game of poker happening at the other end of the table closer to the wood stove. Delilah reaches over to mop up the wine that spilled in front of her. She doesn't know whose it is. Dishes with turkey bones and congealed gravy have been pushed aside, napkins left soaking up spilled beer on the flannel sheet. The twins are climbing on the couch, shrieking, chocolate from the Pot of Gold someone brought smeared over their faces and in their hair.

Most of the adults have been playing poker and arguing about the Berger report, which has been a much-discussed topic at all the get-togethers for months now. Marianne Faithfull is playing on Mac's record player, that warbling, throaty voice that gets under Delilah's skin and makes her squirm. The women, Maggie and Mary Ellen and Louise, are in the kitchen as Maggie says, "Trying to make a dent in the disaster Mac has left in there." Dusty, Louise's kid, didn't come. Louise said she flew him out to Alberta to be with her parents for the holidays. She looks a little too comfortable in the shack tonight, Delilah has noticed. Like it's her party too. Going to the kitchen for extra cups. Telling people where to find clean dishcloths. She even got up and refilled a chip bowl once.

Delilah and Jones could hide out in her room with her comics and her radio, but it's just getting good out there, so they stay put. Jones has snuck some Jack Daniels into both their pops, a tiny splash when the adults had their noses buried in the cards. A slow warm feeling spreads through Delilah as she takes small sips.

"All right, all right, enough of this political bullshit, hand over your fucking pennies," Bear bellows, and the others shove their piles toward him, swearing and laughing. Mac looks happy for the first time in weeks. He catches her eye and winks, his hair a wild mess, sweat beading his forehead. He's wearing his red Christmas T-shirt, and the other men have brushed their hair and put on clean shirts too, though Bear is wearing his work suspenders over an undershirt that barely covers his belly.

Outside the living room window, there are icicles that hang down the entire distance from the eaves to the ground, but the wood stove is glowing red around the top and there are so many people in the tiny shack that Delilah feels like they are cooking in a strange, simmering stew.

"Should we clean up?" Jones asks, pointing at the stacks of plates, the cigarette butts put out in the ice cream.

Delilah shakes her head. "Maybe later."

"What should we do?"

She shrugs and takes a sip of her drink. It's disgusting. The whiskey makes her pop taste rotten.

"Delilah!" Maggie calls from the kitchen door. "Come!" She has a dishtowel over her shoulder, her dress is a crazy swirl of colours that falls to her feet. "You too, my Jonesy! Mary Ellen has something for you." She beckons them and they get up awkwardly, barely able to squeeze between the wall and the table.

Mary Ellen is sitting at the small table in the kitchen. She has two packages in her lap, wrapped in paper with snowmen printed on it. She beams when she sees them. They stand side by side, Jones holding his drink.

"She has a gift for you, isn't this so lovely?" Maggie says.

Louise slides past them to join the men. Delilah can hear her laughing and wonders if she's hanging over Mac like she was earlier, letting her arm brush his at the table while they ate, touching his shoulder when he was talking to her. It's so obvious. Any idiot would be able to see what she was doing.

"Presents," Mary Ellen says solemnly. She hands one to Delilah just as the front door opens and a hail of voices calls out, "Well, well, it's William! Mr. Bilodeau!"

Will is here.

Mary Ellen doesn't hand Jones his present yet. She is waiting for Delilah to open hers. She mimes tearing open an imaginary gift and nods encouragingly. Delilah peels off the tape and opens the paper. It's a pair of leather mitts with intricate beaded pink flowers. There is soft brown fur around the cuffs. They are so beautiful Delilah forgets to breathe for a second. "For me?" she says, even though she knows this is a stupid question. They must have taken Mary Ellen hours and hours.

"Yes, you! Keep you warm," Mary Ellen says.

Maggie is looking over Delilah's shoulder. She clucks her approval. "Oh my, so beautiful. So beautiful, Mary Ellen."

Delilah puts them on and they come up to above her wrists. The insides are lined with fur. They feel like warm silk on her hands. "Thank you," she says. Hot tears are stinging her eyes, but she isn't sure why. She leans down and hugs Mary Ellen, who pats her back like a baby. She imagines her sitting in her rocking chair making these for her, for hours, thinking about Delilah and wanting her to be warm. Jones reaches out a hand to see and she shows him.

"What are they made of?" Maggie asks.

"Caribou," Mary Ellen says, as if it should be obvious.

"The fur?"

"That's beaver. Soft fur for her. Keep her warm." Mary Ellen points at Jones. "You now." She hands him his package.

Jones pulls the paper apart. It's a pair of leather gloves almost identical to Delilah's, except hers are mittens, and his flowers are bright blue and green instead of pink. "Thanks," he says, beaming as he turns them over in his hands.

"Try 'em on," Will says from the doorway.

They all turn to see him towering there, his head almost level with the top of the frame. He's wearing his fringed jacket and clean jeans but he looks haggard and raw. Delilah feels a little red flag waving inside her.

"You gotta try 'em on, Jonesy." Will's slurring.

Jones pulls the gloves on and holds up his hands for them to see.

Mary Ellen claps with excitement.

"Man's gloves," Will says. "Big man now, that's you."

Delilah is now at full attention, watching Will closely, her mittens still on her hands.

Maggie clears her throat and says, "Will, you look hungry. I will get you food. You want some food? Mac cooked a meal fit for kings and queens here."

"Nah, not hungry," Will says. He turns back to the living room and Delilah sees him stumble and catch himself on the door jamb. He's drunk. No doubt about it. She looks at Jones and he raises his eyebrows. They follow Will to the other room.

Will claps his hands together. "Okay, what you folks up to here? Having us a poker game? Deal me in, big man." He takes off his jacket and sits beside Jethro, almost tipping the small folding chair.

Delilah feels like she's watching a train veer off the tracks in slow motion. She is afraid to know what terrible thing made him show up like this on Christmas. Jethro is murmuring to him, but Will swats at him like a fly.

Mac is sitting across from him. "You okay there, buddy?"

Will laughs, a terrible, humourless laugh. "I'm your buddy now, eh? I'm your big buddy now?"

"Hey, hey," Bear growls. "It's Christmas, man, take it easy. Kids here." The chocolate-smeared twins are standing on the couch staring at Will. One of them is wearing only her red tights, her dress tossed to the floor as the room heated up.

Will looks at the twins. Blinks. There's a long silence in the room. Then he laughs. "Okay, how about I take it easy. Good idea, I'll take it easy."

He starts to root clumsily through the pocket of his jacket. Delilah wants to help him because everything in the room is suspended and his fingers aren't working. But she doesn't move from her vigil beside Jones. He is playing with his new gloves, turning them over between his fingers.

Will pulls out his tobacco and rolls a smoke. Jethro goes to the door and gets his jacket. He pulls it on, then walks over to Will.

"Let's get on home, brother," he says quietly. Jethro tries to guide Will from his chair, but Will is slumped forward, spilling tobacco onto his lap. He gives up on rolling his cigarette and sits with his head in his hands.

Jethro goes to the kitchen and calls for Mary Ellen. "Thanks for the hospitality. We'll be going now," he says when he comes back in the room. Mary Ellen is by his side. He stops behind Will. "Let's go."

Will rises unsteadily. "All right, I guess I know when I'm not wanted," he says. "I gotta go anyway, I got shit to do." He starts to head toward the door, a stumbling giant. His leg catches the edge of the plywood table and it scrapes along the sawhorse, plates sliding sideways.

Jethro follows him to the door, Mary Ellen shuffling behind. "You're not going anywhere like this, brother. You got big plans? They can wait till tomorrow. We're walking home now."

Will starts to fumble with the door. Red and Mac come around the table. Delilah can see a look passing between them. Jones pulls her back, and Bear pushes past them to meet Mac and Red at the door. They pull Will back by the shoulders and he tries to shrug them off, furious.

"You get your fucking hands off me! I got shit to take care of!"

Bear holds his arms behind his back while Red tries to talk sense to Will. "Settle down, my man, you can't go out there right now. Too cold. You'll freeze those big balls right off."

Will looks bewildered, trapped, his eyes darting from Mac to Red and over to Jethro. Bear is still holding his arms behind him. The rest stand around him like bodyguards. Chris has gathered his girls and is getting their snow boots on. The women stand in the doorway to the kitchen.

"Got shit to do," Will says, but he relaxes in Bear's grip, and Bear releases him. He stumbles over the tangle of boots and tips forward. His hair has come loose from its ponytail and hangs in strings around his face.

Maggie pulls at Jones and Delilah. "Come back," she whispers. "Come back here." They stand against the wall while she goes back to the kitchen.

Something is breaking in Delilah's chest, a small wave cresting. "Will," she calls.

Jones grabs her arm. He wants her to be quiet. Everyone turns to her from their positions by the door. Will slowly turns to look at her, his hair in his face.

"Stay," she says. "It's a party, right? Just stay."

Maggie whisks through the crowd with a mug. She hands it to Will, who takes it unsteadily.

"Come, chéri," she says, pulling his arm gently. "Come to the kitchen and have some of Mac's cake and drink your coffee. Come, come. It's okay. It's all right."

Bear scratches his bald head and says, "Well, I for one ain't leaving until I win all your goddamned pennies."

Will looks around and then follows Maggie. He doesn't look at Delilah as he passes.

***

AN HOUR LATER JONES is asleep on her bed with an astronomy book he borrowed from Will on his chest. Delilah is curled on the other side of the bed, slowly drifting off in her nest of sleeping bags.

Red comes in through the blanket door. He stoops in

the doorway and whispers, "Hey there, sorry to wake you. Jonesy Boy there needs to come on home now."

"Is everyone gone?" she asks. She wants to sit up, but her arms and legs are like lead.

He nods. "Everyone but Will and Louise. Hey, sleepyhead! Come on, kiddo."

Jones doesn't even flinch. Delilah reaches over and shakes his shoulder lightly, and his eyes fly open. He blinks at her.

"Your dad," she says.

He looks past her and registers his father standing there. He gets up awkwardly, his striped rugby shirt rumpled, and leaves without saying goodbye, still half-asleep.

Red waves at her. "Night, Delilah."

Delilah lies on her back and stares at the ceiling for a minute. Jones has left a boy-sized impression in the bed beside her. She reaches over to the spot where he had been lying and feels its warmth before rolling over and getting up.

Her dad is in the kitchen scrubbing out the turkey pan. He has a red bandana tied around his forehead to keep his hair back. Louise is sitting at the kitchen table packing food into margarine containers.

"Hi Delilah," she says, smiling, her long nails polished and pink as she separates the containers and lays them out.

Delilah ignores her.

Mac turns. "Hey, jeez, Lila, it's three in the morning. Thought you were sleeping. You need something?"

"Is Will still here?"

Her dad is quiet a minute, sloshing suds in the pan. There are countless empty beer bottles lined up on the counter. "Yeah, he's on the back porch, smoking. Maybe just . . . just go to bed. He's had a rough night."

"Is he okay?"

"Yeah, he's okay. Just go to bed." Mac turns the dripping pan upside down on the counter and dries his hands. He smiles at her. "That's what I'm gonna do."

She glances at Louise, who keeps her head down as she dishes the potatoes into a container. She goes back to her room and picks up a sleeping bag from her bed, pulls on two pairs of wool socks and her wool hat, then wraps the sleeping bag around her shoulders and walks back through the kitchen to the back door.

"Lila," her dad says. But he doesn't try to stop her.

"Go to bed," she calls over her shoulder. "If you're tired."

She braces herself and opens the door. She has to take a couple of breaths for her lungs to adjust to the assault of cold. It's so dark it takes a second before she can find the glow of Will's cigarette. He's sitting at the edge of the small porch, his legs dangling. He turns when the door closes. "Hey there, kid."

He sounds like himself again. She sits beside him. There is nothing out there but the towering rock beside them and the dark air. There are no lights on that she can see, just the black, craggy shapes of spindly trees on Joliffe in the far distance. It's a clear night, and the sky is star-filled.

"Hey," she says. "Seen any aurora?"

"Little bit earlier. Died down now."

She pulls the sleeping bag all the way up to her chin and folds her legs under her for more warmth.

"You should go in. Too cold out here for you."

"I'm fine," she says. Her lips have turned to ice. They can barely make the sounds.

"If you say so," he says. He takes a drag.

They sit in silence for a few moments. Delilah watches the stars. She can't hear a single sound. She strains to hear a dog bark or an engine start, anything.

"Will?"

"Mmm?"

"What's the matter?"

She waits so long for him to answer she almost gives up and goes back inside. But then he takes another drag. "She's not coming."

She's momentarily puzzled, but then remembers. "Clementine?" She is greeted by more silence. "You mean for Christmas?"

"No, kid. I don't mean for Christmas."

"Oh. Ever? Why not?"

He laughs, but not like he thinks anything is funny. "Million-dollar question."

"Can you go see her?"

He looks at her now, and she can see a hardness in his eyes that turns her belly cold. "No, kid," he says.

She decides to drop it for now. He won't tell her the parts she wants to know, anyway. All the whys. "Jones was reading your book," she says. "It says there's a storm on Jupiter. Do you know about it?"

He flicks his ash and the glow burns brighter. "Yeah. The storm that never dies."

"What is it?"

He's quiet for a minute. She knows he doesn't feel like talking, about Clem or about anything. But she just wants to hear his voice until she knows he's okay.

"I don't know. It's just a storm. Wind, lightning. Been raging for hundreds of years. Two times the size of Earth, at least. Usually a storm is created by weather systems colliding, interacting. They blow themselves out eventually. That storm sits there. Just keeps going." He stubs out his cigarette.

"Can you see it in a telescope?"

"Yeah. I've seen it. Looks like a dark spot."

She thinks of the last storm they had back in August. The lightning sheets across the lake, the swirling rain, the booming thunder rolling across Yellowknife Bay. She had lain in her bed rigid, counting between thunderclaps until she knew the storm was passing, certain the lightning was going to strike the house and burn it to the ground or that somehow the sound of the thunder could crack the ground beneath her and swallow her whole.

"It'd be terrible to live in a storm like that," she says. "You'd be scared all the time."

He gets slowly to his feet, yawns and stretches his long arms above his head. Surveys the sky.

"Nah," he says. "You get used to anything if you live with it long enough."

January 1978

WILL COMES BANGING ON the door of the shack at one-thirty in the morning. He bangs so hard the windows rattle in their old wooden frames. Delilah wakes with that banging like a fist on her chest. She can hear her dad's feet on the plywood floor, hear him pull the door open, say, "Jesus, Will."

By then she has wrapped her itchy Hudson's Bay blanket around herself and moved through the kitchen. She stands in the living room, rubbing her feet together against the cold. The wood stove has died down to embers.

Mac is in his grey long johns, his hair a mess. He's carrying the kerosene lantern, and light flickers against the walls. Will has burst in wearing a thick sweater and his fringed jacket, his wool hat on his head. The door is wide open behind him, moonlight glittering on the ice crystals painting the small porch.

"What is it?" Mac says. "What is it?"

"Gotta get out there and find it," Will says. He's pointing back toward the open door, the fringe of his jacket hanging like the wing of a large bird. "Ski-Doo's broken down, and Jethro won't come with the dogs. Let's go."

"Find what?" Delilah says. Mac is shaking his head like he's trying to understand.

Will notices Delilah and lowers his arm. "Hi kid," he says. Mac sets the lantern down on the bookshelf.

She raises her hand in a wave. "Find what, Will?"

"Get some warm clothes on," Will tells her. "Come with us. You can ride on the sled."

"She's not going anywhere." Mac pulls the front door shut. "She has school tomorrow. Are you drunk or what?"

Will doesn't answer.

"He isn't drunk, Dad," Delilah says. "Find what, Will?"

"A meteor," Will says. "I saw it fall over the lake. Like the ones I told you about. You'll never see this again. Never. This is once in a lifetime. Once every five lifetimes. Come with us." Snow is melting in his hair, running in fine rivers down his scarred cheek. Small clumps of ice cling to his ponytail.

Delilah nods, but she doesn't move. A meteor? She feels a prickling fear that Will is going crazy. "Maybe it was a falling star. Sometimes they seem big when they're close to Earth. Right? You told me that."

"No, kid. Not a falling star. It was burning red, big." He traces an arc with his hands through the dim light of the room. "I saw it. If we leave now we might find it before anyone else gets out there."

"Will," Mac says. "Come on. This is nuts. A meteor?"

"I know what I saw."

Mac runs a hand through his hair. "Why do you need me? Can't you go on your own? I have to go to work in a few hours."

"No, I need help if we find it. Getting pieces into the sled."

"Listen, man," Mac says, his voice calmer now. "Let's all get a good night's sleep and then maybe I'll take you out tomorrow after work. Whatever it was will still be there."

Will shakes his head. "No, we're going tonight." He starts walking toward the door. "Get your gear on. We're going tonight."

"No. Not now. We'll go later."

Will reaches the door and turns. "You my friend or not?" he says.

Delilah sees the two men look at each other for what seems like a full minute. Her father nods. He picks up his jeans from the back of a chair where they have been drying by the wood stove. "Delilah stays," he says on his way to his room to change.

Delilah hasn't moved. Will stands by the door, looking out the window through the thick plastic film covering the glass. "Shoulda seen it," he says. "Wish you had seen it."

"Will?"

He doesn't answer, his neck craned to see something out of his line of vision.

"Will, are you okay?"

No answer.

Her dad appears fully dressed and pulls on his boots, zips up his blue parka. He grabs his rifle and duffel bag of emergency supplies from the room near the back door. "Back in a couple hours, Delilah. Get some more sleep.

Put wood on the fire before you go back to bed, or you'll freeze your ass off when you get up." He shakes his head and laughs. "Okay, you crazy bastard, let's go find this fucking thing."

Will follows Mac out the door. He turns back to Delilah and gives her a little salute. "See you, kid," he says.

She runs to the window, her blanket falling to her feet. She wants to go now, she doesn't want to let either of them out of her sight. She watches them hook up the sled to the back of the Ski-Doo. Will stands on the sled and holds on as Mac pulls out, his headlamp lighting the way. She sees the snow peel away from the skis as they start down the road.

Will had told her once that sometimes, when you think you're looking for one thing, it's not what you're looking for at all. He was talking about hunting for ptarmigan and secretly hoping for a fox. Or fishing for pike and wishing for a twenty-pound whitefish. But don't kid yourself, kid, he had said. Life is short. Might as well be honest about what you want.

She doesn't know why, but she feels like they are pulling part of her into the night, dragging her behind them as they ride away.

DELILAH WAITS AND WAITS. She should go back to bed, but she waits. She sits on the sofa and watches the blackness outside, waiting for the whine of the Ski-Doo, the sudden glow of headlights coming up the hill. There's nothing out there but dark. She checks her watch: 5:17. They left at 1:35.

At quarter to six, Charlie's headlights send a flash of light through the living room as he starts his truck. Delilah, wrapped in her blanket, rises to add wood to the fire. She pulls on a pair of her dad's wool work socks from the drying rack by the stove. They feel stiff and itchy, and the orange bands around the top come up to her knees over her long johns.

She drags a cushion off the couch and goes to the window by the door so she can see the road outside their house. She pushes aside the boots and shoes and kneels on the cushion on the floor. She puts her elbows on the windowsill and rests her chin in her hands.

Cold radiates out from the window, despite the plastic sheeting stretched tight across the frames. She watches, her blanket around her shoulders. At six-fifteen Martha turns on her porch light and stands on her crumbling front step. She is huge in her cut-off white T-shirt, the sleeves cut jagged around her armpits. Her skirt comes to her knees, her plump round calves shining in the glow of the porch light. Her hair is in black tangles to her waist.

"Charrrlie!" Martha bellows, loud enough for Delilah to hear through the thin windows. "Charlie, you come on home! Where you at, Charlie Boy?"

Charlie is long gone. Delilah's eyes feel heavy. She rests her forehead against the taut plastic, although she's not supposed to in case it breaks or stretches. She closes her eyes for a second. She feels the heaviness beckoning her and sinks into it.

"Charrrlie!"

When she opens her eyes, it's snowing. Hard. Swirling snow that will stick and drift against the side of the shack, pile all the way to the roof on the low side. Delilah checks her watch: 6:22. They should have been back by now. Mac expects her to go to school, but she won't go. Not unless they come back first.

Martha is still standing there on her porch, her hair a wild mass. She stares right at Delilah, right through the window. Delilah's heart hammers in her throat. She glances at the door, knows if Martha wanted to, she could charge across the yard and open it, come right in. But she doesn't move. Just looks at Delilah. Then she calls something, cups her meaty hand to her mouth to help the sound travel through the snow that is now so thick Martha almost seems like a mirage, a form in a pool of light with paper cuttings, confetti, whirling around her.

Delilah wants to know what she's saying. "What?" she whispers. "I can't hear you." She presses her ear to the plastic, covers her other ear.

"Where your dad at, girl?" she hears. Martha is yelling, the sound travelling the short distance between them, muffled by the storm of white. "Where he gone to on that Ski-Doo?"

Delilah presses her hand to the plastic and for one crazy moment considers going over to Martha's house. Asking her to make tea. She wants company, she wants to be in the same house as another person. But Martha turns and goes into her shack, slamming the door behind her.

Delilah thinks of the snow, the cold. Will's suede jacket versus Mac's parka. The rifle. She didn't see Mac pack a single scrap of food, although it would have been insane of him not to after all the stories he has told her of people freezing to death a mile from home in the winter because they ran out of energy and sat in a snowbank and died.

One Good Thing   *179*

At 7:20 she stands and goes to her bedroom. She finds her jeans in a crumpled heap on the floor and puts them on over her long johns and her dad's socks. She pulls on her grey lambswool sweater and grabs her thick toque. Her parka is hanging by the door. She zips it up, flips the hood over her hat. Her mitts from Mary Ellen are on the drying rack, and she slips them on and leaves the house.

Outside the cold is needles pressing up against her skin, stabbing her eyes and her cheeks and her forehead, every inch of exposed skin feels instantly numb. She starts walking down the hill through the piling snow.

When she turns left toward the Flats, she knows she is tracing the same path Mac and Will took, but their tracks are gone. She walks past shacks showing signs of morning life. She smells thick, burnt coffee, hears a dog barking from its pen. A truck sits idling in front of a three-storey house with new siding. Light shines from every window, and Delilah can see the silhouette of a woman downstairs in the kitchen.

She trudges along, her breath white in front of her. The snow has stopped, and she can see better now. She gets to Jones's street. There's a single light burning in the living room window, but the rest of the house is dark.

Delilah watches the house for a minute, but she's getting too cold standing still. She has to go in, but instead she turns toward the lake. She walks to the edge where the ice starts. It looks no different than the land, coated with fresh snow and stretching out as far as she can see. She follows the shore, looking for tracks. She wants to see where they left from, the exact spot they started out on the lake. But the snow has covered everything. She gives up and turns back to Jones's.

When she knocks on the door, she isn't sure what she's going to say when they open it. She isn't sure if this is an emergency or not. But she feels surprisingly calm and cool. It isn't until Red opens the door, a puzzled look on his face, and puts his hand on her shoulder and says, "Oh hey there, it's okay. It's okay, Delilah," and leads her into the warm house that she realizes she's crying, tears frozen in icy trails on her cheeks.

Red feeds her porridge from a big pot on the stove in the kitchen. He pours maple syrup on the top and mixes in some evaporated milk.

She eats the whole bowl in silence, Jones eating his own across the table. He came in while she was on the couch telling Red what happened. She couldn't explain it, why she was so worried. She tried to tell them Will was acting funny, but she couldn't explain how. Jones sat on the couch an arm's length away and listened while Red tried to reassure her that they were seasoned bushmen and would be absolutely fine.

"No," she reminded him. "My dad grew up in Toronto." He had only known the bush for a year, only from a few times with Will. He had only known this kind of cold for two winters.

"Well," Red said. "Will is bushman enough for both of them." But there was an uneasiness in his voice that Delilah didn't miss. "What time did they leave?" he asked, checking his watch.

"Around one-thirty."

He nodded. "It's only eight-forty-five. They could be gone for hours yet. No need to panic. Let's eat. You kids have to get to school. You're already going to be late."

"I'm not going," she said.

"Is that right?" He sounded amused. "Well, I guess your dad going off on an arctic adventure might be reason enough to stay home. Jones can stay too. You can wait here. But you guys will have to keep busy. I got some errands to do in town. I ain't gonna entertain you."

After the oatmeal, Jones and Delilah sit on either end of the couch with comic books. Red comes out in his work clothes and then leaves to start the truck. When he returns he says, "Getting light."

Delilah can see the fiery pink streaks over the lake from where she lies, her head resting on the arm of the couch. She wonders if her dad and Will are watching the sunrise too. How far have they gone? How much gas was in the tank? How far *can* you go on a tank of gas? She opens her mouth to ask Red, but no sound comes out and she closes it again. She watches that sky waking up, the wash of weak golden sun weaving into the fading pink. It's beautiful, but she can't keep her eyes open. Colours blur and go dark as she hears Red say, "Jonesy, I think we're losing her."

✳

RED IS SHAKING HER, but she can't open her eyes. Her head burrows farther into the pillow. "Delilah. They found him. Your dad turned up at Dettah."

Her eyes fly open. Red's face is inches from her own. He stands. "He's okay. He's gonna be okay. He's just cold. Hypothermia. The Ski-Doo broke down. They took him to the hospital for observation."

She tries to process this information, but her mind is fuzzy and heavy, like wet socks. She can't think through it. The terror she has been carrying lifts as she grasps that her father is safe. But she is also thinking, *What about Will?*

Maggie gives Delilah a scalding cup of tea with milk and honey. She tells Delilah that she can't visit her dad until later that day, that the hospital had said he's finally sleeping. "He's going to be fine, chérie," Maggie says, stroking her hair.

"Will wasn't with him," Red says. "But once you're up, I'll take you and Jones to Jethro's to see if he turned up there. Probably just wandered home."

Jones is sitting on the arm of the couch, hovering nervously next to Delilah.

"Okay," she says.

***

"WHOLE FUCKING TOWN HAS gone insane," he tells them on the way. He cranks up the news broadcast on CBC on the truck radio. "That meteor of Will's? Turns out it was a Russian satellite that spun out of orbit and crashed outside of town. It had some sort of small nuclear reactor core on it that was supposed to separate into space if the satellite failed but didn't. They're looking for it. RCMP everywhere, media crews flying in. The whole world knows about it. The goddamned US Army is walking down Franklin right now."

So it's a satellite, not a meteor. Will is going to be disappointed when he finds out. Delilah thinks of Will telling her the story of the Russian satellite that crashed so many years ago, the dog that didn't make it back alive.

***

WILL'S NOT AT JETHRO'S, not at home, not anywhere. On Red's instructions, Delilah and Jones sit in Jethro's shack while Red knocks on doors, and Jethro drives all over Old Town with Mary Ellen. By afternoon they are still there and the neighbours and relatives come and go, buzzing about the satellite and speculating about Will. Someone says they saw a radiation team uptown wearing yellow suits.

Delilah tries to untangle it all in her mind. What does it mean? If Will found this satellite, does that mean he's in danger from the radiation? Or did he walk back to town and go to someone's house? Is he sitting on someone's couch watching the news?

Someone has started a roaring fire. CBC talks non-stop about the satellite from Jethro's small radio, but Delilah is barely listening. She imagines Will trekking through the white blizzard, hunched against the wind, snow drifting on his fringed jacket. Travelling miles through the snow only to find a pile of tangled metal instead of something precious that fell from the galaxy.

Mary Ellen paces back and forth across the rough floors, wringing her hands and wailing softly to herself. Jethro is tracing the shore with a group of Rainbow Valley men, Laska barking at their feet, confused by the excitement. They had found her in the house. For some reason, Will left her behind when he set out the night before.

When the young policeman comes he is too friendly, too patient and calm when he takes Delilah's statement about when Will left, what mental state he was in. He is too slow as he tours the property, stopping at the shore as Delilah watches him through the window from her chair, wrapped in an itchy brown blanket someone pulled off Mary Ellen's bed and gave to her. She feels nothing. She is numb through to her very core. The group of men jog up to the policeman and they stand there together, looking at the lake, gesturing their arms.

The adults talk loudly in the cabin around her, their words colliding, dashing themselves to bits and crumbling around her ears. She hears Muddy say *could live for days out there*. She hears Harry Dean say *just gone for a long walk*.

Still Mary Ellen wails, like the quiet fragments of a broken song. As though she knows something no one else does.

❊

IT'S SEVEN-THIRTY AT NIGHT, and the sky is black and whirling white flakes around the truck as Maggie drives Delilah up the hill to the hospital to see Mac. Delilah stares out at the snow, watches it settling on the drifts by the road, on people's roofs. She thinks of her dad being lost out there in it, and then being found. She thinks of Will. She thinks of how her dad could still be lost too, and the feeling makes the earth below her feel cavernous and dark. Does her mother know? She forgot to ask Maggie and Red.

Uptown looks like a scene from a science-fiction movie. There are people everywhere, some dressed in military clothes. Headlights glaring, news reporters standing in arctic parkas talking into microphones in front of cameras by the fluorescent-lit windows of the Kentucky Fried Chicken.

Maggie has chattered the whole way to the hospital, told Delilah her father would be so happy to see her, that Will is probably fine, that he'll probably waltz back into town any minute now. She said the reporters would go home soon, that this satellite was no big deal, it was far from town, nobody could be hurt by the radiation.

Maggie's arm hooks in Delilah's as she guides her down the mint-painted hallway. Delilah walks in a daze, tiny pieces of ice sliding from the fur trim of her parka and dripping to the hard, shiny floor. Her boots leave instant puddles.

"Two-oh-five . . ." Maggie murmurs, craning her neck to look at the room numbers as they pass. A nurse walks by studying a clipboard, a pen stuck in her swinging blond ponytail.

Maggie hugs Delilah's arm to her. She smells sweet and spicy, like pumpkin pie. Her dark curls are escaping from under her hand-knit purple hat, a pompom dangling from the top. Her skirts graze the floor, moving over her boots. She stops in front of one of the doors. "Here," she says. She knocks lightly.

"Yeah?" a voice croaks from inside.

Maggie pushes the door open and guides Delilah in. "Hello, stranger," she says. "Look who I brought. Look who's here."

Mac is lying on the bed, an IV trailing from his arm. Delilah stays near the door. She looks at her dad's face. His eyes are sunken and dark, his face sickly white. He lifts his hand from the blue hospital blanket and smiles weakly. "Hi, Lila."

"Hi," she says, staying where she is.

She doesn't know why she doesn't just run over to his bed like a normal person would. The whole night he was gone she thought he was dead. She had imagined him out there frozen in the snow, frost in his beard. But here he is. And she doesn't move closer.

Maggie is fussing around his bed, folding a towel, straightening his cups and water jug. "Red brought you the soup, yes? You must eat it all up. I will tell the nurses. Did they put it in the fridge?"

He nods. "Yeah. Thanks, Maggie." He's still looking at Delilah, a puzzled wrinkle between his eyes.

Maggie leaves the room, resting her hand on Delilah's arm for a moment before she goes.

"What is it?" he says. "What's wrong?"

She shakes her head. She can't move. She feels broken, like a glass vase that shattered and was glued back together.

"What?" He tries to sit up. "Are you okay?"

She doesn't answer.

"Come here," he says gently.

"I thought you were dead," she says. She doesn't move. She's afraid a dam might burst inside her if she does.

"Delilah, come over here."

"I thought you were gone."

He reaches out a hand for her. "Delilah."

She takes a few shaky steps until she is within a couple of feet of the bed, then takes his hand.

"I'm sorry I scared you," he says. His lips are chapped, windburned. They look sore. He looks like he hasn't slept in months. His long hair is tangled in knots around his face. "Scared myself too. But I'm okay."

She nods, tears forming.

"I'm sorry," he says. "But I'm fine now. I'm fine." He squeezes her hand. "Okay?"

She nods, hugs him tight, lets herself feel the relief that he's still alive. Rests her head on his chest for a moment before taking a breath and straightening up. Outside his window the lights of town are twinkling. "Dad?"

He reaches for her hand again. "Yes?"

"Where's Will?"

There is a long, terrible silence. He lets go of her hand and puts his head back on the pillow. The light above his head buzzes softly.

"I don't know," he says.

***

SHE SPENDS THE NIGHT at Red and Maggie's playing checkers with Jones and watching TV. Red fiddles with the small black and white TV for an hour, swearing while he jiggles with the antenna and moves the set all over the living room until he gets a signal. When he's done, he leaves to join a search party and Delilah sits with Jones and Maggie eating popcorn and watching *The Beachcombers*. Nobody mentions Mac as they sit there on the couch under blankets. Nobody mentions Will. But every time the phone rings Maggie jumps from the couch to answer it.

Delilah is lying under a heavy pile of blankets on the couch when Red comes in at 3:00 AM. He is quiet, tiptoeing past her, but she's wide awake. She hadn't slept at all. She got up twice to rebuild the fire, but mostly she just lay there in the silence, thinking. A sad, sick feeling in her belly when she thought of the cold outside. Or cracks in the ice and the deadly black water below.

In the morning, they all eat porridge, and Red tells her he'll drive her up to see her dad. He seems exhausted, his eyes puffy, his bright, scruffy hair jammed under a toque. He tells her they searched twenty miles up the lake on Ski-Doos before the snow drove them back.

He drops her outside the hospital and tells her he'll be back for her in an hour. "He won't be in here long," he says. "Just needs a couple of days to recover. He'll be home burning your Kraft Dinner again before you know it."

Delilah walks the long halls until she finds his room. She is holding a basket of blueberry bran muffins Maggie made that morning. Her dad's door is ajar, and she hears an unfamiliar male voice booming from inside. She hesitates, her hand on the silver door handle.

"Feeling better, Mr. MacIntyre? Tough haul, hypothermia. I had a cousin had it very bad once. Fell through a lake skating. Hockey. He would have made Junior, probably, but knocked a girl up at seventeen and things went sideways."

Delilah lets go of the door handle and slides back against the wall, the open door beside her. Her father says something but his voice is not as strong and she can't make it out. She hugs the basket of muffins to her and tilts her head to hear.

"Let's not go that far," the other man says. "You're not a suspect or anything, if that's what you mean. You gotta have a crime before you start going out there looking for suspects."

An RCMP officer? Delilah doesn't like the man's tone. He sounds like he's being nice, but there's a layer of unkindness beneath it. A layer of sneakiness. She slides down to the floor and rests her back against the wall. She sets the muffins beside her.

"I'm sorry," her dad says. "It's just . . . I don't know, did they tell you I can't remember much?"

"Mmm hmm. I was told that, but you did manage to recall a few things. My notes here say you went out at approximately one-thirty AM on January 4 on the Ski-Doo about ten kilometres and that the Ski-Doo broke through the ice. Goddamned things, am I right? Might as well take dogs. Dogs are still more reliable than those goddamned things."

"Yes," says Mac. "We would have taken dogs, but Will's brother didn't want them to go out."

"Okay, Mr. MacIntyre. Now, it's been thirty-nine hours since your friend has been missing. So if he came back to Yellowknife, and he's passed out at the Explorer after a nice bender with some hot chick he picked up at the Gold Range, praise Jesus. Right? Or maybe he hitched a ride out of town and he's on his way to Vancouver to go sailing and eat some salmon. Great. But the thing is, if he's still out there, it's not good."

He didn't, Delilah wants to shout. *He didn't pass out after a bender. He didn't do that.* She hates this man, wants to stand and turn and throw the basket of muffins right in his face.

"The cold," Mac says.

"That's right, the cold. Been thirty below for two days and snowing like a goddamn. Also, it's a simple matter of geography. We're on the edge of so much nothing here. All those folks out there looking for the satellite, plus a few of our guys, so that's good. People have been searching out by

Wool Bay and that, but beyond there there's . . . nothing, really. Can't see why he'd wander out past there."

"But there's still a chance he made it out, though," Mac says. "You're still looking."

A pair of white shoes stop in front of Delilah. She looks up and sees the nurse from earlier. "Are you okay?" the nurse says.

Delilah nods, afraid her dad will hear her voice and know she's listening.

The nurse doesn't look convinced. "Is that your dad in there?" she says, quieter now.

Delilah nods again.

"Well, honey, you can't sit on the floor all day. If you want to wait until he's done talking just go sit in the waiting room. There's a TV in there. Might be cartoons on."

Cartoons? What is she, five? "It's okay, I'll just wait a few more minutes," she whispers politely.

The nurse holds up her hands in defeat and walks away. Delilah sits back against the wall.

"How well are you acquainted with William Charles Bilodeau?" the officer asks.

"We work together."

"At the mine?"

"Yes. And we did some staking when I first got to town."

"I see. Made a few trips out to the Barrens then?"

"Yes. Williams Lake area."

The Barrens. Delilah has a flash of walking in the bursting undergrowth, a flash of her first taste of the charred trout that had been swimming in that lake only an hour before Will caught it.

"Okay. And you know each other outside of work? You're friends?"

"Yes."

"Good friends?"

"Yes."

"Like, you go for beer after a shift? Shoot the shit? Tell each other your lady problems and whatnot?"

"Yes, we're friends, like I said."

Delilah thinks about her dad's bloody nose, how it leaked down his shirt that night Will had punched him. The spots never came out. They didn't rinse it fast enough.

"Were you aware Mr. Bilodeau has a criminal record?"

"Yes," Mac says.

Delilah looks at the dark swirling pattern in the linoleum. She feels dizzy. And hot. She unzips her coat carefully so they don't hear it.

"Did he tell you what for?"

"No, he just told me he can't cross the border."

"It was for aggravated assault. Almost killed a man in Fort Mac. Did you know about that?"

Delilah can't breathe. Her breath is knocked from her. She focusses on bringing air in. She waits for her father to answer.

"No," her dad says.

No, Delilah thinks. *It isn't true.*

There is a brief pause, then the officer says, "So I know you say you don't remember much, but maybe you can tell me what you do remember."

"Okay, well, about one-thirty Will came banging on our door. Woke us up."

"This is your cabin on Old Stope?" the officer asks.

The nurse stops in front of Delilah again. "Honey," she says. "You cannot sit on the floor of the hall. You're going to have to move or go in."

Delilah nods. "Okay," she whispers. She picks up the muffin basket and stands slowly.

The nurse is looking at her with her head tilted sideways.

Delilah clears her throat. "I was just . . . waiting. Until they're done. My dad is . . . he's talking to the police."

"I see," the nurse says, looking at the room number. "Your dad is Mac MacIntyre?"

"James MacIntyre. People call him Mac."

The nurse seems to be thinking. "Okay," she whispers. "Stay here. I'll be right back."

Delilah slides closer to the door so she can hear again.

"He wanted to go out by Wool Bay," Mac says. "Figured it had crashed out there somewhere. We got out about ten miles, and it started snowing. Hard. Couldn't see, so I headed in close to shore. We were a couple miles past Dettah near Horseshoe Island."

"And then you went through?"

"Yes. It was shallow. Must have been a bubble or a strong current there under the ice. The skis went through, and I pitched forward a bit, but the windshield caught me. The whole front end went in, and I got a bit wet through my ski pants. Will pulled me out. Gear got wet. He saved the rifles, I think. I had one on me when I got to Andrew's. Don't know about the other one. Maybe some of the gear."

The officer says, "We recovered some gear at the site. Some could have been swept out by the current. Not sure what all you took out with you, so it's hard to say what's missing. You can confirm that at a later date. So he didn't get wet?"

"No, like I said, he was on the sled. Front end broke through and sank to the bottom, but it was only about four feet deep. Only part of the sled went in. It tilted, and the gear tumbled down because of the angle. That was while Will was pulling me out."

"Here you go, honey," the nurse says, startling Delilah. She has brought a chair, and she's holding a Styrofoam cup in the other hand. She props the chair against the wall. "Have a seat," she whispers.

Delilah sits, and the nurse hands her the cup. "Ginger ale."

"Thank you," Delilah whispers.

". . . It was snowing like anything," her dad is saying. "Couldn't see a foot in front of you. Will had a flashlight, though. I remember . . . I remember sitting on the snow on the shore of the island and seeing the beam. He was standing by the sled, and he was shining that light around him in a circle like he was looking for something. Then he shone it on me, and I could see the snow swirling around all caught in the light. Would have been pretty if it weren't for the circumstances."

"So the Ski-Doo is useless," the officer says. "You're a couple miles from Dettah. You decide to walk?"

"I don't know."

"You don't know?"

"No."

"You don't remember?"

"I don't remember much after the flashlight. After he shone the light on my face."

"So you have no recollection of how you got to Andrew Bell's house?"

"None."

"What's the first thing you remember after this . . . blackout?"

"Andrew carrying me to their truck."

"Carrying you? Strong guy."

"Yes. He's a big man. Six foot five. He told me they were taking me to the hospital. He said they tried to warm me up but they were worried about my heart. Apparently they made me drink tea. Warmed some towels on the wood stove and put them on my belly. But my heart, he said."

"You don't remember the tea and the towels."

"They say it's normal. To have these black spots. It's because of the hypothermia."

"That's what they say, yes. Here's the thing," says the officer. "We've spoken to Madeline, and she says Will never showed up there. She says you were there on her doorstep thumping on the door. Sitting there when she opened it."

"Yes," says Mac. "That's what I hear."

"No sign of Mr. Bilodeau."

"Apparently not."

Delilah takes a sip of ginger ale. The bubbles tickle the tip of her nose. Her heart, she realizes, is tripping in her throat. She has trouble swallowing. She leans over and sets the cup on the linoleum.

"Do you have a theory, Mr. MacIntyre, about why he wouldn't have come back with you? It seems suicide that he would have stayed out there in those conditions."

"Suicide."

"Yes. He was a bushman. Knew the land. Knew not to misread it."

"Yes, that's true."

"So any theories?"

"Maybe he kept going. Got disoriented."

"Kept going," says the officer. "Looking for the meteor, you mean."

"Well, he was . . . like I say, he was agitated. And determined. He wanted to find it. He wasn't acting right. There was something about finding that meteor. It was like he had to or something bad would happen."

"Like what?"

"I don't know. I don't mean something bad would happen. You know what I mean."

"So you say he was agitated, okay. Wanted to find this thing, thought maybe he'd get some fame, some notoriety or something. A bit of cash, maybe."

"Maybe. I don't think that's what he cared about."

"Ah, okay. And what did he care about? I'm guessing you know."

"Pardon?"

"I'm going to be straight with you, Mr. MacIntyre. I haven't been a hundred per cent honest with you. There's some things that didn't make it onto the little file here. Things I've heard around town. It's a small town, and things get around, am I right?"

Delilah sits back against the wall. She doesn't like this. She isn't sure she wants to hear any more.

"I guess so," her dad says.

"Like I said, there's no crime here. Everyone wants the same thing. We're all working together here to find your buddy."

"Okay . . ."

"So what I've heard is your friendship with Mr. Bilodeau, there, has had its ups and downs. Hills and valleys."

"Such as?"

"Such as a fight at the Range a couple months ago. Bloody nose for you. Did you take a punch from your buddy?"

"I did."

"And why was that?"

"Just some . . . business problems."

"Business problems out at the mine? Business problems to do with working the ball mill?"

"No, no. I . . . sorry, I guess I forgot to mention we were thinking of starting a business together. Maybe prospecting a bit in the summer for extra cash."

"Sure, fair enough. So you're having some differences of opinion about something to do with the prospecting business."

"Yes. But it was all worked out. You can ask around. We were fine after that. He was looking after my daughter while I worked night shifts. We had him over for Christmas dinner."

"Glad you worked things out. Like I said, there's no bad guy here yet. Just getting all the pieces of the puzzle."

"*Yet?* You think there's a bad guy? You think somebody did something to him out there?"

"I didn't say that."

"That's what you think, isn't it? That's nuts. No offence, but that's nuts. There was nobody out there. It was a fucking blizzard. It was freezing cold. Nobody was out there."

"Well, the two of you were out there," the officer says. "Despite the circumstances and all that."

"You think I did something to him? I was fucking delirious. He has fifty pounds on me. I can't believe this."

"You need to calm down. Nobody's accusing you. You were the last one to see him. That's all. It's important, what you think and what you say, because you were the last one. My guess? You started walking back together and you got separated. He went the wrong way."

"I didn't do anything to him," Mac says.

"Sit back, you need to relax, Mr. MacIntyre. So do you figure he went the wrong way? What's your theory?"

"My theory? My theory is yes. He just . . . he went the wrong way. He wouldn't have left town without a word to any of us. There's no way. He's out there somewhere."

"Okay. We're on the same page there then. Unlikely that he hitched out of town. But, you know, experienced bushman goes the wrong way . . . also unlikely. Thing is, sometimes people don't always do what you expect of them. That's what makes these mysteries tough to solve. We think of all the things we know about the person, but we can only see what we know. We can't figure on them doing something they would never do. But sometimes that's exactly what happens. So we'll keep looking. But your theory is he went the wrong way."

"That's my theory. Christ," says Mac. "What else, what the hell else could have happened to him?"

The nurse is coming toward her, but Delilah is ready for her.

"It's okay," she says as the nurse approaches. Delilah is already standing. "You can take the chair back. I'm leaving anyhow." She walks down the hall. She isn't sure where she's going, but she keeps walking.

***

DELILAH IS IN HER flannel pyjamas reading in the light of the kerosene lamp at the kitchen table. Mac is on the couch looking out at the icicles hanging in crooked daggers from the gutters, a forgotten cigarette in his hand, ash drifting onto the batik couch cover. He had been rifling through notebooks and maps on the coffee table a few moments before, ignoring the toast and peanut butter Delilah had set down for him.

It's been two days since her dad got out of the hospital. He has spoken nothing about Will's disappearance, has only murmured good morning and good night and how was school.

The first night, after Red dropped Mac at home, he had come into her room and sat at the foot of her bed in the darkness. She knew he wanted to say something, that he felt he should, but all that came out of him were a few heaving breaths and then he patted her blanketed foot and returned to the living room. Annie had phoned that night, and Mac had told her Will was still missing, quietly, in as few words as possible.

Twice Jones has knocked at the door, and both times she has retreated to her room and had Mac tell him she's sleeping. She lies in bed, unable to put into words the cavernous loss she's feeling. It seems like the entire community of Old Town has spent every day trying to retrace Mac's steps on Ski-Doos, despite the almost blizzard-like conditions. Jethro even took the dogs out to Wool Bay hoping they would catch his scent.

Instead of feeling sad, whenever she thinks of Will, there is a small dark animal snarling inside her, angry and violent and dangerous. She hates the not knowing. Is he lying there hurt somewhere? Freezing to death and wishing

One Good Thing

they could find him?

She lies there for what seems like hours. When she's almost asleep, she jolts awake and for a second she sees Will standing in whirling snow, looking at her. She sees Will's face, the small scars that mark his cheeks like tiny moon craters, the ice clinging to his hair. She thinks of Clementine. She is filled up with the feeling of Will, down, down, all the way to the soft centre of her bones. But then he fades. She misses her mother, for the first time since she can remember. She wants Annie to be there, sitting on the bed, singing her an old folk song until she falls asleep. Why doesn't she come back?

The emptiness grips her, opens her up. It splits her in two, her sadness for Will. Her sadness for all of them.

***

DELILAH IS LOOKING FOR Mac's socks, the fancy ones Annie brought him from Vancouver. She had bought them at a Christmas craft fair on Robson Street. Hand-knit with some kind of silky thread. They are thin but warm, and he rarely wears them, so Delilah has adopted them as her own.

The socks aren't on the rack. They aren't on the floor of his room, or at least not that she can tell. It's hard to say with all the clothes and papers scattered over every surface, but she has sifted through most of it in the dim light of the kerosene lamp she brings from room to room.

He's finally back at work. Delilah walks around like a stone, feeling nothing but heaviness. She is cold all the time, even when she stands inches from the fire. Jones has been bringing them Maggie's casseroles, French comfort dishes with meat, thick pungent sauce, and vegetables.

She checks the kitchen, the lamp swinging in her hand by the metal handle, but they aren't there. They aren't by the door with the boots. They aren't in her room. She checks the dark room near the back door. Along with their snowshoes, extra boots, and Mac's rifle, she sees the plastic bag from the hospital, the one with all his belongings from the day he checked out. She sets the lamp down, picks up the bag, reaches in and pulls out his yellow ski hat. There's also his plaid shirt and his grey undershirt, neatly folded. A few magazines people had brought him when they visited. Two oranges. A stuffed cat holding a bunch of plastic balloons that is bewildering to Delilah until she realizes it's probably from Louise. She lays these items neatly beside her on the dusty floor.

Her fingers brush some sort of rough material. She pulls out a glove made of caribou hide, the fingers shiny from use. Will's glove. She stares at it, then roots around and pulls out the other one. Why would her dad have Will's gloves? Did Will give them to him because his were wet? That seems the most likely, but still . . .

She drops them in her lap. The light in the room is getting weak. Shadows sink lower, and she knows she has to turn the key on the lamp to bring up the wick. She doesn't move. She just sits there. Thinking about gloves and Mac's bloody nose from two months before. All those weeks of Mac and Will not getting along. All those things that policeman said.

A while later, there's a knock on the front door, and Jones calls to her through the darkness of the cabin. "Hey!

You up? We're gonna be late."

Delilah stuffs the gloves back in the plastic bag, then piles the other things on top and ties it shut.

"Delilah?" Jones is in the kitchen with his flashlight. He comes in as she's standing, the lamp hanging from her hand. "Oh. You ready?"

"Yeah. I was looking for something."

Jones's eyelashes are sprinkled with frost. "Did you find it?" She brushes past him. "I don't know."

* * *

JANUARY 9, 1978
SEASCAPE ARTIST'S COLONY

Delilah, so much is happening, I wish you would talk to me. I'm sorry to hear about Will. It must have been so scary to see your dad in the hospital.

Do you remember why I call you little bird? Do you remember that day? You were only four or five. It was a terrible rainy, cold Ontario fall day. I was making us tea for a tea party on the living room floor, and you were setting up the blocks for your stuffed animals to sit on when you heard a bird hitting the window. Remember?

"What is it?" you shouted, and I ran to see. There were two grey feathers on the outside of the window. I went out to the small garden outside our window and found the bird heaving in shock. You were

watching the whole thing from the window, your nose pressed to the dirty glass.

I brought it in and found a shoebox. I told you it might be okay. I explained about shock and how sometimes birds just needed to catch their breath.

You sat vigil over that bird until bedtime. You didn't say a word, just watched it. You stroked it so gently on the top of its head with your finger, and I let you, even though people say you shouldn't touch wild birds.

Once when I came in the room I caught you whispering to it. You wouldn't come sit at the table for your dinner, I had to bring it to you. The bird was calm by then. I told you it would probably be fine by morning.

When I said it was time for bed, you screamed, wailing from the depths of your little soul. After half an hour you finally calmed enough for me to rock you in the rocking chair, but when you were almost asleep, you said to yourself, "Little bird . . ."

But in the morning, you woke up and the box was empty. I told you I had taken the bird out in its box, and it had hopped once and lifted itself into the air.

Ever since then I have called you little bird. As a testament to your sensitivity, the love your heart is capable of feeling for such a small creature. Strange though . . . just days after the bird hit our window you had one of the worst asthma attacks of your young life. Three days in the hospital . . . a mother's nightmare to see her baby gasping for breath.

You are at an age where you need your mother, Delilah, you need to have someone to talk to. You are thirteen. What if your period starts? What if a boy asks you to a dance? Will you talk to your father? We must mend this, little bird. You need me. I want to respect your space, even your silence, but please call me. Please write to me. Something.

All my love,

Annie

Delilah was six when the bird hit the window. She remembers because she had just started Grade 1 at a Montessori school in Toronto, three blocks from their basement suite. She remembers because it was fall, and her rubber boots were too tight and too red, and she splashed them in the dirty rainwater all the way to school that first day. Delilah didn't like red. It reminded her of blood, of hurting. It was an angry loud colour.

She also remembers because, the night before, she dreamed that a bird flew at that very window while she watched from inside in her nightgown. In the dream, her hand rushed out to stop it and there was no glass. She reached right through thin air to the outside and caught the bird before it hit. She held it close to her, a small robin, barely filling her childish hand.

The day the bird hit their window, she was home with

asthma and she was not playing with blocks. The blocks had never made it from their apartment in Winnipeg. The blocks, which her father had painted blue like the shell of a robin's egg, had been left behind in the move. She remembers being in her white cotton nightgown, the one with the frayed pink ribbon threaded through the neckline.

She remembers it was late in the afternoon, that it had been a long and quiet day. She was looking out the window to the leaf-clogged gutters and streaming sidewalks and wishing she could run as fast as she could away from the house and down the street. She wished so hard that she could run without losing her breath, wheezing, her lungs constricting to the size of nickels in her chest.

Her mother was making tea in the kitchen when the bird hit. Delilah saw it happen, a dark shape appearing from the gloomy sky, flitting by and then abruptly turning back and heading straight for her. She had slammed her hand to the glass as though to stop it like she had in the dream, but it hit with a rattling thud and disappeared below the window ledge.

It's true she had whispered to it. Sung to it. Told it she was sorry she hadn't caught it like she was supposed to. Told it a small secret when her mother was out of the room. Delilah doesn't remember what it was, only that she was sure this little ruffled bird could keep her secret. But the ending her mother told was all wrong. That little bird didn't fly away with Delilah's secret the next morning, change it to a song that only birds could understand, sing it from the tops of the Ontario maples.

After she was put to bed she tossed and turned. Her mother smoothed her forehead, hummed an old folk song about a ghost and a train. Later, when the house was silent except for cars passing on the rain-soaked streets outside, Delilah snuck out to the living room. The lights were out, but the lamp from her mother's room glowed down the hallway and seeped gold into the main part of the house, and a street light outside their thin-curtained window shone down on the shoebox on the floor.

Delilah had flicked on the lamp by the couch and lifted the top of the box, steeling herself for what she knew she would find. The bird lay on its side, very still, stiller than anything Delilah had ever seen, so still she couldn't imagine it had ever hopped, flown, chirped. Its tiny black eyes were closed, the curved feet were clenched in mid-air by its chest. Delilah pressed her finger to the soft head, felt the coolness that radiates from dead things, a coolness that only things that have been hot and full of life can hold when that life is gone.

On the folded dishcloth beneath the bird's small beak there was a stain of dark blood. It wasn't drops, like when Delilah pricked her finger with the sewing needle, or a pool like when her dad nicked his hand with the wood saw. It was a small, abrupt splash. It hadn't been there before. She couldn't see any blood in the feathers. What had broken inside the bird?

She felt her chest constrict, felt the hand squeeze her lungs, felt the air whistle as she breathed in. There was not enough room in her chest for the air. There was not enough room in Delilah to hold her sadness for this bird and its tiny flower of blood. She removed her hand from the box and pressed the lid back on as tight as she could.

***

DELILAH STANDS ON THE shore of Back Bay. Her breath is white like the snow, but her fingers inside Mary Ellen's mittens are warm. Her blood is singing, and her cheeks, surrounded by the fur of her parka, are hot.

It's been two weeks since Will went missing. One week since she found Will's gloves. She knows there must be an explanation, but the fact that her father hasn't given her one, hasn't mentioned a thing about it, weighs on her like a stone.

Delilah had spent the morning reading, and by noon she was so tired of lying in bed that she got up, got dressed, and wandered down the hill toward Latham, one of the twins passing her on the snow-covered road pulling a toboggan with a doll bundled in the back.

The sky is starting to dim, the light a muted soft yellow over the frozen lake. She has to turn around and head back if she wants to make it home by dark.

The wind has picked up, brushing arctic fingers across her burning cheeks. It blows a few lonely, papery flakes in Delilah's face and they stick to her eyelashes. She blinks them away.

Will?

She can't see a single living thing out on the lake. Will's shack is behind her. She can hear the dogs barking over at Jethro's. Laska is with Jethro and Mary Ellen now, but she roams free. She's showed up at Mac's a few times, at Red's too. She seems lost, like she's looking for Will. Delilah feels lost now too.

At least the snow isn't too high. It's not hard to walk through. Your feet just crunch along. They don't sink in, so you have to march like a toy soldier, like in gym class when they have to snowshoe out back of the school. Mr. Mallory yelling "Knees up! Knees up!" Will had laughed when she told him. *He think you kids are in the army, or what?*

She hasn't been back since that day he went missing. There is still wood piled in the back of Will's truck. Six inches of snow on it. It's good wood. She's surprised someone hasn't taken it.

She walks out on the lake. It's getting darker. She wonders if there will be stars. She doesn't mind walking in the dark if it's bright, if there's at least a moon.

She takes twenty long strides and stops. Her toes have started to tingle sharply, her fingers cramped with cold. She can see the shoreline running back all the way to Peace River Flats. She could walk home across the ice if she wanted to.

Better get on home, kid.

She knows.

But first she kneels and clears the snow from the ice. She pushes and scoops with Mary Ellen's mittens. It isn't hard. It's like moving shredded paper, light and agreeable. She clears a Delilah-sized area and peers down.

The ice is opaque here, creamy. Sometimes it's clear for a few feet and then that deep-sea green. She lets her breath out. Looks around. The pink shack is just sitting there. But there are lights on at Jethro's. There are some kids about a mile away on the ice now, racing their dogs. There are living things out here.

She watches the dogs run like silver streaks and thinks of Jethro's dogs pulling her and Jones on the old wooden sled while Mac and Will stood on the lake and smoked. She lies belly down, her parka flat against the ice. She presses her ear to the frozen lake and closes her eyes. Her arms and legs are spread wide, as though she were making a snow angel in reverse. She imagines Will out walking on that ice. The fringe of his jacket moving in the breeze, the red beads of the wild roses shining like quivering fish eggs in the winter sun. She tries, but she can't see his face. Only that jacket.

Will?

She listens through her parka hood, listens for anything, even the groaning cracks of shifting ice.

Nothing.

She lies there as long as she can stand it, until the cold starts seeping into her veins, and then she sits up.

"Delilah?"

She turns. Jethro is standing by Will's shack carrying a cardboard box. He's hunched forward, his grey hair showing beneath his knitted cap.

"What are you doing out there?"

He waits for her to come over to him. She feels foolish as she brushes the snow from the front of her parka.

"Sorry," she says. "I was just . . . I just wanted to come here."

He nods, the corners of his dark eyes crinkling as he looks out at the lake and the patch she cleared.

"What's the box for?" she asks.

"Tidying up," Jethro says. "Cousin Elizabeth is gonna

move in to Will's for a bit. Needs a place to stay. You can come along in if you like. No bother to me."

He turns toward the shack and goes inside. She follows him. It's dark in there, and freezing cold. Jethro sets his box down beside Will's small dresser and pulls the canvas sheet aside to let in the daylight.

Delilah can see the dark outline of the star atlas on the wall by the table. The counters are clear, there are no dishes piled up. The table has been wiped clean.

Jethro starts piling some of Will's clothing from the dresser into the box. To make space for Cousin Elizabeth's things, she guesses. But she doesn't want him to. She wants every single thing in that room to stay exactly where it is.

Jethro's watching her, one of Will's shirts in his hands. "You can help," he says. "You can get those dirty dishes there." He points to the shelf above Will's bed. There is a Scooby-Doo mug that says "Zoinks! It's morning!" and a plastic glass half-full of water.

She walks numbly to the bed and climbs the short ladder. She sits on the shiny sleeping bag and looks at the books on the rough shelf lining the wall beside the bed. They are mostly about astronomy, as well as some geology texts that look like they belonged to a university. She picks up the mug and notices it has three inches of frozen coffee in it. The mug was resting on a book about the phases of the moon. There are some papers sticking out the side. She slides them out of the book, glancing up to see if Jethro is watching her. He isn't. He's busy stacking some wood by the airtight.

Delilah looks at the top page. It's wrinkled, as though it had been crumpled and then laid flat again. She holds it up to the light from the window.

December 12, 1977
Maitland and Associates
Attorneys at Law
2733 Bloor Street West
Toronto, Ontario

Dear Mr. Bilodeau,

Please be advised that our clients, John and Lorraine Clark, acting on behalf of Sarah Clark, have put in a petition to become the legal guardians of Clementine Bilodeau-Clark. The Clarks are asking you to relinquish your parental privileges as of January 1, 1978, and they are prepared to take the matter to court if you do not comply.

Once this becomes a legal issue, as you can imagine, many factors, including background and criminal history, are used in reviewing a defendant's acceptability as a parent in the eyes of the judge.

As a gesture of good will, and the family is aware that this might cause some hardship for you, they have offered a one-time-only payment of $10,000 to cover any emotional damages incurred. The cheque will be sent as soon as you sign the enclosed papers and return them to us. As you will see, there is also a copy of the no-contact order they have placed against you. Please read it carefully, as breaching this order is a serious offence that could result in imprisonment.

Be advised, Mr. Bilodeau, that the family feels this is in the best interest of the child.

Sincerely,

Grant Maitland

The words start swimming in front of Delilah, sliding sideways off the page.

"Jethro," she says.

* * *

JONES IS OVER STUDYING with Delilah for a geometry test. She is hopeless, and even after forty-five minutes, she still doesn't get all those strange angles and complex fractions. She can't concentrate, not since everything that had happened. Finding the letter has cemented something inside her, some unspoken worry she hadn't wanted to feel. The letter means things were hopeless for Will. The letter means Clementine isn't coming back to him. And he knew that.

She's glad Jones is there tonight. It means she doesn't have to talk to her father. She has not said a word to him about what she overheard at the hospital.

She's wearing the mood ring Jones got her on her birthday. She wears it every day now because it reminds her that he thought of her that moment in the drugstore and wanted her to have something she liked. It seems significant to her that her moods, all of them, the black ones and the blue ones and the light ones, are something he thought would be fun to keep track of.

Mac is cooking, frying pork chops and Campbell's mushroom soup on the stove, a pile of peeled potatoes bubbling in the pot.

There's a knock, and Jethro comes in and calls hello. Mary Ellen is standing behind him. Mac shuts off the potatoes and walks out to the living room. Delilah puts her pencil down and follows him, Jones close behind.

"Come in, come in," Mac says. "You guys eaten?" He walks toward them, smiling, but stops short when he sees Jethro's face.

"Seen Ezra Justice's wife in town," Jethro says.

Mac has a dishcloth over his shoulder and he uses it to mop his forehead.

Nobody says anything for a minute. Delilah doesn't know who Ezra is or why it would matter that Jethro had seen his wife, but she can feel that it's important. Mary Ellen rocks in place, humming to herself by the door. Normally she would have come over to Delilah right away and smiled and held her hands and patted her head.

"What'd she have to say?" Mac asks.

"Said Ezra saw Will out on the lake that night Andrew found you. She's been telling everyone. Told the RCMP too. They talked to him today."

"Saw Will?" Mac says. "Out by Dettah?"

Delilah sits on the arm of the couch, the ground shaky beneath her. "Why?" she says. "Why would he be out there?"

Jethro scratches his head under his thick wool hat. He shrugs. "Don't know. Gonna head out and talk to Ezra. Thought I'd let you all know."

Mac nods. Delilah sees he's only half there, turning things around in his mind. "Guess I'll head out too," he says.

"We got room for you in the truck if you want to come

with us," Jethro says.

"I'm coming," Delilah says. "I want to go."

* * *

THEY ARE ALL CRAMMED into Jethro's Chevy crew cab, Jones and Delilah and Mary Ellen on the bench seat in the back. Delilah stares out the window the whole way. They drive through swirling snow all the way past the sci-fi city of Giant and then through nothing but darkness again. They cross the Yellowknife River, frozen on its journey out to Back Bay in the moonlight, the lights of Giant reflecting off the white lake.

Delilah has the insane thought that they will get there and find Will sitting on Ezra's couch, drinking a cup of tea and eating some bannock and blueberry jam. Wearing his jacket, rolling a smoke, and saying, "That so?" when Delilah tells him a story about school.

When they reach Dettah, it's dinnertime and the small cluster of homes is lit up, everyone inside and eating with their families. Delilah, who had been looking forward to Mac's pork chops all afternoon, has lost her appetite completely.

They stop in front of a waterfront shack at the farthest edge of the village and get out. It's set apart from the other homes, resting on the edge of a small frozen bay that curves in from the lake. As Delilah walks up to the door she can see the lights of Yellowknife beyond the house, far off in the distance across the lake.

Ezra's wife, Rose, greets them at the door, a plump

woman in her sixties, and invites them in. Ezra is making coffee, she tells them. He is a small man, barely over five feet, wearing denim overalls and a work shirt. He doesn't look surprised to see two teenagers and Mac along with Jethro and Mary Ellen.

"Been a big day," he says, laughing as he pours coffee into mugs. They sit on two couches draped with white wolfskins. There are other skins hanging from walls. Delilah sees fox, mink, muskrat. The coffee table between them is a wooden crate scattered with old newspapers and *National Geographic*s. "Talk talk talk, that's all I done today."

"Big news, I guess," Jethro says. "Rose said you saw him out here."

"Yeah, yeah, I saw him. Left that morning for trapping so never heard the fuss till I got back yesterday."

Rose sets a plate of store-bought chocolate chip cookies on the table and nudges them toward Jones and Delilah. "Eat, eat. You had your supper yet?"

"Yes," Delilah mumbles. She doesn't want Rose to heat her up some stew or soup that she won't be able to eat. "Thank you." They each take a cookie. Delilah sets hers in her lap.

"What did you see?" Mac asks. "Was I there too? Was he walking with me?"

Ezra looks at him more closely, the deep lines in the corner of his eyes crinkling. "Ohh, you the one? Yeah, you two were together, walking. He had a light, here." He taps his forehead with a wrinkled hand. "Was about two-thirty, three in the morning. Walked up to Andrew's. That's the next house over. I was getting ready to go out in a couple hours, so I was loading up my gear on the sled out by the side of the house." He points toward where the small, isolated bay sits. "You were walking together. He was talking to you, couldn't hear what he was saying. Maybe a hundred yards away or so. He didn't see me, neither. I didn't think nothing of it."

Delilah's heart is thudding in her throat. He was here. Right next door, right there outside that kitchen window. Here where it was warm. Where there was hot coffee and hot water and blankets and clothes and people who would bring him back home to the ones who loved him. Where did he go?

"You saw him walk over that way?" Jethro traces the path with a finger behind him. "Over to Andrew's?"

Mary Ellen is playing with the fringe on her mitts, humming to herself. She hasn't looked up once that Delilah could see. Her coffee and cookie are untouched.

Ezra shakes his head. "No no, I seen him again. Going right back the way he come, but alone this time. Heading straight out on the lake. Still had the light." He taps his forehead again.

"Back the way he came?" Mac says. "Why?"

It's a question Delilah knows he doesn't expect anyone to answer, that maybe he didn't even mean to say out loud.

"Don't know," Ezra says. "At the time, I thought he maybe forgot something on a sled out there or dropped something in the snow. I had to go find my Thermos, see if Rose sewed up my socks. Didn't think another thing about it until today."

Mac is looking out across the room to the black windows facing the lake. "He brought me back," he says. "He walked me back so I didn't get lost. He must have walked me to Andrew's and then turned around and gone back out. Why Andrew's, though? Why not just here?"

Jethro is working his weathered hands together in his lap. "He knew Andrew since he was a kid. Friend of his when they were young."

"Why wouldn't they have gone out to get him?" Delilah says to her dad. "Why wouldn't you have told them he was out there?"

He shrugs slowly. "I was freezing by the time they let me in. Probably couldn't say anything. Couldn't think straight. I don't remember getting to the door . . ."

"Might be he meant to go in with you," Ezra says. "Maybe he forgot something out there on the lake. Wanted to go get it first."

There is a stillness, a deadness in the room. Mary Ellen hums, running her fingers down the length of fringe, releasing it, doing it again.

"He walked away, I guess," Mac says. "That's just what he did. He walked away. All that legal stuff with Sarah . . ."

"No, but it doesn't solve anything." Delilah stands up. She needs to get out of here. She needs to get outside. She wants to go look again now that she knows he was here. "We still don't know where he is. We need to . . ."

"Yes," Mary Ellen says firmly, looking up from her fringe. "Yes." She points at Delilah and says, "You sit."

Delilah feels like she has been slapped. She sits. "Yes what?" she says. "Yes, we know?"

Mary Ellen nods gravely. "Yes."

"Where is he?" Delilah knows she sounds like a child and that everything she is saying and doing is ridiculous. But she can't seem to stop it. She's glad she sat down. She feels like she might faint.

Mary Ellen holds her hands apart, upturned. Lovingly, like they are carrying something invisible and precious. She just holds them like that. Weighing the emptiness.

"Gone," she says.

※※※

JONES AND DELILAH ARE on the couch watching *The Beachcombers*, despite the intermittent reception on the old TV. Mac is at work, and Maggie had insisted Delilah join them instead of staying home alone all night in the drafty green shack. There was whitefish and boiled potatoes for dinner, and now Red and Maggie were doing the dishes and drinking wine in the kitchen. The show is funny and reminds Delilah of Vancouver's towering trees and temperamental ocean, but while Jones seems riveted, leaning forward, his thin body swimming in one of Red's old cable-knit sweaters, Delilah's attention wanders toward the big window and the frozen lake.

When the show ends, Delilah and Jones play a listless game of checkers on the floor by the wood stove. He is whittling a small piece of firewood with his Swiss Army knife between moves, a can of root beer by his knee.

"My mom says City Jane didn't go to work for four days after Will disappeared," Jones says, chipping at the wood with the tip of his knife. Delilah imagines the knife closing on his finger, the blood dripping onto the chipped squares of linoleum.

"Yeah, I heard that too," Delilah says. She knows

City Jane went out looking too, borrowing a neighbour's Ski-Doo to join the search party. Delilah thinks of her alone in her little dollhouse with all her books, lying in her bed wondering where he went.

"You ever know anyone else who died?" Jones asks.

She hugs her knees closer. "He might not be dead."

He looks up at her. "I know."

She thinks about it. "I guess my Grandpa Pete. But he was pretty old. Like, seventy, I think." She had only three real memories of him: his hand guiding hers while she held a pearl-handled steak knife and carved a crooked triangle into a pumpkin, her sitting on his feet while he tried to walk through the kitchen, and finally, the last time she saw him, in their apartment in Winnipeg when they had flown out unexpectedly, him and her Grandma Ellen. Her father's parents. She remembers the first words they said when they walked in the door.

"Well, we tracked you down! Our nomadic son!"

She remembers the shock on her father's face, then the pure joy. She remembers too how her mother raised her eyebrow and how she made ginseng tea when even Delilah knew her Grandma Ellen only drank orange pekoe.

"Yeah, my grandpa died too," Jones says. "Last year. I never met him, though."

"Why not?"

Jones shrugs. Whittles.

"It's not the same," Delilah says.

"What isn't?"

"Will." She means because they don't know where he is. He might be dead, but where? It's not the same at all.

"They're gonna burn his stuff if he's dead," Jones says.

"What?"

"The family. That's what my dad said. They might wait a bit longer, but if they think he's dead they'll burn all his stuff. That's what they do in Rainbow Valley when someone dies."

Delilah imagines his fringed jacket lying on a pile of charred wood, his star atlas curling in the flames. She hears a roaring in her ears like the ocean has gone wild. She stands. She's suddenly too hot, the airtight is a howling furnace beside her. She stumbles toward the pile of shoes and boots by the door.

"Don't go outside. It's too cold." There's a matter-of-factness in his voice that she's grateful for. But she can't breathe in this heat. She hauls on her boots, still damp from the walk there, and yanks open the door.

Outside is a black, still cold that slams the heat from her body with a vicious slap. She shivers, her knees shaking violently in her thin dress and long johns, but out here she can breathe, her lungs expanding in the crystal-clear air, her chest no longer silently heaving.

She leans against the rough logs of the shack and looks up at the stars. And like Will says, she does feel small. She feels so small she's barely there at all.

The stars sit there, still and silent, as though they aren't doing a thing. But she knows they are hot and blazing with life, impossible to contain. She imagines them in pairs, holding tightly to each other's hands as they spin, their long hair flying like comet tails.

**

LATER, DELILAH LIES WITH her head at one end of the lumpy green sofa, while Jones lies with his head at the other end, both of them curled on their sides. They were reading *Archie* comics, but it's late, and they were starting to nod off when Maggie covered them with a heavy patchwork quilt. Jones could have gotten up and gone to bed in his room, but he hasn't. Delilah notes this. They have been careful not to bump each other, and Jones has been still now for at least ten minutes, his breath deep and even. Delilah's eyes drift shut, listening to the muted sounds of Red and Maggie talking in the kitchen.

Delilah exhales. There's a restlessness beneath her fatigue. Part of her wants to throw the blanket down and run out into the cold night, to run and run, fast as the dogs, flying across the moonlit lake. Her foot shifts and bumps Jones's lightly. Without thinking, she presses the soles of her socked feet to his. He doesn't move. She presses harder, gently pushing against him, until he's pressing back. She can feel the roughness of Jones's socks through her own, his toes slightly damp where snow must have gotten into his boots.

The room glows in the flickering light of the oil lamp. They lie like that under the quilt, feet pressed together, finding solid ground.

***

DELILAH EATS HER CAP'N Crunch, a book propped against the salt shaker. The cereal is ridiculously syrupy sweet. Mac's trying to be nice by buying it. He has been trying extra hard, making real meals for dinner, sticking close to home when he isn't working. He even asked her to play Scrabble the night before, but she had complained of a headache and gone to bed.

Mac stirs sugar into his coffee. "You want some coffee?" he asks.

Delilah looks up, bewildered by the offer. She shakes her head.

"Okay." He clears his throat. "So listen, Lila. I have some news."

Her hand freezes, milk dripping to the table below. "What?"

He takes a sip, winces, then blows on the steaming cup. "Your mom and I have been talking, and we have decided it's time you and I headed on down there. To California."

She drops the spoon and a small wave of milk laps out of the bowl. "What? Will is still missing! We can't just leave."

"Delilah, I know you care about Will. We all do. But he has been gone weeks now."

"But there's still a chance. You still go out there looking."

"We're not . . . we're not looking to find him alive out there. When they found me, I was fifteen minutes away from being dead." Mac reaches across the table for Delilah's hand, but she pulls it away. "He just . . . he must have gone the wrong way. I know it's sad. But we need to carry on with our lives."

She can't believe this. That he would just bring up moving to California like it's no big deal. When he knows it's the last place she wants to go. And like Will being missing isn't even a thing anymore. That it's something they should get over.

She looks at her father, his hollowed-out face, thin from stress. Grey streaks shooting through his beard.

"Why?" she says. "Why did he bring you back and go back out again?"

Mac sits back in his chair. "I have no idea. You know that."

"You have no idea because you don't remember."

"That's right. I don't remember."

"But you remember some stuff. You remember waking up. You remember walking in the snow. Why don't you remember where he went?"

She tries not to think about the gloves stuffed in that bag in the back room. The bag isn't there anymore; she doesn't know where it's gone. Delilah hasn't seen her dad wear either of the shirts that were in it since.

"That's how these things work. I can't decide what I want to remember."

She stands, grabs her bowl, turns and dumps it clattering into the sink, soggy cereal and all.

He takes a deep breath behind her. "What is it? What's going on with you?"

Ice crystals have formed on the kitchen window. She can't see through it. Even if she could, all she would see was white.

"He knew about the bush," she says. "He knew how to survive in the bush."

"Yes."

"And you didn't."

He doesn't answer.

She turns. "He knew, but he didn't survive, and you didn't know but you did survive." She says it like the fact that it is.

"Jesus." Mac stands and faces her. His eyes are wild, wounded. "Do you wish I was the one who died out there? Is that what you wish?"

She shakes her head, tears trickling down her cheeks.

"What then? Because it sure as hell sounds like it." He takes her shoulders, tries to make her look at him, but she won't. "It was an accident, Delilah, a fucking awful, terrible tragedy. Nobody wanted it to happen. You think I wouldn't do anything I could to change it?" Delilah doesn't answer. He stands there like that, holding on to her. His hands are bricks on her shoulders.

"Let go," she says. "I am *not* going to California."

"Well, yes. You are," he says, holding her gaze, his arms dropping to his side. "It's the best thing for you after everything that's happened up here. I already booked the tickets. I have saved enough money for a down payment on a house in the town your mom is living in. And that's where we're going."

"Well, have fun," she says, fury flashing through her. "But I'm not going to live with Mom and all her crazy artist colony friends. I'm staying here."

He shakes his head, frustrated. "Yeah? With who, Delilah? Who do you think wants to take in somebody else's snotty thirteen-year-old? Come on. We are a family." His hand smashes down on the table when he says this, and Delilah jumps, startled. "We have been through a lot, and we are going to be together again. Like a real family."

A real family? Annie left them. Annie betrayed Mac with Marcel. Is that what family does to each other? She shakes her head, but no words come out of her mouth. She turns and runs to her room, pulling the blanket closed behind her.

"We leave in two weeks, Lila," he calls. "I'm sorry." He sounds tired now, all the fight drained out of him.

✱✱✱

DELILAH TRIES TO GET through the school day without having to talk to anyone. When she woke up that morning she noticed he had packed some banana boxes and stacked them in a corner of the living room. He was already getting ready to leave.

She keeps her eyes cast down and brushes past people in the halls. A raging furnace burns inside her. She has visions of the school blowing up around her from her own sheer desire, splinters of blackened wood falling in the snow.

In Socials, Delilah watches Misty apply lip gloss using a small heart-shaped mirror. Misty fluffs her feathered bangs, and Delilah wants to stand and start shouting at the kids in the room about how ridiculous and stupid they all are. How the things they care about don't matter at all. She feels like doing something drastic, dangerous. Something she will regret like hell later.

After last bell, Jones catches up in the hall. Delilah is walking swiftly, moving like a shark through the milling bodies. She is heading for the back door by the library.

"Where are you going?" he asks.

"Smokers' pit."

"Seriously?" He slows down. "I can get you a smoke if you want one. From my dad."

"Just come. They'll give us one."

He shakes his head. "No."

"Fine. I'll see you later then."

"Okay . . ." he seems taken aback at her abruptness. "Hey, I'm going out to the cabin one day this week. Do you want to come?"

"You are?" she stops, the cigarette momentarily forgotten.

"Yeah. Maybe Sunday after—"

"Tonight?"

"Tonight? No, my mom won't let me go at night. Not in the winter." He looks at her like she's nuts.

Her eyes flicker down the hall past the retreating backs of the students to the doors, where the sun has already started to sink into a grey twilight.

"So we don't tell her," she says.

"What?"

"We tell your mom you're at my place and my dad we're at your place."

"I don't know . . ." He looks tempted, but anxious. Weighing things.

She sighs, irritated with his caution. "Forget it." She turns to go, continuing her mission to the smokers' pit.

"Fine," he calls after her. "But they'll kill us if they find out."

"Whatever," she says without looking back. "See you after school."

She walks to the door. Takes a deep breath and pushes. They're out there, the girls with their sprayed hair, their roach clips dangling from barrettes. The guys with their army jackets decorated with black felt pens that announce their favourite bands—Led Zeppelin, Pink Floyd, the Who. Delilah stands there in her bell-bottoms with the rainbow on the back pocket, her virginal white sweater under her red parka. She hugs her books to her chest. The guy closest to her is taking a cigarette out of a new pack, crumpling the foil. His black hair hangs in his pink-rimmed eyes.

"You want one?" he asks.

She nods. Reaches out and takes one clumsily and lets him light it for her. It takes her three tries before she realizes she needs to inhale for the cigarette to light. He smells faintly like stale booze.

"Never seen you before," he says. "You just starting out here?"

She takes a drag and it burns her mouth, her throat, her lungs. It tastes terrible, her mouth feels coated in toxic ash, she wants to cough and gag, but she doesn't. She lets the smoke out slowly and takes another drag.

"Yes," she says. "My parents just bought a big house uptown. There's, like, a giant Jacuzzi. It's as big as a hot tub. They work for the government. We're staying here until I finish high school." The next drag goes down smooth. She's already got the hang of it.

***

SHE GOES FOR ANOTHER smoke after the last bell rings, so she's late meeting Jones. By the time she gets to their meeting spot in front of the school, she can see he's already a block away, heading down the hill. He's carrying a Coke, so he must have stopped at the drugstore. She quickens her pace, almost slipping on a slick patch of ice on the sidewalk. He stops to look in the window at the hardware store and she gains a block.

"Hey," she calls when she's only a few stores away. "Wait up."

He glances at her, takes a swig of his drink and looks back at the window.

She catches up. They stand facing the hardware store window. "What are you looking at?"

He points. "Camp stove." There's an arctic camping scene set up on a platform. A below-zero tent, some puffy sleeping bags, the green metal cook stove with the detachable propane tank, some enamel plates and cups, and metal forks. A few cotton-batten clouds drifting from fishing line.

"Oh. For the fort?"

"Cabin," Jones says. "You smell like smoke."

Delilah smells her hand. "Oh yeah, I do." She smiles. "How come you didn't come with me? Those guys aren't so bad."

Jones snorts, takes another swig, and tosses his can on the sidewalk, crushing it with his boot.

"I have to get home. See ya." He takes one last look at the camp stove and then starts walking.

Streaks of grey and that surreal twilight blue that make Delilah feel like she's in a waking dream are already washing out the afternoon sun.

"Hey," she calls, angry. She can feel the furnace start up again. Whatever good it did her to smoke that cigarette has worn off already. "What's your problem?"

"Nothing," he calls over his shoulder. "What's yours?"

His loping back retreats. She notices the patch on the back of his parka sleeve. A small red plaid square against the green, cut from one of Red's work jackets. She looks off down the hill, and she can see Joliffe with its sparse dark trees and the white ice surrounding it.

"Jones," she calls.

"What?"

"I still want to go. I'm sorry I was late meeting you."

He stops. Waits for her. "You're the one who wanted to go." He sounds sulky.

"I know."

"It's . . . cold, you know. And kinda, like, dangerous."

"I know. I don't care."

He watches her for a moment. "Okay. It will be really cold. Even with a fire. It's still not insulated that good."

"So? We can bring lots of blankets."

He chews the thumb of his mitten, looking at his boots. "I don't want to have to bring you back in the middle of the night."

"You won't have to. Oh my God, relax."

Like she would be that much of a baby to make him take her home. They walk down the hill in silence. Delilah wonders what shape the cabin will be in. She thinks of the wind whistling through the crack in the walls they haven't filled yet. The roof is precarious, too. They did a lot of work on it in the summer, but the heavy snow could have collapsed it by now. Then she thinks of the one single mattress they hauled out there on the sled a few weeks before. One mattress. Not big enough for two.

When they get to Jones's after school, nobody is there but Laska, who is curled by the airtight and perks up when they enter the house. Jethro had started letting her wander because every time he puts her in the pen, she howls for hours and keeps the neighbours up. He was afraid someone was going to shoot her.

Jones scrawls his mom a note saying he is staying over at Delilah's. They make a Thermos of tea and load some bread, cheese, and canned chicken noodle soup into a plastic grocery bag. They pack extra parkas, sleeping bags, and firewood into the sled outside the door.

Laska at their heels, Jones pulls the sled down to the frozen lake. The sky is clear and dark, the moon lighting a path to Joliffe. They had tried to tie Laska to it so she could pull it for them, but she wouldn't do it. She sat back as soon as they harnessed her.

They follow the silver, glittering glow of the moon to the island, pulling the sled easily over the smooth snow, then trek across the rock to the cabin. Smoke curls from Old Tom's shack at the southern tip of the island. This makes Delilah feel safer, even though Tom is a strange old trapper with missing teeth and a long yellow beard like one of the seven dwarfs. There are rumours about how he used to stand in front of the Yellowknife Inn and preach to people who walked by about the evils of alcohol and the sins of the flesh.

Once they are on the island, the sled keeps getting stuck in the snow or snagged on hidden shrubs. They have to stop many times to pull it free. Once, it overturns and they must repack everything, sweeping around with their flashlight beams in the snow to make sure they don't leave anything behind.

Delilah's legs ache from the walk and she is sweaty and itchy under her parka. She wishes she had gone home, thinking it might have been better to sneak some of her dad's beer and listen to Janis Joplin records.

The cabin is eerily dark and quiet. Nothing much has changed since they were there last. There are dead leaves on the plywood floor. The old mattress rests against the wall. The table, crooked but standing, is still there. They are both breathing hard from the walk, white wisps illuminated in the harsh light of their flashlights. She could live here, she thinks. If everything goes to hell, she could just live here.

"Looks okay," Jones says. He brings the dry wood they brought with them over to the rusty old stove and kneels to start a fire.

Delilah shines her flashlight on the one narrow mattress again. How will they decide who sleeps where? "Yeah. It looks fine."

They play cards by the light of the kerosene lamp, sitting at the table with chipped mugs of tea. The fire is roaring in the airtight and although they are still wearing their parkas, they aren't cold anymore.

Jones sets his cards down. "Rummy."

Delilah sighs, then stifles a yawn with the back of her hand. Her watch tells her it's after eleven. She glances over at the mattress again. It's lying flat now, piled high with the sleeping bags. They still haven't discussed the bed situation.

"Tired?" Jones says.

She shrugs.

He reaches into the bag at his feet and pulls out a small blue bottle and sets it on the table.

"What's that?" she asks. "Vodka?"

"Gin," he says. "I took it from the cabinet at home."

Delilah has that same feeling she had when she opened the doors to the smoke pit, when she took that cigarette from the boy with the black hair.

Jones is waiting. His parka is unzipped, and he's wearing the sweater she likes with the thick blue and white stripes.

One Good Thing

It makes her think of a French sailor. He won't drink it without her, she knows that. He's waiting to see what she wants to do. She drains her tea in one gulp and sets the cup down beside the bottle.

"Fill 'er up," she says.

***

AN HOUR LATER THEY are lying on the rough wood floor, laughing. Jones rolls to his side to catch his breath, tears stream from Delilah's eyes. Their parkas are discarded on the floor by their chairs. Laska is asleep between them, probably tired of their foolishness now. The bottle is half-empty on the table. They have had enough sense to stop.

"Charrrlie!" Jones says, rolling onto his back again. "Charrrlie, come back, so I can beat on you again!"

"With a two-by-four!" Delilah gasps. They have been doing impressions of all the Old Towners, amusing themselves for at least half an hour. Delilah feels deliciously, deliriously happy. She has a slight, persistent cramp in her stomach, but chalks it up to gin consumption. She doesn't feel a single ounce of the anxiety she felt before, about anything. She's not even worried about where to sleep. She's not worried if they both crash on the mattress. But the sudden thought of Jones's arm or leg brushing against her accidentally in his sleep makes her cheeks flush and she turns her face away so he can't see.

"Hey," she says. "I think we need some artwork in here or something. Like, on the walls." *Shomething.*

"We could make some!" he says. "Let's nail some old

tin cans to the wall like Timmy Fisher does to the outside of his shack."

"That would be pretty," Delilah says. "And maybe an old wagon wheel too."

"Yeah." Jones turns toward Delilah and rests his head on his hand. "Hey," he says. "Why did you go out to the smoke pit?"

She gazes up at the ceiling, the rough patchwork of wood and the army-green tarp above them. She wishes there were no roof at all, wishes she could see the stars.

"I don't know," she says. "I wanted to do something different. I wanted things to be different for a minute."

"You know that guy? The one you took the smoke from?"

"Yeah. Al, right?"

"Right." He's watching her. She glances over, catches his green eyes. "Did he say anything about me?"

"No. Why?"

All she had talked about with Al was how much school sucked. How much the teachers sucked. How much Yellowknife sucked. It had become immediately clear that, in the smoke pit, it wasn't cool to like anything.

Jones is silent.

"Why?" she says.

"Some stuff happened with me and him last year," Jones says.

She feels that insistent pain in her abdomen, all the way down the inside of her thighs, little nails scratching, the tip of a knife on her skin. It must be the gin. She hopes, hopes to *God* she doesn't throw up tonight. She will die if that happens.

"What kind of stuff?"

It takes Jones a minute before he talks, and in that minute Delilah thinks of every possible scenario she can. Stole something from him? Called him names in the hallway? Tripped him at Mr. Mike's so he fell into the salad bar? This last one almost makes her laugh but she catches herself in time.

"We used to be friends," Jones says. "From when we were kids. Like, four or five. We were in kindergarten together. His folks used to live in Old Town. His dad worked at Giant, and then he got promoted to a big-shot job. They moved uptown and Al . . . I don't know. It was, like, his mom didn't want me to come over anymore. Mom says it was like they got a shot at the high life and they didn't want their past dragging them down or something. I don't know what it was. But anyways, we stopped hanging out."

"Oh." Delilah is trying to wrap her head around Jones having a friend. At least, aside from her. It's hard to imagine. She places a hand on her stomach to try to quell the rising pain. What is it? She closes her eyes and tries to focus on what Jones is saying.

"That's too bad."

"Yeah." He hesitates, and Delilah knows that Al not being his friend isn't the whole story. "So last fall at the beginning of Grade 7 I was down by the water in Peace River Flats, throwing rocks and stuff. And Al comes by on his bike with Damian and George. Damian, he never liked me. Not since Grade 3. He's always calling me, like, faggot. And loser."

Delilah opens her eyes. The room has become dim in the flickering light of the kerosene lantern. She tries to breathe around the cramps. This is the most Jones has ever talked about himself, ever. She is afraid to even make a sound in case he stops.

"I'm standing there by the shore. Just . . . I don't even know what I was doing, just standing there. And Damian says, 'Hey, maybe Jonesy needs to go for a swim.' And George goes, 'Yeah, I think he does.' Al didn't say anything, I could tell he wasn't into it at first. He looked kinda nervous and stuff."

Delilah listens with every cell.

"So they . . . they made me go in."

"Into the water?"

"Yeah."

"Wasn't it cold?"

"Yeah. It was late September."

"Jones?"

"Yeah."

"What do you mean, they made you go in?"

Silence. It's getting cold now. Delilah shivers on that hard floor. She wants her parka, but she doesn't want to move. She wants to hear Jones's story. She wants the room to stop spinning. She wants the pain to stop. It is creeping up to her chest now and her head is aching.

"They pushed me in from the shore. Held my head down."

She turns toward him, all her pains forgotten. "They held you *under*?"

Laska stirs between them. She shifts her body and rests her head on Jones's chest, looking up at him. He lays a hand on her head.

"Yes," he says.

"For how long?"

"Too long."

Delilah imagines the scene, the tumble of bodies jostling

in the cold water, rough hands on Jones's skinny arms, the shock of the water on his face, a hand pressing on the back of his head, the boys shouting at him, saying terrible things. Laughing as he tries to turn his face to get air.

"How'd you get away?"

"Johnny Cole came down to the shore. Heard the yelling, I guess. He broke it up."

She's still watching Jones. A terrible thought grips her. "Do you think they would have . . . ?"

"I don't know."

She flips onto her back again. The ache in her stomach has crept around to her lower back. What would it be like? she wonders. To think someone wanted you dead. Wanted to kill you, even for a minute, for nothing but the fleeting thrill of it. To know that you were that insignificant to someone, like a little kid who lets an ant burst into flames under a magnifying glass on a hot day just to see it burn.

The room sways and lurches, and Delilah sees fragments, images of Jones, his Atari shirt soaked with September lake water, her father stumbling through the snow toward Dettah, Annie smiling at her at the Wildcat, her long hair smelling like roses. And suddenly Delilah feels nothing but the sadness ripping through her. She curls into a fetal position and tries to catch her breath, to breathe past it.

Jones sits up. "Delilah? What's wrong?"

She says nothing; all she can do is cry.

"Delilah?" He has a tentative hand on her arm. He sounds terrified.

She stops and tries to get some words out. "I have to leave."

"Here? You want to go back? Okay, I can . . ."

She shakes her head clumsily against the rough floor. "No, I have to leave. Yellowknife. My dad is making me go."

His face is swimming above hers, bobbing in and out of her line of vision. She can't tell if he is moving or if the room is just wavering around him.

"What? Like, move?" Now he sounds confused.

She nods. She can hardly hear him anymore, and her stomach is starting to hurt again.

"When?" His voice is disembodied.

"Soon. Really soon." As soon as she says this, she feels a thick, unfamiliar wetness spread between her legs, soaking through the front of her jeans, she finally knows why her stomach is trying to kill her, and she wishes the dirty floor of that cabin would open like a black hole and suck her through so she never had to see Jones or her dad or Annie or anyone ever again.

***

DELILAH OPENS ONE EYE, the other still pressed into the pillow. Cold light bleeds under the grey army blanket nailed to Jones's bedroom window. She is trembling, and her feet, even in their thick socks, are brittle ice. She pulls the layers of rough wool blankets and sleeping bag up over her head.

Her body feels empty, like all that's left of her is aching bone. Her throat is paper that cracks and tears when she breathes. When she moves even slightly, her stomach lurches to her chest, and the terrible, searing cramps still ricochet through her thighs and abdomen despite the dose of Tylenol Maggie gave her a few hours ago when Jones brought her back.

Jones. She could die. She wants to die. The blood and that terrible, ripping pain. Why had no one told her it could be like that? How could her mother not have warned her it would feel like someone was trying to tear you open from the inside? Maggie had to calm her down on the bathroom floor, show her how to use the pad, convince her she wasn't bleeding to death. With all the school nurse speeches, all the talks from Annie, Delilah never would have thought she would act like such a stupid, crying child when it happened.

She hears Red down the hall. Maybe getting ready for work. He laughs a short seal-bark laugh, and then Delilah hears another voice trickle down toward the bedroom. There are a few people out there. They sound loud, excited. She blinks at the alarm clock by Jones's bed. The glow-in-the-dark hands read 8:15.

It dawns on her that she's in Jones's bed, in Jones's room. That on top of all the other humiliations of the night before she has also taken his room and forced him to sleep somewhere else in the house, most likely on one of the lumpy couches. What does he think of her now? Drunk and sloppy, crying like a baby. *Take me home. Take me home . . .* and then . . . oh God. He had run for Old Tom, who took Delilah back on his snowmobile. She had clung to his filthy parka, smelling the kerosene and smoke in his hair the whole way back to Jones's.

She hears Red talking again, Maggie laughing. What is going on? She was expecting a stern talking-to about safety. She thought she and Jones would be roasted over the coals. She rolls over gingerly and tries to sit up, just as Jones bursts into the room wearing only his sweatpant bottoms, his hair standing on end like he just bolted out of bed.

"It's Will," he says, his face breaking open with joy. "Are you awake yet? It's Will. I just woke up and he's here in the house."

Sure enough, there is Will's unmistakable laugh filling up every crack in the house around Delilah. Everything in her line of vision tilts at an impossible angle, and she covers her mouth, sure she's going to throw up. She notices Maggie's soup pot on the floor, surrounded by socks and jeans and comic books. "Come on," he tells her.

She stumbles to her feet, shivering. She's wearing a pair of soft pink sweatpants that must be Maggie's, and Jones's blue hooded sweatshirt with the white zipper. She pulls the sleeping bag off the bed and wraps it around her, then turns toward the door. Is it really him?

She opens the door, and the smell of toast and coffee and fried meat accosts her. She grabs the jamb to steady herself. She wonders if this is how animals feel, forced to smell every smell so keenly, against their will.

Maggie is chirping away in French, probably on the phone, and when Delilah finally emerges from the dark hallway, she can see her father and Red sitting on the couch holding coffee cups. Jones is huddled in a chair by the fire, his back to Delilah. And there is Will. Sitting in a chair at the table, a cigarette in his hand. Looking like he has been there all along.

He grins at her as she stands there wrapped in her sleeping bag, her hair a mess, her skin probably blotchy from crying.

"Rough night, kid?"

Everyone laughs, and she feels her knees buckle as she slowly crumples to the floor, the light dimming until it's gone entirely.

***

WHEN SHE COMES TO, she is lying on the couch. Mac is shaking her awake. "Lila. Lila! You okay?"

She struggles to clear her head and sits bolt upright when she remembers Will. He's still there, sitting at the table. She looks back at her dad, who is wearing his work coveralls.

"You okay?" he asks again.

She nods and looks back at Will. Jones is showing him the Swiss Army knife he got for Christmas.

Red comes in the room with two steaming mugs. He hands one to Delilah and one to her dad, who sits beside her on the couch. She looks into the cup and sees blackness.

"Coffee," Red says, settling down across from Will at the table. "Old enough for a hangover, you're old enough for coffee."

He laughs, and Delilah wants to disappear into the couch.

"Where were you?" she croaks in Will's direction. He doesn't hear her, turning Jones's knife in his hands. "Where were you?" she says louder. It comes out like a bark, like an angry demand.

He looks up at her. "That's right, you missed the big homecoming this morning."

She's confused.

"He came in around five," Red says. "Been catching up

since then. You need something to eat?" he asks, the faintest twinkle in his eye as he takes a swig of coffee.

She shakes her head.

From the kitchen, Maggie chirps on, banging dishes as she talks.

"Jesus, Delilah. You could have died out there," Mac says to her.

"I'm fine." Died? How could she have died? She was ten minutes from Jones's house.

"Where did you go?" she asks Will again.

"Here and there," Will says. "Stayed at some old trapper's cabin out there. Kinda holed up looking for the meteor. Turns out . . ." He laughs. "Turns out it wasn't a meteor at all. Guess you guys know that, eh? Found out before I did. I was the chump out there trekking through the snow looking for a hunk of metal. Never even found that. Hear some other guy did, though."

Delilah shakes her head. "It's not funny."

He quiets down. Everyone does. Mac even stops his cup halfway to his mouth.

"I thought you were dead," she says, tears pricking her eyes.

He looks down at his hands. "I know."

"Delilah," Mac says. "Let's be grateful Will is—"

"I thought you were dead." She stands, the sleeping bag falling away from her and pooling at her feet.

He looks back up at her. Nods. "I know."

She has to get out of this room. Everyone is staring at her. They already all know what happened, they have had time to get used to Will sitting there like he's a normal, living man. To her, he's still a ghost.

She steps over the sleeping bag and runs down the hall and into Jones's room, slamming the door as hard as she can behind her. She burrows back under the blankets on Jones's bed, her heart slamming under her ribs. A few minutes later the door opens, and Will comes in. She covers her face with the blanket. He sits beside her on the bed and places her mug of coffee on the small table.

"Hey, kid?"

She doesn't answer.

"Drink that coffee," he says. "You don't look so good. Don't think partying agrees with you."

"You're not funny," she mumbles under the blanket. But then she sits up, avoiding his large body as she pulls her knees up to her chest. She picks up the mug and takes a small sip of the strong, lukewarm coffee.

Will scratches behind his ear.

He looks exactly the same, she thinks. He doesn't look skinny or malnourished or frostbitten or like he almost died of hypothermia. He doesn't look like he was lost at all.

"So what, you mad at me or something?"

Mad? Is she mad? She tries to untangle the ball of many-coloured wool that is her feelings. She shakes her head. "I don't think so. Maybe. I don't know."

"Didn't mean to make you worry, kid. I was just . . . I had to do some thinking. I thought I had to find that thing, you know."

"The meteor?"

He nods, his gaze fixed on Jones's Millennium Falcon poster on the back of the door. "Yeah. Guess I thought it was something it wasn't."

She sets her coffee down again. Her guts are churning from the alcohol and all the Tylenol Maggie gave her. "The meteor, you mean?"

"Yeah."

"Why couldn't anyone find you? They looked for you."

He shrugged. "Don't know. Lots of snow, for one. Stayed the first night out at Wool Bay in a fishing cabin. Then I headed inland and stayed at some trapper's cabins here and there. Had some gear with me. My .22. Not hard to live out there if you have what you need. Most of the cabins leave wood and a bit of food. Shot some rabbits. I guess I didn't want to be found is why nobody found me. Didn't spend much time out during the day. I could see signs folks were out there. Saw the helicopters too when the sky cleared. They were looking for that satellite."

She takes a shaky breath, afraid to ask him what she wants to ask. He is coming more alive in front of her. She's starting to believe he's really there. He smells like tobacco and wet wool.

"I thought you gave up. Because of Clementine."

His eyes are tinged with sadness. "Yeah," he says. "Guess I almost did."

"But . . . you came back."

"Yeah, I did. Got too cold out there." He smiles at her. "Just joking. No, came back because I gotta get back to work. Save up for some fancy lawyer, I guess."

"Lawyer?" She brightens. "You're fighting back?"

"Oh yeah, kid." He laughs that laugh she's missed so much. "You met me? I'm fighting back. Ain't gonna win, but I ain't going down without trying."

***

"JONESY KNOWS BETTER," RED says, lighting a cigarette. "You don't fuck around when it's fifteen below. Good way to get yourself killed."

Mac nods his agreement, looking pissed right off at Delilah and Jones, who are on the couch, facing the music. The excitement has died down, and Will has gone back home with Jethro and Mary Ellen. Delilah had missed their reunion when she was in the shower, but she had heard Mary Ellen's joyful singsong from the bathroom.

"We had a fire," Jones says. "We weren't cold."

"Sure, everything was fine until the plan went to hell," Mac says. "And the plan went to hell because you guys got shit-faced, and then one of you got sick. That's how people die. Making stupid mistakes like that. You're lucky you lived to tell us about it."

Jones's eyes flicker to Delilah and she looks away. He's reminding her it was her idea. She knows.

"Dad," she says. "He brought me back. It's not a big deal."

Mac looks exhausted. He was working a night shift, so he hasn't slept since the previous morning. "Okay. Okay, guys. Just don't do it again. I mean . . ." He smiles. "I guess you won't really have a chance to. Delilah won't, anyway. Not like you can freeze to death in California."

There's a crackle in the air as Delilah stares at her dad. Red is looking at his lap and Jones shifts uncomfortably beside Delilah. She stands.

"Can we go home? I'm tired."

* * *

DELILAH SLEEPS STRAIGHT THROUGH until the next morning. When she wakes up, she wraps herself in a blanket and finds Mac sitting at the kitchen table reading, the lamp beside him.

"Hey Lila," he says. "You hungry? I can heat up some stew."

"It's okay," she says. There is a frailty between them, like china with a hairline crack.

It's warm, the wood stove roaring. "Dad?"

"Yeah?" He arranges some papers beside his coffee cup, stacking them neatly and placing them in the book.

"Why do you have Will's gloves?" It comes out before she even has a chance to think about it.

He stops, his hand still gripping the cover of the book. "What?"

"You had Will's gloves in that bag from the hospital. Why?"

"What are you talking about? What bag from the hospital?" He looks so genuinely confused that Delilah instantly knows he doesn't have a clue what she's talking about.

"The white plastic one. You . . . it was in the back room. And then it was gone. It wasn't there anymore."

He runs his hands through his hair. "His gloves were in there? I never even looked in that bag after I got home."

He goes into the living room and she hears him rustling in his room. She waits for him to return, but he doesn't. She stands and heads tentatively into his room. He's sitting on his bed, just a dark shadow lit by a single candle flickering from the bookshelf in the living room. He's holding Will's gloves in his hands. He doesn't look up at her.

She sits beside him.

He turns the gloves over in his hands. "I didn't look in the bag. I didn't want to. I thought it was just . . . my clothes. From that night. I didn't want to see them again. Andrew and his wife had taken off all my wet clothes to warm me up. I was wrapped in blankets. They must have put these in a bag and brought them to the hospital. Never even saw them."

"Oh. I thought you hid them."

He turns to her. "Hid them? Why?"

She doesn't answer. It all seems so foolish now that Will's back. Everything she thought. She can't even say it out loud.

"You thought I hurt him?" He sounds broken. "You really thought that?"

"Well . . . well, obviously you didn't. But I just . . . I guess I didn't know why you had them."

"I don't know. He must have given them to me," he says. "I don't remember. I'll ask him. He told me last night that he told me where he had gone. That he was going back out to look for the meteor. He said I seemed okay, that I was having a normal conversation with him. He feels bad he didn't walk me right up. He got to the edge of the lake and told me to walk in to Andrew's, that he was going back out. But I didn't remember." He laughs softly. "All that time I knew, but I couldn't remember."

"Sorry," she says, "I didn't mean anything . . . I just . . . I didn't know why you were fighting all the time. And he punched you. Why did he punch you?"

He looks at her, holding her gaze. "We were working on trying to get some samples tested from that site in the Barrens," he says, his voice hollow. "We had a . . . disagreement. About some things related to that."

"What things?"

"Delilah, sometimes adults do things they shouldn't do. They make mistakes. And sometimes they do those things because it will make a significant difference in their—"

"What things?"

"We stole," he says quietly.

"Stole? What? What do you mean?"

"Gold."

"You stole *gold*?"

"From Giant. We were working the ball mill after hours. Me and Will and Muddy. Crushing up the discarded ore. We got about five ounces and then Will wanted out."

"You stole from the mine?" Delilah can't believe the words she's hearing. All the ethical stuff, the "work hard for what you believe in," things her father has been saying to her since she was a child are void. Erased.

"Yes. It's not okay. I'm not excusing it, but that ore . . . it gets tossed. They don't process it, or if they do, not for a long time. It's not okay, but they are a massive, multi-million-dollar company. They aren't missing it. It was five ounces. That's all. I've heard stories. There are lots of guys that have done it. We needed the money. We were sitting on something very promising, and I needed the money for the down payment so your mother—"

"Will stole?" She's breaking apart.

Mac rubs his forehead. "Yes. But he wanted out. He

didn't want to steal. He was never okay with it. I wasn't either, but Muddy convinced us it would be fine. Will got panicky because he was afraid if he got caught it would ruin any chance he had of seeing Clementine again. He wanted to pull out of the whole deal, but it was tricky. We already had some people interested in checking it out. So we were trying to find a way to buy him out if it took off. But we didn't have enough money to pay our expenses. It's all over now. It's done. I gave my notice at Giant, and Will never took his share. So it's all fine. I needed it, Delilah. Your mom wants us down there, but I didn't want to show up with nothing. Do you understand?"

Delilah lets all of this sink in. How Mac would steal for Annie. How he would do anything to be with her. How he falls apart without her. Falls into a black hole just like one of those binary stars. Yes. She is finally understanding.

"Dad?"

"Yes, Lila? I'm so sorry. I'm so . . ." He has tears in his voice. She can feel his shame and desperation.

She puts a hand over his hand on the bed. "It's okay."

Martha's voice carries across their yard and through the house. "Charrrlie . . . Charlie Boy!"

Mac stands.

"Dad?"

"Yes, Lila?"

"Do you remember what I told you about Marcel?"

His face is pinched. "There are sometimes just . . . things that happen between adults, Delilah. It's . . . complicated."

"I know," she says. "But I don't want to leave Old Town."

Mac crouches down and looks at her. He puts a gentle hand on the top of her head.

"I know," he says. "But we're a family. I can't leave you behind." He still has tears in his eyes, somehow at odds with his ragged beard, his weather-beaten face with the crinkles by the eyes.

"It's okay," she tells him gently. "Just let me finish the school year here. Please. I can stay with Maggie and Red."

"Delilah, I—"

"Please? Just until June. You can go down and see her and then who knows? Maybe you can even get her to move up here instead of buying a house down there." She's grasping at straws, but he needs a reason to let her do this.

"You aren't going to let this go, are you?" He wipes his eyes. Nods. "We might be able to work that out. It's only four months. But after that, we all live together as a family. Whether it's there or here."

Delilah nods her agreement, allowing herself to feel the thrill of this small victory. If that's really what it is. All she knows is, she isn't going to California. She isn't moving. At least right now.

"Charrrlie . . ." Martha calls from outside.

Delilah exhales. Then she reaches over and hugs her dad before getting up and walking to the front door.

"Don't," Mac says, following her.

She swings the door open to the eerie blue morning and walks out on the snow-covered porch in her socks. She can't even feel the cold. She is burning up. Her father stands behind her and touches her shoulder.

"He's out for a walk!" she calls.

Martha is on her porch in a long velour bathrobe, the edges jagged and torn. She peers at Delilah. "Who's that?"

"He just went for coffee at Nettie's," Delilah says.

One Good Thing

Mac tries to guide her back inside. "Come on, now. She's a crazy old woman."

Delilah shakes him off. She walks closer to the edge of the porch, and Martha does the same on her own porch. "What you saying there, girl?"

"He's only at coffee, Martha. He's coming back. He's just having coffee."

"Who, Charlie?"

"Yes. He's coming back. He's not gone." Her voice is shaking. It's important to her that Martha understands this. That grieving for someone who isn't even gone is a waste of her time.

Martha scratches the back of her head and looks up at the sky. "Gonna be sunny today," she says.

Delilah looks up too, feels a few loose flakes fall onto her face. There are some patches of blue breaking through. Delilah breathes in the freezing air, deep down into her lungs, and lets it out.

Martha is watching her, standing there in her worn bathrobe, snow settling in her wild black hair. "You got any comics?" she says.

Delilah can suddenly feel the cold burning like a hot iron up through her legs and it makes her feel alive. "Yeah," she says. "I have some comics."

***

DELILAH FEELS LIKE SOMETHING has broken between her and her father now, but not in a bad way. More like a fever. Like all the confusion and delirium of the past few months is finally over. For the last week that he's there she doesn't go to her room the second he walks in the house. She says more than three words to him at dinner. She even helps him trim his hair when she found him trying to hold the mirror up to his face in the lamplight and the light kept catching and reflecting off the scissors so he couldn't see. She knows he wants to look his best for Annie.

* * *

ON SUNDAY, THE NIGHT that Annie calls, Mac and Delilah have just finished packing up the belongings they won't be using and piling them into Delilah's bedroom. He will still pay the rent until springtime, just in case he can convince Annie to come back.

Delilah and Mac have had their dinner of beans on toast, and Mac is reading on the couch when the phone starts to ring. Usually he answers right away, but not this time. He's absorbed in his book. Delilah is doing homework at the table and she looks up. She sets down her pencil. Without thinking, she stands up. She walks over to the bookshelf and looks at the phone. She hasn't spoken to her mother in nine months. Not a word. She isn't sure what she would even say to her.

She reaches her hand out, hovering over the receiver. She can feel her father watching her. She picks it up and holds it to her ear.

"Hello?" she says.

February

DELILAH STANDS ON THE frozen bay looking back at Red and Maggie's house. There is a massive bonfire lighting up the black night, engulfing the old scraps of wood and broken furniture Red is trying to get rid of. Maggie made pea soup, and people are sitting around the fire in parkas with mugs and spoons and chunks of homemade sourdough bread. City Jane is next to Will under a blanket on the front steps. Jones is over by the shed trying to harness Laska so they can go for a sled ride. Will laughs at something Red says, and it booms and echoes across the ice to Delilah.

"Come on back now," Maggie calls out to her from the fire. "You've been out there so long."

Delilah turns back toward the lake. The wind has died, the snow has stopped swirling and is settled at her feet. The sky is clearing, the clouds blown away. The air bites her cheeks.

Look up, Will had told them that night at the movie.

She does. She looks up at those millions and millions of stars, the moon a pale crescent above the bay. But this time she doesn't feel small like he said she would. She thinks of Jones and Maggie and Red. Jethro and Mary Ellen. She thinks of how they belong to her now, and she belongs to them. How even this lake belongs to her. This town. She thinks of how Will was gone, but he came back. She thinks of Annie and Mac, who might come back too, and she feels like she's expanding, growing every second. She feels like a giant in her red parka and Mary Ellen's mittens, a giant down there on this vast frozen lake.

I'm here, she thinks. *I'm right here.*

She's not small. She is something you could see for miles.

acknowledgements

HEARTFELT GRATITUDE TO THOSE who offered their wisdom and insight on the manuscript: Gaël Géneau, Hal Wake, Joseph Denham, Ruth Linka, Lizette Fischer, Justin Gilbert, Dana Woolliams, Mary Louise Hendry, Maria Kojic, Koree Rogers, Rochelle Fairfield and Rashmi Singh.

To Betty Keller, who I am proud to call my mentor: This book would not exist if it weren't for your encouragement and guidance. Thanks also to Rosella Leslie, Erin Whalen, Kim Clark, Diane Foley and the other writing group folks who helped me untie the knots.

Fran Hurcomb, thank you for reading the manuscript as well as being such a patient resource when I asked you question after question. Also, thanks to Dave Smith, Bob Carroll, Tamara Carroll and the coffee shop guys in Yellowknife for their tips and ideas.

Thanks to my sharp-eyed editors Kate Kennedy, Warren Layberry, and Janine Alyson Young for helping me find the cracks and repair them. And a huge thanks to Taryn Boyd, Renée Layberry, Tori Elliott and the team at Brindle & Glass for launching this book out into the world, as well as to Tree Abraham for the perfect cover.

Thanks, as always, to my beloved kids, my family, and my friends for listening to me talk about this story for so long—and to my parents for bringing me to Yellowknife all those years ago.

Thanks to the thousands of people who have posted on the Facebook group YK Memories for sharing their knowledge and photos about Yellowknife in the seventies. Greg Loftus, you are missed.

And finally, thanks to the residents of Old Town, past and present, who know exactly why that unique place is worthy of having entire books written about it.

BORN IN OTTAWA TO a hippie mother and a poet father, Rebecca Hendry moved to a new city or town across Canada every year until she was eleven, when she settled on the Sunshine Coast in BC. Her first novel, *Grace River*, was published by Brindle & Glass in 2009, and her short fiction has appeared in the *Dalhousie Review*, *Wascana Review*, *Event*, *Windsor Review*, and other literary journals. She lives in Gibsons, BC, with her two children.

Photo by Justin Gilbert